AUTUMN'S GRACE

AUTUMN'S GRACE

A NOVEL BY
SARA MEISINGER

© 2016 Sara Meisinger

Published by Wings of Hope Publishing Group
Established 2013
www.wingsofhopepublishing.com
Find us on Facebook: Search "Wings of Hope"

Printed in the United States of America

All rights reserved. No part of this publication may be reproduced, stored in a retrieval system, or transmitted in any form or by any means—for example, electronic, photocopy, recording—without the prior written permission of the publisher. The only exception is brief quotations in printed reviews.

Meisinger, Sara
    Autumn's Grace / Sara Meisinger
    Wings of Hope Publishing Group
    ISBN-13: 978-1-944309-08-4
    ISBN-10: 1-944309-08-X
    eBook ISBN-13: 978-1-944309-09-1
    eBook ISBN-10: 1-944309-09-8

This is a work of fiction. Names, characters, incidents, and dialogues are products of the author's imagination and are not to be construed as real. Any resemblance to actual events or people, living or dead, is entirely coincidental.

Cover design and typesetting by Vogel Design in Hillsboro, Kansas.

To **MARK**, who has encouraged me from the beginning.
You have made it possible for me to follow this dream.
I am so blessed to be your wife.

And to **KRISTI GORMAN**, the first one to inform me that everyone
didn't have a story playing in their heads. Then you asked what
I thought God wanted me to do with the stories in mine.
Thank you.

Galations 6:9 NKJV
And let us not grow weary while doing good,
for in due season we shall reap if we do not lose heart.

CHAPTER ONE

Struggling to take in a deep breath, Hailey scanned the crowded ballroom. Why had she volunteered to accept this award? Dim lights created intimacy to the room, a contrast to the harsh fluorescents used earlier during the business meeting. The faces circling the tables had grown familiar over the past three days, some even friendly. But not all.

She looked toward the third table in the fourth row. Even from this distance, Trey's blue-eyed gaze beneath the slash of dark brows narrowed with hostility. Her legs trembled. She gripped the podium. What was he doing here? She hadn't seen him since the morning she took him to the airport two-and-a-half years ago.

His raised eyebrows mocked her silence. With an open hand, he motioned for her to speak. Heat washed over her face. The words on her white note card blurred. She had to get through this speech—and leave.

"On beha—" Her breath caught on the first words. The clinking of glass resonated through the spacious room. She closed her eyes to steady her nerves and began again. "On behalf of the Harper family, I'd like to thank you for this honor. This award could have gone to any of the other nominees. Like all of us in Agritourism, a plan to support our families while preserving our values and way of life is key. We also strive to educate the growing urban community."

She glanced at the fourth row and met impassive eyes. The white card shook in her hand.

"Fourteen years ago, my parents began a pumpkin patch on five acres of land. Their goal was to supplement the family income enough that Mom wouldn't have to work in town. Today, that pumpkin patch is a thriving Agritourism business. It covers fifty acres and averages twenty-seven thousand visitors each fall.

"Since the accident that took my mother's life and left Dad in a wheelchair, we have learned what it is to come together as a family." A single cough echoed through the cavernous room. She knew its source and the scorn it represented. She shuffled her feet, trying to stop her legs from shaking. "The farm has allowed each of us time to adjust and heal. We are honored, and we thank you for this award."

The room filled with polite applause. Hailey stared at the smeared and mangled note card in her hand. How could one small piece of paper represent her life so well?

Trey gripped the cool glass in his hand. How much pressure would it take before it shattered? The prime rib he'd eaten sat like a stone in his stomach. A door behind him opened with a groan. He should leave before the night became any more personal.

Senator Rob Bryant pushed his chair back as the lights came up and the noise in the room increased. "Mind telling me what that was all about? That poor woman looked like she was on trial, and you seemed to be the judge." He glanced pointedly at the amber liquid in Trey's glass. "I haven't seen you drink at one of these events for a couple of years."

Trey downed the last swallow. "I haven't wanted a drink until now."

Hailey stood in front of the podium, talking to the man who had presented her with the plaque. She looked good. Why did he still notice? Time had done nothing but improve what was already perfect, in his opinion. Hailey's trim build carried the silver sheath dress with an understated elegance. Soft, dark brown curls danced around her shoulders when she laughed at something the man said.

Had she come to Washington alone? Trey threw his twisted napkin on the table.

"I'm going to go talk with Ms. Harper."

Ms. *Harper?*

Senator Bryant tapped his fingers on the back of the chair. "I suggest you wait here." He hurried toward Hailey, leaving Trey at the table.

The Harper family picture still loomed, larger-than-life, on the screen at the back of the stage. He studied the three faces of the family he'd called his own. Hailey's brother Todd smiled confidently, his arm wrapped around a pretty—and very pregnant—redhead. A beautiful, blond-haired baby sat on Jim Harper's lap. Trey shook his head at Todd's good fortune. A beautiful wife, daughter, and one on the way. Did Todd realize he had it all?

Trey moved his gaze to the other woman in the photo and reached for his glass. Empty. He studied the half melted orbs of ice. The burning liquid hadn't been enough to numb his senses. He should've refused to come tonight. No job was worth this. The panic in Hailey's eyes had been more than stage fright. An odd mix of anger and sympathy warred within him. He hoped she only saw the anger.

Raising his head, he searched the crowd until he found her standing with his boss. He pulled on his tie to loosen the knot and took a deep breath. Had the hotel staff already turned off the air conditioning? For three years he'd imagined what it would be like to see Hailey again. He planned to appear detached and indifferent. Instead sweat ran down his back and his gut churned.

Hailey shook Senator Bryant's hand and hastened toward a side door with her head down—and the plaque against her chest like a shield.

"Excuse me." Trey pushed through a group of people hovering near the exit. In the hall, she wove her way around the people talking before disappearing around the corner. He hurried to keep her in sight. When he entered the lobby, Trey stopped, frantically scanning the mass of people. She had to be somewhere. He edged around the perimeter. A glimpse of silver slipped into the elevator.

"Hold the elevator, please." He rushed into the elevator, smiled at an older couple, and brushed past Hailey to the back. "Thank you for waiting. I wanted to catch up with my wife." Mirrors decorated the panels and reflected Hailey's pale face. Trey stared at the face in the mirror, willing her to lift her eyes.

"Floor?" The man pointed to the numbered buttons.

Trey glanced at the top number. "Twenty-fourth." The doors whispered to a close and stale air surrounded them. Hailey bit her bottom lip. A nervous habit he remembered so well. Resting his shoulder against the wall, he took in the woman he once knew. By the time his eyes met hers, a blush crept up her neck. The elevator came to a gentle stop. When the doors opened, her defiant eyes met his, and Hailey took a step. Trey gambled that she wouldn't cause a scene.

"Wait, honey." He stepped toward her and wrapped his arm around her waist, pulling her back from the door. "This isn't our floor." He breathed in the familiar scent of her perfume. Her body stiffened under his arm. The doors closed as the other couple turned with questioning eyes.

Trey grinned and shrugged. "We were on the fourteenth floor at the last hotel we stayed in." His years of working with politicians served him well.

The elevator doors slid open at the next floor. Trey smiled at the couple. "Enjoy your evening." The other man nodded before the doors shut.

Silence roared as the elevator moved. Hailey jerked out of his arm and stood in the front corner for a quick escape. Trey forced his body to relax against the back wall again.

"You look great" He sent his gaze from her toes to her head.

She wrapped her arms around her waist, the plaque becoming a familiar shield. "What do you want?"

"It's been a long time." He slowly brought his eyes back to meet hers, raising his eyebrow—hoping she wouldn't see the pain that threatened to overwhelm him. "Can't we catch up?"

A gasp escaped her lips. "Why are you here?"

"Perhaps I wanted to celebrate this evening with my wife. I didn't see anyone else with you, and I wouldn't want you to be alone." He swallowed against the tightness in his throat. "Where is Daddy tonight?"

Hailey's chest rose as her breathing quickened. He tamped down the remorse that crept through him.

"You know it's hard for him to travel."

The doors opened, revealing an empty hall. Trey pressed the button to close the door, then hit the STOP button.

"What do you want, Trey?" Her pulse beat at the hollow of her neck.

"I might not see you for two more years. Better get caught up on the family now, right?" How could he let her walk away from him again? "Todd didn't want to come?"

"His wife's expecting."

"Looks like he has a nice family." They could have had a family if Hailey hadn't left.

She pointed to the elevator controls. "How long are you going to keep me trapped in here? Alarms are probably going off by now."

"We could discuss this in your room."

Her face blanched. "No."

"Are you sure? We have a lot to catch up on."

"I'll ask one more time—what do you want?" Her eyes glistened as she met his gaze.

"I want to move on with my life." The lie escaped his lips. The choking feeling intensified. "If there's no chance for our marriage, then it's time to end this." He couldn't bring himself to say the word. He never imagined he'd be at this place.

Hailey turned her back on him and faced the doors. Her fingers trembled as she gripped the hand rail. "I leave early in the morning."

"I'll have the papers sent to you." He paused, relaxed his clenched hands.

She nodded once.

"You can have the things you left in the apartment. It should be easy." Bile rose in his throat. He focused on the carpet before the pattern blurred.

"An easy divorce." Her voice broke on the ugly word. "That's how every marriage should end." She pushed button fourteen, keeping her back to him.

His senses filled one last time with this woman he had vowed to love until death parted them.

The doors opened for Hailey's escape.

"Why wasn't I enough?" He whispered as she stepped into the hall.

She stopped and turned. The dark eyes that had flashed fear moments before were filled with pain. The grief on her face so strong it took his breath away.

"Send the papers, Trey. I'll sign them."

CHAPTER TWO

Hailey slipped off her heeled sandals, hooked the straps over her fingers, and hurried to her room. A muffled sob escaped her tight throat as she jammed the card into her door and pushed it open. Letting the door swing shut behind her, she tossed the wooden award into her suitcase in the closet and watched as it hit the edge and fell to the floor with a muffled thud.

"Mommy!" Sophie toddled towards her wearing a purple pony nightgown. Her blue eyes sparkled.

Hailey knelt and drew her daughter into her arms, breathing in the smell of her baby shampoo. Tears ran down her cheeks and got lost in her daughter's blonde curls.

"Mommy sad?" The toddler touched a tear on Hailey's cheek.

She wrapped the child into her arms again. "Something must have gotten in my eye." It wasn't a lie. Trey had gotten in her eye. She'd keep the image of him long after she left Washington in the morning. "I'm so glad you're ready for bed."

Across the room, her aunt stood by the window, concern etched on her lined face. "You and your mommy have to wake up early to get to the airport in the morning, don't you, Sophie?"

Hailey rose, her hand trailed through the curls that hung around her daughter's shoulders. "Were you good for Aunt Joni?"

"Of course. She's always good for me, aren't you, sweet girl?"

Aunt Joni tucked a piece of graying dark hair behind her ear, apprehension in her eyes. "We were just getting ready to lie down. Let's let Mommy change and I'll read to you." The older woman pulled the covers down on Sophie's side of the bed.

"Night-night, Mommy." Her child reached up.

Hailey lifted Sophie into her embrace. She sighed as the arms tightened around her neck. "Thank you for being such a good girl tonight," she whispered into Sophie's ear. At least someone in the Williams' family had behaved well.

Hailey turned off the light in the bathroom and stepped into the dark room. Aunt Joni sat by the window, looking out on the city's lights. Pulling her robe tighter, Hailey sank into the other chair and tucked her legs under her.

"Better?" Aunt Joni's question emerged on a barely discernible sigh.

Hailey studied the paths the raindrops made on the outside window, distorting the view. "I can't believe Trey was there tonight."

Aunt Joni pursed her lips. The lines between her brows deepened.

"It's a good thing you kept Sophie up here. All I could think of was how close he was to her. I don't even know if my speech made sense." Hailey rubbed at the growing headache.

Rain beat against the window.

"He has a right to know." Aunt Joni's firm whisper penetrated the dark.

"How could I tell him now?" Hailey's head snapped in her aunt's direction, her hand balling into a fist. "He would–"

"He needs to know."

"He's sending divorce papers." Hailey took a breath to calm her stomach.

"Maybe he'd change his mind if–"

"He would expect to be a part of her life. He'd want her to be with him. Here. He'd take her away from me. I can't live without her, and he'd take her away, just to hurt me."

Aunt Joni shook her head. "You don't know that."

"You didn't see him tonight! He's different. He's angry." Hailey shivered. "Angry at *me*." She took a shuddered breath and voiced the thought she'd kept for so long. "If Trey would have come back one more time he would have known about Sophie." Hailey stole a glance at Aunt Joni who stared into the distance. "You don't understand."

The older woman looked out the window for several moments before she leaned forward and covered Hailey's hand with her own. In the dark of the room, with only the glow of the city beneath them, Hailey could almost pretend her mother sat across from her.

"You won't like what I'm going to say, but your place is with your husband. Not your dad."

Hailey jerked away and moved to the window. She rested her forehead against the cool glass and looked at the distorted car lights on the street below. "What kind of daughter would I have been to leave Dad? He lost Mom and his way of life. Who else could keep the pumpkin patch going? Todd couldn't do everything himself, even if Dad would've let him."

A heavy silence filled the room. Hailey fought to keep her breathing even—trying to calm the nerves that made her stomach hurt. How could she make her aunt understand? Was it possible to make someone comprehend something she did not?

Pushing back from the window, she knelt in front of her aunt and took her hand. "Please, listen. This marriage is out of control. There is no way to stop what's going to happen. It's hopeless. . ." Hailey's voice broke. "But he can't have my daughter."

Joni cupped Hailey's face in her soft hands. "Nothing is hopeless. Not if you are willing to fight."

Frustration boiled. Didn't she get it? "Trey will never forgive me for keeping Sophie from him. Never."

"He might not. It's a lot to forgive. He still has the right to know the truth."

A cold surge of fear rushed through Hailey. "I can't. I can't lose her."

"I'm afraid if you don't tell him, you will lose her." Joni stood and moved to the bed. She took her time to pull back the striped comforter. "You're scared he'll do exactly what you've done to him."

"He can't if he doesn't know."

"Somehow, before the divorce is final, he will find out. I don't know much about law, but I can't imagine that a judge would go easily on you for hiding that kind of information."

Hailey slid to the floor in defeat. Her elbows rested on bent knees and sobs racked her body.

Warm arms wrapped around her. "Oh, Hailey. You've got to trust God with this and do what is right."

Hailey buried her face in her aunt's shoulder. "I don't think I can."

"You can. He wants the best for each of you." Aunt Joni pulled back and smiled through her tears.

How could both she and Trey have God's best? They only had one daughter.

"Good morning," The bed squeaked as Aunt Joni rolled over and stretched out her arms. A sliver of morning light touched her worried face.

Hailey looked up from where she dressed her sleeping daughter on the other bed.

Aunt Joni pulled the blanket around her shoulders. "Did you get any sleep last night?"

Hailey shrugged. "A little, I think. Maybe I'll sleep on the plane." She folded the tiny nightgown and tossed it into the open suitcase on the bed. "I think we're almost ready to leave."

"Have you thought about our conversation last night?"

Hailey sensed her aunt's gaze on her, but she refused to look up. "Yes."

The zipper on the suitcase got stuck on Sophie's swimsuit. Hailey worked to release the fabric without tearing it, grateful for the distraction. The discomfort she felt made her sick. When had she slipped so far away from the faith she'd cherished most of her life? There had been a time when she believed God could take care of any problem, when she trusted Him with everything. She still trusted Him, just not with her daughter.

"What if God takes her from me as punishment?" She pulled the suitcase off the bed. A soft knock at the door brought a sigh of relief. The bellboy had come for their luggage. She propped the door open and pointed at the luggage stacked near the door.

Hailey faced her aunt. "Thank you for meeting us here. I know Sophie had a great time with you, and I loved having you here."

Disappointment shown in Aunt Joni's dark brown eyes. She pushed the covers back and stood. "He needs to know."

Hailey scooped Sophie into her arms. "I don't want to leave with you upset with me."

"Ma'am?" The bellboy spoke from the threshold. "Your taxi's waiting."

Hailey looked over her shoulder at him before turning her attention back to her aunt. "We've got to catch our plane. You'll still come and help with the pumpkin patch this fall?"

"I'll be there in time to help with the wedding at the end of August."

"You'll be alright?"

"I'll be fine. My flight doesn't leave until after lunch." Aunt Joni stood and embraced Hailey and Sophie. "I love you, Hailey. Like my own daughter. That won't change. But I cannot agree with you."

Hailey closed her eyes to hold back the tears that threatened. "I love you, too. I just can't do what you're asking."

CHAPTER THREE

Trey rolled onto his back, groaning as he stretched the cramped muscles that tightened with each move. The arm of the sofa had served as his pillow for the few hours he slept, leaving him with a stiff neck and a pounding headache. He rubbed the sleep from his eyes and hoped the previous evening had been a dream. The fact that he still had on his clothes assured him it hadn't been.

He picked up the wedding photo on the coffee table. Last night he'd brought it out from the bedroom, longing to find some sign of what had gone wrong. Even in the early morning light, he saw nothing but love shining from their young faces. Had they married too early? Their parents had wanted him to finished law school first, but he and Hailey thought they had waited long enough.

A knock at the door startled him. Neighbors rarely came by for a missing ingredient since it was public knowledge that he kept very few food items fresh—or even edible—in his kitchen. Mrs. Nelson had probably locked herself out again. Trey set the photo on the couch.

"Just a minute." He tried to smooth the wrinkles out of his pale green shirt. The more he pulled and pressed the worse the shirt looked. The knock came again.

"I'm coming." He reached for the door. "Good morning, Mrs.–"

The smile Trey had ready for his seventy-year-old neighbor froze on his face. "Joni."

"May I come in?"

He let the door swing open and groaned as he looked around the room and saw everything he wished he'd put away before opening the door. The blanket, his tie and coat thrown over the top of the kitchen chair, the wedding picture.

She closed the door behind her. "I won't ask how you slept." Joni looked sympathetic. Dark circles shadowed her eyes. "Can we talk for a few minutes?"

Trey moved into the kitchen and pulled out a chair for her. He felt like an actor in a lousy movie. He pointed toward the single cup coffee maker. "Coffee?" He needed a cup to clear the fog from his brain.

"If you're having some." Joni set her purse on the chair beside her.

A thousand thoughts raced through his head while he waited for the two cups to brew. The silence grew heavier with each passing second. Setting a steaming cup down in front of his uninvited guest, he moved to the chair across from her. He studied her as she turned the cup in her hands, wishing he felt as calm as she appeared.

"How'd you find me?"

"I took a chance that you hadn't moved." The cup continued to turn. "Jenny and I visited you and Hailey right after you moved here."

Trey nodded slowly. He preferred not to acknowledge any remembrance of those years.

Joni closed her eyes for a moment before she spoke. "Hailey said you were at the banquet last night."

He nodded.

"You want a divorce?"

Another nod. "I never thought I'd be divorced. But I can't compete with Jim."

"You knew the kind of man he was before you married her." Joni lifted the mug to her lips, watching him over the rim.

"Yes, but Hailey had wanted to get away from that."

"I'm not making an excuse, and Jim has always been a hard man, but he's lost a lot. Losing his firstborn right as Brandon was becoming an adult knocked the wind out of him. But Jenny worked hard to bring him through that. When he lost her and the use of his legs it hardened his heart even more. Hailey believes she's the only thing holding that family together. Maybe you could have been more compassionate."

Trey rubbed the back of his neck. "More compassionate? Between the weekend of the wreck and July Fourth, I made seven trips back to Kansas. On every trip but one, I stayed in a hotel alone while Hailey slept at the hospital so she could be closer to Jim. In case he needed anything."

"You should have gone back again."

Trey focused on the bitter coffee in his mug. "I gave Hailey a ticket to come back with me. She accused me of trying to control her." His breath caught on the words. He closed his eyes against the flood of hurt. "She said she needed time and she'd call me when she felt ready to talk. I left with the senator that next week and I had to be out of the country for months working on a foreign trade bill. I called so many times, but Jim finally answered and told me she wasn't ready to come back and to leave her alone."

Joni took a deep breath and lifted the mug to her mouth for a quick sip. "Trey, there's more that you don't know, things you haven't seen. Don't send those papers until you do."

Trey leaned back in his chair. "What don't I know?"

"I've said more than anyone would want me to. Believe me though, Trey. You need to go back before you do anything."

Trey's chair scraped across the floor as he stood. He took three steps to the counter and dumped his coffee down the drain. Turning, he found Joni behind him. He took her cup and poured it out.

"Is this some type of game we're playing now?" He kept his back to her, hands gripping the edge of the sink. "Now that I want out of this marriage, I'm supposed to go back to Kansas? Are you kidding me?"

"This isn't a game. It seems to me if you would have gone back to Kansas before now, you probably wouldn't be getting a divorce." She kept her voice even and quiet.

Trey whirled around and glared at her. His insides quivered in anger. "This is my fault?"

Joni met his gaze. "I think both of you have shown how stubborn you can be." She looped her purse over her shoulder and walked to the door. "I'd better go. Thank you for the coffee."

"That's it? You're leaving?"

Joni turned and faced him. "Trey, I came to tell you that you don't have the whole story. I'm not playing games, and Hailey would disown me if she knew I was here. Honestly, it will take a miracle to save your marriage, but there are things you have the right to know before you end everything." She pulled the door open.

"I'm leaving in the morning with Senator Bryant. We'll be overseas for a week." Why had he told her that?

Keeping her hand on the door, she looked over her shoulder. Her smile never reached her eyes. "Have a safe trip."

The door closed, leaving his apartment empty. Trey returned to the kitchen and slumped down in the wooden chair.

What did he have the right to know? He couldn't imagine anything that would change his mind, but the shock it would give Hailey if he showed up might be worth the trip.

Dry brown grass rustled over the Kansas prairie, testimony to the lack of rain since early spring. Heat waves shimmered above the silver ribbon of highway stretching towards the horizon.

"Come on." Hailey chewed on her bottom lip. "Just get us

home." Her brown Explorer jerked as she pressed on the gas pedal. "You can't go out now." A silver sports car shot around her and honked. "I can't help it!" She smacked the steering wheel and glared at the receding vehicle.

The SUV slowed on its own as it chugged down the road. Hailey guided it onto the gravel shoulder and turned the key to off.

A hot, late July wind rushed through the open windows.

"You okay, honey?" Hailey turned to peek at her daughter, strapped into her carseat in the middle of the back seat. "Welcome home, right?"

"Home, home." Sophie giggled and pushed against the straps of her carseat.

"Just wait, okay? Mommy will call Uncle Todd to come help us." When he didn't answer, she left a message. That only left her dad to help. She pressed his name in her contact list and listened to it ring. Where was everyone? She left a message on his phone, too.

"Well, Sophie girl, what do we do now?" She laid her head on the steering wheel and tried to think. Who else should she call? They were only fifteen miles from home, but she couldn't keep Sophie in this heat for long.

The phone chimed, and Dad's number popped on the screen. She sighed and hit the accept button. "Hi, Dad. I can't get a hold of Todd."

"Ellen had a doctor's appointment today, and he thought he needed to go to with her." His voice was gruff with annoyance. "Grant is here delivering some seed. He said he'd come and get you."

"I don't want to bother him. Maybe Todd can pick us up when he goes by. We could get the Explorer later." She wasn't ready to see their neighbor.

"We don't have time to go back for it later, Hailey. Grant offered to bring his trailer. He'll get it loaded and bring you home." Dad left no room for argument. Would she always feel like a child when she talked with her father?

"Okay, thanks." She ended the call and tossed the phone onto the passenger seat. It had been just over two years since the accident. One day had changed every part of the life she knew. Dad had always lived with high expectations. His whole life revolved around the farm, and he expected his family to feel the same way. There wasn't a man in Hartford County who worked harder than he did. He demanded that his fields be planted and harvested before any other farm around. If they weren't first to the CO-OP during harvest, it was an embarrassment. Hailey heard the comments from other farmers and secretly agreed—if Jim Harper could, he'd be farming a year ahead of everyone else.

The car accident had taken more than just Mom. Her dad had also been lost that day. Just like the pumpkins they grew, he had become a hard, tough shell—hollow on the inside.

They kept the farm going, but she lost her marriage, dearest friend, and Sophie's father. Would she ever come to believe it had been worth the cost?

"Welcome back." Grant Thurston walked to the stalled vehicle and smiled at the woman inside. Relief filled him. He'd argued for weeks with Jim that she shouldn't go to Washington alone. Not out of concern for her safety. She'd lived in D.C. for several years. But what if she ran into her no-account husband? None of those concerns mattered now. She was home.

He opened the squeaky door and grinned. "If I'd known I was the greeting party for the National Farm Family of the Year recipient, I'd have cleaned up a little."

Hailey glanced at his dusty work clothes before meeting his gaze. "I've seen enough suits to last me a long time." Her smile didn't diminish the sadness in her eyes.

"Good trip?"

She nodded. "It's good to be home. Thanks for coming to get us. Right, Sophie?"

"Go home." The child's sweet voice squealed from the back seat.

"Hey, little lady." Grant opened the back door. "Let's get you out of this hot car." He slid the car seat toward him and pulled the child out. Thin arms stretched around his neck. Her warm breath played across his cheek. Instinctively he hugged her tighter. He might not be allowed to show her mother how he felt, but nothing could stop him from sharing his love with this little girl. "You've been gone too long, Sophie. I think you've grown into a young lady." He kissed her cheek.

A grin covered her face when she leaned back to look at him. She jabbered something he couldn't understand.

"Will we be able to drive that old thing onto the trailer?" He shot a teasing grin at Hailey as he strode across the hot asphalt to settle Sophie in the truck. "Think your momma will ever get a new car?"

"I heard that." Hailey hollered from behind him. "This is still a great vehicle."

Grant strapped the carseat into the backseat of the cab. "You know, eventually, a new vehicle will cost less than fixing that thing."

"Probably, but I doubt it's anything too costly."

He turned around to see if she really believed what she said. " Costly? Hailey, it's probably the transmission. I've been telling you that for weeks."

She winced.

"Let me talk to your dad. He'll agree if I tell him. We can go tomorrow and find you a car that's reliable." He pushed his cap farther back on his head. "I don't mind rescuing beautiful ladies, but what if I'm not around next time?"

Hailey returned to the vehicle and paused with her hand on the driver's door. "You don't know that it's anything serious, right? Until I know it can't be fixed, I'm going to wait. Now, do you want me to drive this up or will you?"

Grant pulled the ramps down and bit his tongue. It wouldn't make a difference if he argued with her. He'd lost count of the times he'd suggested replacing the old clunker. The cost of a vehicle didn't prevent her from buying a new one. She wouldn't let go of the memories the old one represented.

He shrugged. "Go ahead. You seem to be able to do everything by yourself." He let the second ramp fall to the ground with a thud and moved out of her way. The sun reflected off the windshield making it impossible to see her in the driver's seat. When the engine didn't start, he jogged up to the car door. "Won't it start?"

"You do it." She slid out from behind the wheel and stalked to his truck..

He shook his head as she climbed in. "Women... Life has got to be easier without them."

As soon as he had the Explorer loaded and strapped down, he joined Sophie and Hailey in the truck. Hailey kept her face toward the window so he looked back at Sophie who rewarded him with a big smile.

"Did you have fun, Sophie? Did you meet the president?" Grant pulled out onto the road and smiled as the little girl chattered in her own language. She carried the conversation for several miles with an occasional word from him.

"You really think I have to do everything by myself?" Hailey finally broke her silence.

Grant glanced at her. Maybe he should have considered the comment before he spoke. "I think you've worked hard to show your independence."

"And you think that's wrong?" She continued to stare out the window.

"I didn't say it was wrong, but it might not hurt if you let me help you and Sophie more."

"That's not your place."

He squeezed the steering wheel in frustration. As long as she wore that wedding ring, it wasn't his place. But what happened to the man who gave her the ring? Changing the subject would be easier than continuing on this line. "Did you have a good trip?"

"We did. We loved having Aunt Joni there. She reminds me so much of Mom."

"See anything special or historical?" He smiled when she grinned at him.

"We spent an entire day at the Smithsonian and didn't see everything. That place is amazing."

"How was the banquet? Did your speech go well?"

She fell silent again. Tension filled the cab.

He shot a quick glance to the serious look on her face. "Did you forget what you wanted to say? Or trip going up the steps?"

"No, I didn't trip. I was nervous, so it didn't go as well as I'd hoped." She gave him a little smile. "But it's over now. The plaque is in my bag, and I'm glad to be home."

If she was so glad to be home, why'd she seem so sad? He pulled into the drive of Harper Farms. Gray metal buildings of varying sizes stood against the backdrop of trees that separated the buildings from the fields of growing pumpkins. Colorful blooms and green textured leaves outlined the base of each building in an explosion of yellow, orange, and burgundy chrysanthemums. As usual, the neat appearance of the place sent a rush of pride. He stopped in front of the shed where they kept the tractors.

"Some things never change." She pointed to the shop entrance. Jim sat in his wheelchair with a scowl darkening his face, and Todd rushed around the swather, making adjustments. "Do you think if Brandon was still here those two would get along better?"

Grant stretched his arm across the seat and rubbed the back of her neck. The image of his best friend at nineteen crossed his mind. Even this many years after the accident he still wondered daily what he could have done differently. "I think if Brandon was here Todd would have found his own way in the world."

Hailey gathered her bags from around her feet. "I didn't miss being the mediator between the two while I was gone." She slid out of the cab. "Thanks for helping us out."

Grant lifted Sophie from her seat and set her on the ground. He followed her to the shop. The little girl ran and climbed onto Jim's lifeless legs while Hailey leaned down to hug her dad.

"Thanks for bringing the girls home." Jim spoke through Sophie's hair that blew across his face. "It's nice to know I can depend on someone."

Grant glanced at the younger man. Todd's nostrils flared as his lips pressed together in a tight line. "If I had a pregnant wife, I wouldn't have been here today either."

"You would have been." Jim squinted his eyes while jabbing his finger at Grant. "You're like Brandon. He knew what running this place took."

"Don't you want to see the award?" Hailey dug through her bag with shaking hands. The plaque caught on the handle. She jerked it loose and held it in front of her. "See?"

Todd slapped an allen wrench in Grant's hand. "Since you're so much like Brandon, make yourself useful and check the blades."

"I thought you might like to keep this up here." Hailey strode into the gloomy room and stood beside her dad's chair. The heavy curtains had been pulled since the day she'd brought Dad home from the hospital. The evening news blared from the television.

Jim reached for the glossy wood plaque and held it in front of him. "You had a good time?"

"We did. Thanks for letting Aunt Joni join us." She sat on the edge of the couch. "She'll be here in a couple of weeks."

"I don't know why you think she needs to come. We'd get along fine without her." His grey eyes challenged her to argue.

"She likes to come, and I like having her around. I guess she reminds me of Mom."

"Joni's nothing like your mom. Joni is headstrong, opinionated, and stubborn."

Why had she said anything about Mom? Hailey swallowed a protest. "Sophie had a fun time. She made a great little tourist."

"That's good." He stared at the screen.

Some days she wished she could throw out the TV. How many times in the last two years had that box replaced any conversation she might have with her father? If he wanted to tell her something, he demanded her undivided attention. He, on the other hand, never thought she had anything worth giving his attention to.

Defeat crept in. Hailey shuffled to the doorway.

"It's good you're back." Dad spoke from behind her. "Todd can't run this place without your help."

She froze. "He could if you'd give him a chance."

"He needs to grow up. Be a man, like his brother."

She turned and glared at the back of Dad's gray head of hair. "He needs to be his own person. Brandon died when he was nineteen. How do you know what kind of man he'd have become?"

"I know what kind of man Brandon would have been, and I know what kind of man Todd is." Dad's voice lowered to a dangerous calm. "He needs to be pushed or he won't accomplish a thing." He reached for the remote and turned up the volume on the TV.

She ground a fisted hand into the wooden door frame. "I'm going to bed." Hailey hurried down the hall to the steps, determined to ignore any other comments he might make. But no raging followed, and she paused at the stairs, unsure whether his silence surprised her or if it frightened her.

CHAPTER FOUR

Hailey straightened from her bent over position at the work shed table and eyed the colorful wooden sign critically. DON'T GET CORN-FUSED. STAY ON THE PATH. The orange background made the letters stand out, but they wouldn't guarantee anyone would read it. Every year she wanted to cry when she saw the damage made by those cutting across the corn maze in search of a quick exit.

Had she really been home two weeks? The trip, award, and Trey seemed like a lifetime away. Well, maybe not Trey. He remained an open wound, a hurt that grew daily, knowing the deceit she harbored.

She turned her attention back to the sign. The scarecrow's overalls still needed to be painted blue. Rubbing the cramp from the small of her back, she twisted enough to see her father come through the open double doors of the wood framed building.

"Need something?" She pushed her brush into the plastic cup of water.

"This came today." His chair rolled to a stop next to her. A farm magazine hit the table beside the painted board.

Photos from the awards banquet last week lay before her. "Did you read the article yet?"

"Just the caption under those two photos." He pointed to the one of her and Senator Bryant talking and another of the senator at his table. "You never mentioned Senator Bryant being there." He tapped the photo of the man sitting beside the Senator. "Was he there, too?"

Hailey reached up and pushed a curl off her forehead. The knot that had been a constant companion in her stomach since returning home constricted. Foolishness made her think she could keep that information to herself. Lifting the brush from the cup, she turned back to the board and reached for the bottle of blue paint.

"Did you talk with him?" Her father's fierce glare demanded an answer.

She squirted a blob of paint onto the Styrofoam plate. "For a few minutes."

"Where was Sophie?" An edge of fear wove through his terseness.

"With Aunt Joni. In the hotel room."

"What did he say?"

"Daddy..." She sighed and gave him her full attention. "I don't want to talk about it. Please just leave it alone, okay?"

"Hailey, he's never coming back here. Men like him have dreams that don't include anyone but themselves. This is where you belong. As much as I'm against divorce, it's time for you to do something. Get on with your life. You can bet he has."

The image of Trey in the elevator filled her thoughts. She turned back to her project, blocking the tears that threatened from her father's prying eyes. "I'll think about it."

"Honey, I know you don't want to break the vows you took, but there are times when it's okay. You know, if you two would've listened, it would have saved you all this heartache. You should have married Grant. He's a part of this family and understands what the land is all about."

Her fingernails dug into the palm of her clenched hand. She tried to focus on the pain rather than the rising anger that tightened her chest. She didn't want Sophie to see her crying again. "Where is Sophie? I thought you were watching her."

Dad looked around the building. "She asked to come out here with you."

Hailey put down the brush. "I'll go find her." The door seemed miles away as she hurried to put distance between them.

"Sophie?" She hollered as she ran down the path to the fish pond. Only weeds dotted the banks around the pond. If Sophie was outside, their faithful collie, Zoe, would be with her. The dog gave Hailey a measure of peace. Zoe always guarded Sophie if she managed to slip away from them.

"Sophie? Zoe?" She stopped to listen. A sharp bark sounded from behind the house, and relief flooded her. Hailey jogged up a different path that led behind the food building. Another bark from Zoe encouraged her to continue through the backyard.

"Sophie? Zoe?" A bark came from the other side of their personal driveway. Once past the house, she saw the black and white dog standing on her back legs, front paws clawing up the old tree.

"Is she up there?" Hailey scratched Zoe on the head and looked up at the old treehouse. "Sophie, are you up there?" Could she even climb that high? Sophie's cherub face, outlined with soft curls, peeked down from the weathered wooden railing.

"No-no, Mama."

Hailey climbed the rickety ladder, gaze fixed on her daughter. "Get away from the ladder, Sophie. Mommy will get you." Her legs threatened to give out. What if she hadn't found her this soon?

"No-no."

Hailey grabbed the railing and pulled herself onto the deck. She knelt down and reached for Sophie. "Oh, Sophie! You scared Mommy so much." Hailey breathed into the baby-fine hair. "Don't ever go away from Mommy or Poppa."

"Zo-Zo." Sophie turned her head and smiled into Hailey's eyes.

"No, Zo-Zo can't help you down. You don't leave again. Do you understand?"

"Bad no-no." Sophie pulled her arm free and pointed in the door.

"What?" Hailey leaned back on her heels and studied the child. "What's in there?"

Sophie's small hand wrapped around Hailey's and pulled her through the door. Sophie pointed to a spot beneath the window. "No-no."

Hailey looked at the spot that had captured Sophie's attention. Tears blurred her vision. She moved to the board and touched the carved words with her paint-stained finger tips.

BUILT BY HAILEY AND TREY. BEST FRIENDS.

Her eyes closed as the memory of that day washed over her.

Trey held the board with one hand while trying to grab the hammer from her. "You hammer like a girl. I could have had this treehouse finished hours ago."

"And it would've fallen apart by now." She swiped at the hair that blew into her face when she glanced up at him. "You just don't want to admit that I'm doing as well as a boy. Or better, even."

"Hardly." A teasing smile softened the word. "It's a good thing we're finishing up today. I don't think your dad likes me being around so much."

Hailey gave the nail one more pound and stood up. "Looks pretty good to me." She leaned back on the rail she'd just finished. A flat roof, two windows, hole for the door, and a deck completed the project they had worked on each evening for the past two weeks.

Trey gripped the railing with one hand while pulling her away from the edge with the other. "I'm not sure I'd trust our work quite that much."

"You mean like this?" She jerked away and leaned out over the rail.

"Cut it out. You're gonna hurt yourself." He edged against the solid wooden structure and folded his arms. "You're crazy, Hailey Harper." His smile warmed her. "Let's eat those cookies your mom brought out." Trey's twelve-year-old body sprawled on the floor inside the little hut. The smell of fresh pine boards mixed with the aroma of homemade chocolate chip cookies.

Hailey reached over and took the cookie he offered and sat down across from him. "This is great! We can put a table in here and do our homework. I hear Mrs. Nelson really lays it on in seventh grade. You can ride your bike over and we'll do it together. Don't you think?"

"Fine with me."

She stretched out on the uneven boards and put her hands behind her head. "Look at what we did, Trey. This is so cool. We should make a sign or have a plaque made that says"—she held up her hand and pretended to write the words in the air—"'Trey and Hailey built this.' Oh, and the date. What do you think? That way everyone will know it's ours."

"We could just scratch it into one of these boards with a nail." He pulled a nail from his shorts pocket and looked around. "Where should it go?"

"Right there." She pointed at the board below the window.

Trey worked for several minutes carving the information into the new wood. When he finished, he stood back and let Hailey studied the inscription.

"There's just one thing missing." She jumped up and yanked the nail from his fingers.

She finished and stepped back. A smile covered his face as he read her addition—BEST FRIENDS.

A tug on Hailey's hand brought her to the present.

"Bad." Sophie touched the words.

With the back of her hand Hailey brushed at the tears running down her cheeks. "It's okay. Just in here." Her fingers traced over the other words listed beneath Trey's nail-scratched words. Each line held a book full of memories that Hailey fought to keep closed.

"Hailey? You up there?" Concern edged Todd's voice.

She jerked away from the board and picked up her daughter. "I found Sophie."

"You need to get down here. You've got a visitor."

Todd's tone filled her with dread. Glancing over the railing, she saw the sheriff's car at the edge of the drive. With one arm wrapped around Sophie, she moved down the ladder.

Her brother stood with his fists planted at his hips. Beside him the county sheriff, Will Hastings, looked away when Hailey's gaze met his.

"Somehow this little scamp made it up into the treehouse on her own." Nervousness made her prattle. "What brings you out here, Will? Come to help us get ready for opening weekend?"

Will shook his head and smiled. "'Fraid I'm on duty for the rest of the day. Otherwise, I'd be more than happy to come out." He nodded toward the field behind the tree where bright orange pumpkins dotted the bed of foliage. "It's looking real good. Think you'll be ready by the middle of September?"

"We'd better be." She lowered Sophie to the ground and smiled when the child grabbed hold of Todd's jean covered legs. "Is there something else you wanted to talk to us about?"

The gray haired man cleared his throat and looked at the ground before speaking. "Actually, Hailey, I'm here to talk with you." He glanced up at Todd.

Todd nodded. In one swoop, he picked up Sophie and swung her onto his broad shoulders. "Let's go find something to drink, Sophie-girl. Good to see you, Will. Come out opening weekend and we'll give you a pass." His eyes relayed unspoken concern.

"Might just do that. Thanks for the invite." Will watched the two walk away. "Cute little girl you've got." He turned to her, his face pinched into lines of regret. "Sometimes there are parts of this job that make me want to quit. This is one of them." He reached for the envelope sticking out of his shirt pocket. "I'm here to serve these papers to you, Hailey."

She stared, unable to raise her hand high enough to accept the packet. Loneliness and shame melded together and wrapped around her like a suffocating blanket. Tears burned her eyes as she bit her bottom lip to stop its quivering.

Will cleared his throat again. "I'm sorry it's come to this. I'll admit, when you and Trey got married, Ruth and I figured you two would make it."

Her hand shook as he laid the envelope in her palm. She read the name of the law office listed in the left hand corner.

He sniffed. "I'd guess the last couple of years haven't helped much."

The kindness in his voice broke her silence. "I wish I knew if I've made the best choices." Her thumb caressed the typed lettering, spelling out her name for the world to see.

"It's none of my business, but a man who doesn't fight harder for his wife and daughter isn't much of a husband and father."

Hailey's head jerked up at the harsh words and fought the urge to defend Trey and his ignorance concerning Sophie. "We're probably both responsible for this." She waved the envelope between them. "I'm rather new to these kinds of situations. Do I thank you for coming by?"

The corners of the man's mouth turned up. "You've already been more polite than most of the responses I receive. I'm real sorry, Hailey." He paused. "You two had something special."

"Things happened that neither of us expected. Thank you for coming."

Will squeezed her shoulder then turned to walk back to his car. The weight of the letter in her hand increased with each step he took.

Memories called her back to the treehouse. Unable to resist, she climbed the ladder once more. Kneeling beneath the window, her tears fell. With shaky fingers she traced the other words scratched into the wood plank.

SENIOR PROM 4-21-02
FIRST KISS 4-22-02
ENGAGED 12-31-08
MARRIED 6-23-09

Did one add divorce to the list? Or just put a big X through the others, crossing them out like an un-erasable mistake?

"Trey, I'd like to see you in my office before you leave." Senator Bryant's voice echoed through the empty room.

Trey grabbed a notebook and followed him. "I thought you had a school recital tonight."

Rob Bryant looked at his watch and grimaced. "I'm leaving as soon as we finish here. Mallory doesn't play until the second half, so I should be fine." He pulled a file toward him. "Kevin has suggested we need to get a new commercial out. Something that's more down-home and will resonate with the voters."

"I glanced over the polls this morning and things look good for you to beat Kline."

"I hope we can sustain that lead." Senator Bryant opened the folder but continued to look at Trey. "I suggested looking into Harper Farms and Pumpkin Patch as our filming location."

Trey bit his tongue and looked at the wall behind the Senator's shoulder. He had to keep from showing any emotion. "I'm sure it would look good on film."

Senator Bryant raised his eyebrows. "I'm not sure they'd welcome us after your reaction to Ms. Harper last week."

Trey shifted in the leather chair before meeting the eyes of his boss. "She isn't Ms. Harper. Her name is Hailey Williams."

Senator Bryant rocked back in his chair, staring at Trey. After several drawn out seconds he leaned forward with his elbows on the desk and tented his fingers under his chin. "As in Mrs. Trey Williams?"

"For seven years." The admission twisted his insides.

"I've wondered when your estranged wife would surface." Sympathy showed on the Senator's face. "What happened?"

"Hailey went home for her brother's graduation the spring I came on staff. She was driving her parent's car and another car ran the intersection. The accident killed her mom and left her dad paralyzed. Between her grief and his manipulation, she never came back."

"I'm sorry." Senator Bryant shook his head. "Would you rather we find some other place? You wouldn't have to be a part of this. I'd send someone else to make arrangements and scout out the place."

Trey stared at the lamp on the desk and considered his next words. "You can't let my personal life interfere with your campaign. Actually, I need to go back. Check out a few things before we finalize the divorce. This would give me a reason to be there."

Senator Bryant angled his head. "You might also ruin any chance of us filming there."

"Jim Harper will see the value of having his business in your commercials."

"How many days do you need?"

"A few. I could be back the first part of next week. Maybe earlier."

"Let me know what you get planned." The senator pushed back from the desk. "I'm sorry about your marriage. I wouldn't have twisted your arm to go the other night if I'd have known."

"It helped to force some issues. The time has come to admit defeat and move on."

Senator Bryant stood and reached for his brief case. "Let me know your itinerary for the next few days."

Trey followed him to the door.

Senator Bryant stopped short and turned. "Washington is hard on marriages—even the ones we think are strong. Let me know if I can do anything to help."

Hailey grabbed the stack of envelopes from her cluttered desk in the kitchen of the food building and hurried to the door. A blast of hot, dry air hit her face when she stepped outside.

"Hailey, wait." Todd yelled from the shop across the drive. "I can drop the mail off in town later."

"That's okay. I'll just run it out to the box." She didn't want him to hear the panic speeding her pulse. If she could get to the mailbox right before the mailman came by, no one would know about the manila envelope addressed to the law firm in Washington.

She pushed questions from her mind. This was the best place for her and Sophie. Here Sophie had acres of land to roam. The highway that ran to the west of Harper Farms brought thousands of strangers to their place each fall, but the white iron fence bordering the property kept the boundaries well defined. Here, neighbors weren't just unknown people next door. They were your community, your family. She had made the best choice for them.

The orange and red floral bursts of color seemed to mock her as she walked towards the limestone-lined, raised flower beds on each side of the driveway entrance. Every week gardeners spent hours tending to these plants and watering them, working to keep them alive until the first visitors would arrive the second weekend in September. Three more weeks and the pumpkin patch would be officially open, and Harper Farms would look beautiful dressed in its fall colors.

She glanced at her watch. Just a few minutes before the mailman would drive up. It amazed her as a child that he came at the same time each day. Nothing changed. She could still set her watch by the mailman. Hailey sat on the edge of the flowerbed and pulled the brown envelope from the pile and slid her finger under the loose flap.

"Ouch!" Her hand jerked back as bright red blood formed a thin line across the top of her index finger. What would Preston, Howard, and Moore think if she left blood all over the envelope? Would they understand that a part of her had died when she signed her name on those lines? The papers eased from the envelope and she read them once more with her finger in her mouth.

Trey said it would be an easy divorce. But he if he knew about Sophie, things would never be easy for any of them. Hailey pushed the papers back into the envelope and licked the flap.

"Those for me, Hailey?"

She jolted. The blue Jeep, with its familiar driver inside, sat at the mailbox. How had he arrived without her realizing it? "Yes, they are." She stood and hurried forward. "My mind was somewhere else, and I wasn't paying attention."

"That's all right." He reached out the window. "Sure looks good around here. I can't imagine the gallons of water you folks put on this place to keep it looking like this all summer."

"It's good we have our own wells or we wouldn't be able too. People appreciate the flowers and the green grass almost as much as the pumpkins by the middle of September."

"Well, it looks really nice. My wife comments on it every time we drive by."

"Thanks, Mr. Olson. Have a good day." Hailey step away from the Jeep.

"Uh, Hailey, did you want me to take those letters from you?" He chuckled softly.

She looked at the envelopes clasped in her hands and forced a laugh. "I guess I forgot."

"Thanks." He pulled the mail from her hand and waved. "Enjoy your day."

The Jeep eased onto the pavement. Hailey took a deep breath and exhaled. She'd done it. Tears filled her eyes. The brake lights on the vehicle lit up. Slowly, it backed to where she waited. Hailey wiped the tears off her cheeks.

Mr. Olson pulled into the drive with a smile on his face and held out the manila envelope. "Just noticed this one doesn't have any postage on it."

Hailey grabbed the package and pulled it to her, hoping he hadn't read the address. "I guess I was in too big of a hurry to get the mail out here this morning. I'll take care of it later when I go to town."

"I don't mind taking it now if you want to send some money along."

"It's fine, really." She gave a small wave to send him on his way. "I have to run in for milk."

CHAPTER FIVE

The chatter around the long table in the Windsor Café changed quicker than the town's only blinking light. Self-proclaimed experts on a multitude of topics filled the chairs each morning.

"What do you think, Grant? You're mighty quiet down there."

Grant glanced up from his half-eaten stack of pancakes to find the over-seventy audience looking at him. "What do I think about what? The president? Friday night's game? The price of corn? A guy can't keep up with all the wisdom in this room."

The men laughed then launched into the next subject on their ever-changing discussion list.

It was an honor to be included at the table. These men had welcomed him to sit every morning since he'd come home from college twelve years ago. Each lined face told a story of hard work—of making a life for their families off the land.

Jingling bells above the door announced the arrival of a newcomer, silencing the nine men around Grant's table. No greetings were called out. No sound of scraping chairs moving to make room. Just silence. Even with his back to the door, he knew that whoever had just come in wasn't a regular. He always felt sorry for the person who chose to eat at the local diner. Did anything scream "outsider" more than silence?

The men resumed their conversation. Grant put another forkful of pancakes in his mouth and reached for his coffee cup when a gentle nudge pushed against his boot. He looked across the table at Ken Bartel, his former seventh grade math teacher. Over the years of eating breakfast here, Grant's appreciation had grown for the older man's quiet comments and good humor. This morning, concern showed in Ken's gray eyes as he leaned over the table.

"I think you'll be interested in seeing who just came in."

Grant put down his cup and nonchalantly surveyed the room. The pancakes stuck in his throat. Turning back to the table he pushed the plate of uneaten food away. He took a drink of coffee, welcoming the hot liquid that burned all the way down. "What's he doing here?" Grant met the older man's gaze, which conveyed more sympathy than Grant would've liked.

Ken shrugged. "Guess the only way to know is to go and ask him."

The scrape of his chair across the floor grabbed the attention of several men.

"Leaving already?" the one beside him asked.

"Marybeth looks busy so I thought I'd get my own refill." He reached for his cup and moved to the front of the room. The coffee pot shook as he poured. Words and emotions collided inside him—what should he say? Time ran out when he turned and found the smiling face and proffered hand of the man he wished gone.

"Grant, it's good to see you. Have time to join me?"

He met the man's grip and forced a polite smile. "Trey Williams. What brings you back to Windsor?"

Only a corpse could miss the exasperation radiating from the man across the table. Regardless of Grant's attitude, Trey appreciated seeing a familiar face. In any city he visited, it never bothered him to walk into a restaurant alone. Here, the patrons of the only diner in town had let him know he was a stranger. It might be better if they kept thinking of him that way. Otherwise he might be sent out of town tarred and feathered.

Grant had been in college when Trey and Hailey started dating. Trey realized the first time he met Grant that he filled the gaping hole after Brandon's death. Surrogate son and big brother. What brought him back to Windsor? Trey wished he knew. "Mostly business. Still farming with your dad?"

"He retired last fall, but he comes out daily. Where're your folks now?"

"They live in a small town outside of Colorado Springs. That church has been good for Dad."

Grant's wary stare never wavered as he took a drink of coffee. "What kind of business do you have here?"

"Bryant's looking for a place to shoot a new campaign ad."

"And you're just passing through."

"Sorry this took so long." The waitress's approach gave Trey time to think. How much did he want to tell this man?

The waitress set a plate in front of him and reached over and poured coffee into both their cups. Her eyes twinkled when she smiled at Grant. "I saw you had to get your own refill, Grant. If you'd settle down and marry that cute neighbor of yours, you wouldn't have to wait on my poor service every day. Let me know if you need anything else."

Trey shoved his plate to the middle of the table. Hunger gave way to a flood of heavy anger. Elbows on the table, he tented his fingers in front of him and glared at the other man. Grant had the decency to look uncomfortable. "Someone new moved in?"

Grant's eyes flashed. "Why don't you divorce her and let everyone get on with their lives?"

Trey paused. It appeared Grant wasn't aware that the papers had been served earlier in the week to Hailey. If she hadn't told Grant, he certainly wouldn't be the one to share the news.

"Anything going on between you and my wife that would make me think I should divorce her?" The question made him sick.

"You don't know Hailey at all if you have to ask that."

"She's the one who left me."

"They deserve so much better than you."

"They have been the problem. What happened to leaving your father and becoming one with your husband? Jim Harper deserves nothing from me." Years of resentment boiled inside him.

Disgust covered the other man's face. "What kind of man doesn't even acknowledge his own–" Grant's jaw hung open on the last word, shock flooding his features. He grabbed his cup and took a long drink.

"My own wife? I came back two years ago and tried to convince her to come home with me. She couldn't leave her dad, and Daddy did nothing but encourage her to stay here." He slid out of the booth and pulled out his wallet. Throwing a ten dollar bill on the table, he bent over to look directly into Grant's eyes. "It's a good thing you live a mile away from Harper farms. When our divorce is final, and you can finally marry her, you'll be close enough to visit her daddy anytime she wants."

The clanging bells reverberated through the diner, marking Trey's departure. Grant leaned back in the booth and looked around the room. The six-thirty crowd changed into the eight o'clock group as one man after another left, only to be replaced by a new one.

What had Hailey done? Did Trey even know he had a daughter?

"Your friend left mighty quick." Marybeth held the glass coffee pot and motioned toward his cup. "Refill?"

"No, thanks." His stomach churned with this new information.

"Things looked pretty tense over here." She put the ten dollar bill in her pocket and reached for the plate of uneaten food. "He didn't even take a bite. You scare him off?"

Grant could imagine how quickly the news of Trey's visit would spread and grow if he said anything. Twenty months ago, an outcry of sympathy greeted the birth of Sophie Harper Williams. How could the father not even show up? What kind of man did that? The breakfast groups had discussed the issue thoroughly for days. Without the presence of the defendant, Trey had been tried, convicted, and sentenced in this café courtroom.

How quickly would the tide of sympathy turn if Hailey had indeed never told Trey about the baby?

CHAPTER SIX

Hydraulic fluid sprayed from the broken hose, covering the back window of the John Deere tractor. The contrast between the dark soil and the clear blue sky blurred as narrow streams of fluid ran down the glass.

"Can't anything go right today?" Hailey wrenched the key to off, grabbed her gloves, and pushed against the heavy door. "If something didn't break down every day I wouldn't know what to do."

"No mad, Mommy."

Hailey's frustration grew with her daughter's reprimand. "Stay in here while I fix it."

"Down." Sophie knelt on the seat and reached her arms out.

"It won't take me long, and I don't want you to get filthy. We have a lot to do today, and I don't have time to give you a bath before lunch. Stay in the seat and don't touch anything." Hailey jumped off the last step. Her mood improved a bit when she discovered the extra hose in the tool box. Todd must have known this one would break soon and left a spare. Too bad it hadn't broken the last time he used the tractor.

"Go down." Sophie's curls danced around her shoulders as she jumped up and down.

"My hands are covered with this stuff." She looked back down and focused on removing the hose.

"Mommy. Go down!"

The shrill cry caused Hailey to jerk, spraying excess fluid over her face. Wiping her eyes clean on her sleeve, Hailey blew out an exasperated breath. "Okay, honey. Until I fix this hose. Then you have to get back in the tractor."

Hailey ran her hands down her jeans to remove some of the fluid. If only Dad would have been willing to keep Sophie with him that morning, she would almost be finished working the field. There were days he volunteered to keep Sophie at home, but not when she needed to be doing fieldwork. He blamed her because he couldn't get in a tractor anymore. Hadn't he always told her there were no accidents, just careless people? She hadn't been the drunk driver that night, but she'd been the one behind the wheel of her parent's car.

She stepped around the ladder of the tractor and looked up. A tiny smile tugged at the corners of her mouth. Arms raised like a bird ready to fly from its perch, Sophie stood in all her princess glory. The rosebuds embroidered on her pale pink satin bodice had started to unravel. The tulle on the skirt had holes in several places and was short enough to reveal her other passion, brown and John Deere green cowboy boots.

Hailey reached up and pulled the waiting child into her arms. "You about lost your tiara, princess." She set Sophie on the soft soil and straightened the crown. "Let's hurry so Mommy can get this tractor fixed and we can finish the field before Uncle Todd gets home from the doctor."

"Baby?" Sophie flipped her tulle skirt and twirled around.

"Not today. Just another week or so." Hailey grabbed at the dancer when she tripped over a clod. "Here now, be careful."

Sophie squealed and pointed toward the road.

Grant's blue truck turned into the field and drove up beside her. He sauntered over. "Got problems?" His customary smile seemed trapped behind clamped lips.

"Broken hose."

Sophie reached out until he took her into his arms.

"Need me to run to town and get another one made?" He bent over and looked at the problem.

"Thanks for the offer, but Todd already had an extra one made, so I'm okay." Hailey smiled up at him and met his blank stare. "You probably think all you do is rescue me from broken down things." She shoved her hands into her back pockets while he searched her face. "You okay? Did your breakfast buddies upset you this morning?"

Grant moved to his truck and set Sophie inside. When he turned around he held a magazine in his hand. "This came in the mail yesterday. It seems you omitted a few details when you told me about your trip." He pushed the magazine at her. "I'd have thought you'd be more excited about Senator Bryant being there. Did you enjoy meeting him?"

Unexpectedly, Hailey's defenses rose. "He seemed excited about what we're doing here."

Grant stepped closer and put his finger on the picture of the senator at the table. "Is that Trey sitting beside him? I don't remember you mentioning you saw him."

"Good grief, what's got you all worked up this morning?" She shoved the magazine back and hurried to his truck. "Come on, Sophie, we've got to get busy." She lifted Sophie out. "I didn't realize I had to report back to you on every detail of my trip." Her anger increased with each word.

"That seems like a pretty big detail to leave out." He grabbed her arm. Hailey looked up at the disappointment in his eyes. "And Sophie? What did he think about his daughter?"

Anger turned to dread as she backed away. "He—he didn't see her."

"Really? Wasn't he a little curious about his own child?" Grant followed her to the tractor ladder.

She pushed Sophie to the top. "Go sit on the seat." Hailey

stalked to where the hose hung, still half-attached to the tractor. "I don't know, Grant. Why don't you call him if you're so curious?" She prayed he wouldn't take her up on the suggestion. The broken hose came off with one last yank. Hailey reached down to get the new one, only to find it in Grant's hand.

Nudging her over, he went to work fitting it on the nozzle. "Did you talk to him?"

"What does it matter? It was over two weeks ago."

Finished with the hose, he walked back to his truck and pulled a rag from under the seat. Wiping his hands, he turned and glared at her. "You can't hide out here forever, Hailey. It's time to move on with your life."

His words brought tears of anger. She pretended to be busy putting tools away until the truck drove out of the field. In a fit of anger she threw the broken hose as far as she could. "There's nothing left to move on to."

Trey stepped out of his rental SUV and took a deep breath to calm his nerves. The afternoon had barely begun and heat waves already shimmered above the parking lot pavement. Things had changed since the last time he'd been here. He'd never paid much attention to this area—always just followed the driveway to the left and parked by the house. For the first time in his life, he was a visitor at Harper Farms. All of its joy died with Jenny Harper, and the thrill of seeing Hailey had turned cold.

A gray-haired woman stood up from the flower bed beside the shed. She wiped at the sweat on her forehead with her sleeve. "It's a scorcher today. I thought I'd get this bed finished, but I think I'm going to have to quit for now. What can I do for you?"

"It looks good around here. Are you responsible for all the flower beds?"

"Heavens, no. Hailey has an eye for that, but I come in a few hours each morning and weed. Once we hit September, there's no time, so I try to get it all done before we open."

"I need to talk to someone about an event." A twinge of guilt coursed through him for pretending to be a stranger.

"Oh, it's a real good time and great food." Her eyes lit up as she talked. "Ellen's over in that building working. You might check with her."

Trey looked to where she pointed and nodded. "I appreciate your help. Have a good day."

"You bet I will. I'm going home to rest for a few hours. If it cools down this evening, I'll come back."

Trey followed the paved path to the building marked with a General Store sign. A cool blast of air hit him in the face when he opened the door. Long tables cluttered with different craft projects in various stages stretched the length of the room. The woman he'd seen in the photo at the banquet came around from behind the table, led by her big belly.

"Sorry about the mess. I promise that by opening day this will look like a store, but right now you'll have to use your imagination."

Trey chuckled and glanced up and down the tables. "Do you make all this?"

"A lot of it. We'll add a few things we bought at market, but for the most part, we try to utilize what's available here." She leaned down and picked up a basket. "Whew! That small chore gets harder each day." She smiled and patted her extended stomach. "Sorry, little one, you probably don't like it either, do you?"

The same envy he'd experienced toward Todd at the awards ceremony filled him. "Congratulations. When's the baby due?"

"Next week." Her eyes glowed. "But I'm hoping sooner."

"Baby?" A small voice drew Trey's attention. The little beauty he'd seen in the family picture sat at a short plastic table beside the long one.

"That's right, Sophie. Pretty soon, you'll have a baby to play with."

The child smiled up at him, her clear blue eyes holding fast to his. A silver plastic tiara with large fake diamonds held back her tangled mass of curls.

Trey couldn't resist smiling at the little girl. "She's beautiful."

"And ornery." Ellen laughed. "Can you show this nice man what you're painting?"

The toddler pushed her plastic yellow chair back and marched around the table, holding her project. He knelt as she came near. She wore a Disney princess dress. Paint spattered the pink top, adding to the disheveled look. Her tiny feet slid down into the front strap of matching heeled slippers with pink flowers.

"Are you Princess Sophie?"

She wrinkled her nose and giggled.

"You are lovely." He pointed to her project. "What's that?"

"Good."

"Good?" He looked at her mom.

"Gourd." Ellen explained. "After they dry, we paint them into characters to sell. We have jack-o-lanterns, Santas, cats, frogs—just about anything you can make into that shape."

"What's yours going to be?" A smear of rainbow of colors coated one side, while the other had colorful fingerprints covering it. "Is this one for sale?"

Sophie giggled.

"May I buy this from you?" He pulled his wallet from his pocket.

Ellen cleared her throat, reminding him that she stood there. "You don't have to buy anything. I doubt that's why you're here." The woman's easy smile had disappeared. Uncertainty filled her eyes. "I don't think you told me what you needed."

Trey stood and faced her. "No, we got sidetracked. I have a business proposal I need to discuss with someone."

"My sister-in-law is the one who schedules events." Ellen looked back and forth between him and Sophie. "She's not here right now. If you leave your name and number, I'll have her call you."

Trey knew what would happen to that information. "Is there a better time to get a hold of her?"

"What do you want?"

How should he answer? Had she recognized him? Something had changed her easy attitude. "Senator Bryant would like to make a television ad here with him meeting other Kansans. I need to make arrangements."

Ellen pushed herself up, moved around the table, and stood behind her daughter. "I could have Hailey call you when she gets in." The woman's green eyes probed his.

Not willing to offer any information, he bent down to Sophie. "It's been nice to meet you, Princess Sophie. If you decide to sell your artwork, I'd like to buy it." He touched a spot of green paint on her cheek. "Take care of your mommy and that new baby."

"Baby." Sophie smiled at him and covered his hand with her little paint covered one.

Trey stood and backed away. "You and Todd have a beautiful family." Ellen's lack of surprise at his slip in mentioning Todd's name affirmed that she knew his identity. "I'll call and make arrangements."

Closing the door behind him, Trey gulped in deep breaths of the hot air. What had he been thinking? He could still feel the warmth of his niece's hand on his. Running his hand through his hair, he hurried past the freshly weeded flower bed.

"Trey. Trey, wait."

He stopped as Ellen hastened toward him, her gait awkward. Damp eyelashes framed her eyes. She licked her lips and looked down at the painted gourd in a shoebox that she held. "I think Sophie wants you to have this."

Trey swallowed the emotion rising in his throat and tried to smile. "Tell her Uncle Trey says thanks."

Ellen glanced over her shoulder, as if uncertain, but when she faced him her lips were set in a determined line. "Hailey usually spends her mornings getting the pumpkin patches cleaned up.

She'll be in the one across the swinging bridge early tomorrow. I've got to get back to Sophie."

"Thank you." What had Joni expected him to find? He turned slowly, taking in each area of Harper Farms. What was he missing?

Remembering the box in his hands, Trey looked down. How quickly the little girl found a place in his heart. He held the gourd by its dried stem to examine the artwork. When he came to an unpainted spot, he stopped. Two words, apparently added by Ellen, glared up in black ink.

Love, Sophie.

CHAPTER SEVEN

"Sophie is asleep in her room." Hailey stood at the door to her dad's office and spoke over the blaring television. Did he ever turn that thing off? "I need to finish some things up outside."

He looked up from his desk. "It's a good thing one of you kids got my work ethic. Your brother is going to get behind in the field work if he doesn't start staying home more. Between doctor appointments and church meetings, he's rarely where he should be."

"It's their first baby. He wants to be with Ellen."

"Ellen needs to toughen up if she's going to make it as a farmer's wife. You were born in the middle of wheat harvest, and–"

"I know, Dad." Hailey didn't need to hear the story again. "Mom drove herself to the hospital so you could keep cutting."

"That's what it took then, and it's a lot tougher nowadays. You understand what it takes."

"Todd does, too. Maybe if you weren't so hard on him all the time, you'd see everything he does."

"You watch what you say, Hailey. You're under my roof."

The coldness in his tone left her shaking. She hurried out of the house and slammed the back door behind her.

The setting sun cast the sky into a painted canvas of pink,

purple, and orange. The humid hot air blew across her tired body. After a long day the thought of spending hours upstairs with her dad or alone in her basement room drove her outside.

Didn't he realize why she still lived under his roof? She'd walked away from her own home to take care of him. The papers sitting in her room reminded her daily of all she'd given up.

Hailey pushed open the side doors on the shop. If she were lucky, the breeze would cool the stale air inside. She gathered her paints and brushes as the overhead lights buzzed and then settled at the table to paint over the faded letters on the WELCOME sign.

"Trying to make me look bad?"

She gave a start. She aimed a teasing grin at her brother. "Ha. I don't think you need any help."

Todd perched on the table beside her board. "If you would work from nine to five, Dad wouldn't think I was such a slacker."

"Ellen said her appointment went well?"

"Yep. Hopefully, by this time next week, I'll be a dad."

She looked up from her project and grinned. "You'll be a great dad." Hailey dabbed at the orange paint on one of the pumpkins, comfortable with the silence between them.

After several minutes Todd sighed. "You know, I think having this baby is the most exciting thing that's ever happened to me."

Hailey nodded and continued to paint.

"It's made me wonder what would keep a man from his child."

Hailey fought to keep her breathing even and her hand still.

"It's always bothered me that Trey showed no interested in Sophie. Now that we're a week away, nothing would keep me from being there. Unless...I didn't know about the baby."

Hailey refused to look up. What would her brother think of her if she confirmed his suspicion? Her eyes burned with tears.

"Trey was here today. He knelt down and touched Sophie on the cheek. He told Ellen she and I had a beautiful daughter."

Trey had seen Sophie? Hailey dropped the paint brush. Her legs shook. She turned an old bucket upside down and sat on it.

Todd rubbed his forehead and expelled a deep breath. "What have you done? You had no right to keep her from him."

Humiliated by her own deceit, Hailey stared at the ground sorting out her reasons—ones that would convince Todd she hadn't been wrong—but she knew none would change his mind. "I tried when I found out, but he had already left for South America. By the time he came back I had so many things to do here. He refused to understand that I couldn't just leave Dad." She wiped her tears. "Dad still needed me, and if Trey knew about the pregnancy, he would have demanded I come back. After she was born, I was too scared to tell him. Scared he'd take her and leave me."

"You let us all believe that he didn't care." Todd yanked off his cap and rubbed his forehead. "Does anyone know the truth?"

"Dad. Aunt Joni figured it out while we were in D.C."

"How much of this did Dad put you up to?"

She crossed her arms across her chest. Tension pounded in her temples. "He needed me, Todd. You know what it's been like. He's lost so much."

"Hailey, Dad will ruin us all if we let him. This has got to stop. You need to be with Trey. You have to tell him."

"It's too late." She covered her face with her hands as a sob escaped her throat. "Sheriff Hastings served me the divorce papers last week."

"He still has to know about Sophie. It's not an option."

She shook her head. "He'll take her. I can't lose my daughter."

Todd slid off the table and knelt in front of her. He gently squeezed her shoulders. "You've woven a tangled web. I don't know how you're going to get out of this, but Sophie deserves to grow up knowing her father is a good man." Todd lifted her chin and waited until her gaze met his. The disappointment in his eyes brought fresh tears. "Tell him the truth. If you don't, I will." His tone left little doubt he meant it.

Panic flooded her. "You can't tell him. It's not your place!"

"If I'd have known, I would have gone to him two years ago."

"Don't you understand?" She grabbed his arm. "Do you want me to lose Sophie?"

Todd pulled away. "Of course I don't want you to lose Sophie, but what you've done is wrong. You can't believe that he isn't going to hear about it from someone else." He walked to the door and seemed to stare across the grounds. "What happened to make you hate him so much?"

"I don't hate him." She pressed her hand over her heart. "Everything happened so fast. Trey never understood why I needed to stay here. Time has gone by, and now it's too late."

Todd hung his head. "Ellen and I will be praying for you and Trey. But, I am serious, Hailey. Tell him the truth."

Lack of sleep pressed on Hailey. She yawned as she rolled a basketball sized pumpkin halfway. After watching each hour change from midnight on, she'd headed to the pumpkin patch when the sky lightened. She longed for a nap, but she needed to get the rest of the pumpkins turned to avoid rotten spots. Unfortunately, the tedious chore allowed Todd's words to play over and over in her mind. He was right, but how could she not feel betrayed by his loyalty to Trey?

Two months after the accident, Trey asked her to come back with him. Hailey closed her eyes. That weekend rolled through her mind like scenes from a movie. Her excitement at seeing him, their night together, Trey handing her the plane ticket and asking her to leave with him, his angry words, then finally his promise that he wouldn't come back again.

At the crackle of dry weeds, Hailey twisted around. Trey stood a few feet away with his hands shoved into the pockets of his faded jeans. The white athletic t-shirt stretched across his chest, and accentuated his tanned, muscular arms. Trey the business-suited politician looked good, but this was the Trey she'd fallen in love with.

His steel blue eyes held hers. "You once said this would be the biggest pumpkin patch in the state."

"And I think you sarcastically said that would be a real claim to fame." His face didn't give any sign that he already knew about Sophie. Nerves exploded within her. All night, she'd tried to imagine what she would say. She still didn't have an idea. "This is as close as I get to an office, but you're welcome to sit down." Hailey pointed to the pumpkin beside his leg. The silence grew as thick as the humid morning air. "Can I . . . um . . . is there something you wanted?"

He raised his hand to rub the back of his neck. "I'm here on official business for the senator." The silver ring on his left hand caught in the morning light.

"He sent you?" She glanced down at the glove covering her own ring.

"Senator Bryant would like to film parts of a campaign ad here."

"Why?" Did Trey notice the tremble in her voice?

"You and this business impressed him. It would make a good place to show him meeting people, back to his Kansas roots type of thing."

"I can't imagine he's very impressed with me. You must have had a lot to tell him."

His stare never wavered. "My personal life is my own business. Before October first would be best for us. Maybe offer a cookout, at the campaign's expense. Are you interested?"

Hailey struggled to listen. Todd's threat to tell Trey about Sophie if she didn't taunted her, making it hard to concentrate on what he was saying, much less remember what events were marked on her calendar.

"Would you be coming back?" She pulled at the dry weeds.

"There's nothing left for me here."

The words sliced her heart. She turned her head so he wouldn't see how the loathing in his voice affected her.

"It's a business deal. You let Bryant use this place, and you get some free advertising. I'm only here doing my job."

Keeping her head down, Hailey's breath shuddered. She rolled another pumpkin, needing time to corral her emotions. "If you have time, I could run up and check which day might work best." Hailey stood and passed him on her way to the ATV. In her nervousness, her shoe caught on a vine and she stumbled. Trey grabbed her, and her skin burned where his hands held her arms.

She looked up and recognized deep sadness in his eyes. "That's why I drive down here. I'd probably break a leg if I had to walk too far." Trey's expression never changed. She needed to put distance between them. "Do you want a ride back to the office?" Her legs were like jelly but she managed not to trip again as she made her way to the waiting ATV. Trey followed. Would he take her up on the offer? So much for the distance idea.

The key dropped from her shaking hand. How was she going to tell him about Sophie? If she told him now, what would happen by the end of the day? How would her confession change everyone's world? Nausea welled inside her.

Trey reached under the dash for the fallen key and put it in the ignition.

"Need me to drive?" He turned the key and the engine hummed.

She had to get away from him, give herself time to think. How she told him might make a difference in his response. Without looking at him, she stepped out of the vehicle. "Why don't you drive? I think I'll walk and meet you up there." She took off before he could reply. A few minutes later, Trey drove past her.

Should she apologize first or ask him to try and understand before she told him? How in the world was she going to admit what she had done? The desire to forget the whole confession grew stronger. She could tell one more lie and say he didn't care. Trey would be gone before anyone would know. She grimaced. Todd wouldn't let her get by with that. He'd make sure Trey knew. Hailey's breaths came in short gasps as she hurried up the hill, fighting for control.

"God, help me." She whispered the prayer. She hadn't prayed in months, but she needed Him now. "Don't let him take her from me. I don't know how to tell him." Fear overtook her, and nausea attacked. She turned off the path and bent over, losing the breakfast she'd forced down earlier. She wiped her mouth on the back of her hand and stood up.

"I don't know what to say. Give me the words, please." Old habits were hard to break. She doubted her prayers had even been heard. What did she expect? She'd walked away from God and Trey on the same day.

Forcing her legs to move, she trudged the rest of the way up the hill. The ATV sat in front of the main building, but she didn't see Trey. Had he left? The thought gave her a thread of hope. Maybe he'd decided this could be done on the phone. As she neared the building, Trey's voice drifted back to her.

"Did you help plant these? They sure are pretty."

Bile rose in her throat again.

Trey looked up from where he leaned over the ledge of the flower bed and gave her a smile she remembered from years ago. "Look who I found out here weeding"—he hooked his fingers into quotes—"the garden."

A small pile of petals littered the ground beside the toddler. Sophie jumped off the railroad tie that made up the edge and ran towards her. "Mommy!"

Trey's gaze followed Sophie as she passed him on unsteady legs. The smile melted into a frown of disbelief. He stood, hurt pinching the features of his face. "What did she call you?" His eyes flashed as they bore into hers. "Whose...?"

"Yours." She knelt beside Sophie and pulled the child into her arms.

"Kitty." Sophie pointed at their black cat, Snippet, strutting by.

"Can you feed Snippet his breakfast?" She nudged the child towards the cat, hoping she'd leave.

"I feed." Sophie ran after the cat and disappeared around the corner of the shed.

Hailey moved close enough to Trey to put her hand on his arm. "I wanted to tell you. I was going to tell you. I am so sorry, Trey. I never should have–"

His head jolted up. His face had drained to a chalky white, and his jaw twitched as he stared at her. "You kept my child from me? What were you thinking?" Wrenching his arm from her hand, he took several steps back. He grasped his head between his hands and squeezed his eyes shut. "When did you think you'd tell me? When she needed a father to walk her down the aisle at her wedding?" Trey staggered away, then whirled and pointed at her. "I will fight for her, and you will lose."

"Trey, please, please don't do this. I'm her mother." Tears streamed down her face. Dizziness struck. She collapsed beside the flower bed. "You can't take her from me. Please."

He stalked back to her and reached for her chin, forcing her to look at him. "Did you forget what it takes to have a child? I'm her father, and you...you deceived me." His hand fell away as he rose and marched toward the parking lot. Several feet from her, he pivoted on his heel. "What happened to my best friend? The girl I've loved since I was twelve? What did you do with her?"

CHAPTER EIGHT

"Hailey? You up there?" Grant stood at the base of the oak tree with one foot on the first rung of the ladder. Her sobs gave her away, but he wanted to warn her before he got to the top.

"Go away, Grant. I don't need you to yell at me too."

Three rungs later, Hailey came into view—her back against the far wall and her head resting on bent knees.

"I won't yell." He pulled himself the rest of the way up and joined her in the small hut. "You okay?" He sat down and leaned against the wall.

"He's going to take her from me." She pushed her hands through her dark hair and squeezed her head.

"Trey?" His heart hammered.

Fear flashed in her eyes. "How do you know? Todd told you, didn't he?"

"Tell me what?"

She shook her head. "I can't tell you—you wouldn't understand. Todd had no right to tell you anything."

Grant stared at the warped wood floor. Her confirmation of deceit sickened him. "I talked with Trey at the restaurant yesterday morning. By the things he said I realized he had ever been told about Sophie. Did you really believe you'd get by with that?"

"I don't know." She covered her face and sobbed. "Just leave, okay?"

Disbelief and sympathy surged through him. Nothing weakened his resolve faster than tears. "He almost ran the stop sign in town. You told him about Sophie?"

"No, she did." Her words were muffled. "She called me Mommy, and he wanted to know who her father was."

"You could have said me." The knot in his stomach tightened.

Hailey snorted. "And add adultery to his list against me?"

Grant put his arm around her. "You were wrong to not tell him. A man has the right to know about his child. Somehow we'll figure a way out of this mess." No matter his opinion of her deception, he'd help her.

"I can't fight him—he's her father and I didn't tell him. What judge is going to reward me for that?" Fresh tears ran down her face when she looked at him. "What was I thinking? He hates me now."

Could he blame the man? Her head rested on his shoulder. The tears soaked through his shirt while her sobs broke his heart. "Do you know where he went?"

"He said he'd fight me and I'd lose." Her body shuddered beneath his hand. "He asked what happened to me."

A car wreck of guilt had happened. He understood Trey's anger and hurt—if he'd lost his wife and child he'd be just as angry—but Hailey had been put in a tough place. The choices she made weren't the best ones, but was there a right choice?

"I'm going to be left alone." She wiped her nose on the shoulder of her t-shirt.

"You're not going to be alone." He brushed the tears off her cheek with his thumb. She raised her swollen eyes to his. "I'll be here for you Hailey. We will fight him together. Let's go see the lawyer your dad uses and find out what you need to do to end your marriage and keep Sophie."

"I've already signed the divorce papers." She pulled away and leaned back. "I even messed that up and forgot to put stamps on the envelope so Mr. Olson brought it back. I never made it to town to put it in the mail." She pointed to the opposite wall. "Do you think I should add divorce to that list?" A sob cut through the last word.

Grant read the list. He'd like to suggest they tear the treehouse down. With reminders carved into the wood, would Hailey ever completely be his?

"Trey and I came here after the all night prom party. We ate donuts and watched the sun rise. He kissed me for the first time that morning."

He didn't want to take this trip down memory lane. "Let's go see the lawyer and explain about Sophie. That way we'll know what we're dealing with."

Trey pulled his car into the parking lot of the church his dad pastored in the small Colorado town. He stepped from the car and looked around. Families on summer vacation strolled the wooden sidewalks connecting gift and antique stores to ice cream shops. They all seemed so carefree. He envied them.

He aimed himself for the church. After leaving Hailey, he'd given little thought to where he'd go. He just he had to get away from her. As he drove, the need to talk to his father grew, pushing him beyond the speed limit on the flat stretch of I70 through western Kansas until he turned south toward the Colorado Springs area. Maybe talking to his dad first would make telling his mom easier. Trey took a deep breath of the clean mountain air and opened the church's office door.

Dad's secretary, Ruthie Anderson, peered over her reading glasses at him from her chair behind the desk. "Well, this is an unexpected surprise." The woman had been a fixture in this office since before Trey's dad had become head pastor thirteen years earlier. "Your daddy didn't say anything about you coming to visit." She pulled off the glasses and let them fall from the beaded cord around her neck. Standing, she held out her arms in welcome.

Trey accepted the embrace as the familiar scent of wintergreen on her breath wafted about them. He swallowed against the emotion growing in his chest. How long had it been since he'd been held by someone who loved him? She had no idea the solace she offered.

"This will be a surprise to Dad, too." Trey kept his voice low in case Dad was studying. "Is he in his office?"

"Ruthie Anderson," boomed a deep voice from the doorway, "what are you doing in that young man's arms?"

The woman snorted and stepped aside. "Pastor Sam, he's the best looking fella I've seen in here in a long time. It's good to get some young blood in this place."

In four steps his father crossed the carpeted floor and pulled him into an embrace. "Trey, it's good to see you. Your mother will be shocked. How long can you stay?"

Stepping back, Trey recognized concern in his father's discerning eyes even though his words were upbeat. "I'm not sure."

"I'm finished here in the office for today. I need to run some things out to Steve Patton. Ruthie, you go on home, and I'll lock up."

The woman pulled her purse out of her desk drawer and bustled to the door. "That's fine with me. I need to get things set up for Bunko tonight. The ladies will be there by seven. Good to see you, Trey. Don't make yourself so scarce. Next time, bring that pretty wife of yours. We haven't seen her for so long." With the wave of her hand, she hurried out the door.

"Are you ever going to let her retire?" Trey watched through the window as she got into her mid-eighties Crown Victoria.

"I think the woman believes the church will shut down when she's not the secretary anymore." Dad motioned toward his office door. "Let me grab this box and we'll go. You don't mind riding out to the Patton place with me, do you?"

Trey took the box when his dad came out and followed him. Sliding into the truck, he smiled at the familiar fishing pole and tackle box sitting on the floor at his feet. "Any good fishing?"

"Not recently. The weather's been too hot. Next week your mom and I are planning to get away for a few days—go to Lake City. I'm hoping to find some good fishing there." His dad turned onto the busy street. "It's good to see you, Trey. Did you fly in from Washington?"

Trey rubbed his forehead and took a deep breath. All day, he'd felt suffocated by the weight of Hailey's deception. No wonder Joni had encouraged him to go back to Kansas.

"I drove from Hailey's. I needed to talk with you." How could he say the words to the one man he'd always worked to make proud? "Hailey and I are getting a divorce."

"Oh, son... Have you tried—"

"There's more." Trey pulled his phone from his pocket and brought up the photo of the Harper family that he'd found on the drive here. He swallowed against the boulder that had taken up residency in his throat. At the only four-way stop in town he handed the phone to his father. "That little girl? She's mine."

His dad drew in a sharp breath before he grabbed the phone and pulled the screen closer. "She looks like you." The light changed, and he drove into the Get-N-Go parking lot. "How long have you known?" Dad stared at the small screen.

"About nine hours."

Dad's head wrenched to look at Trey. "Nine hours? The child is how old?"

"I dunno, maybe two? She's talking and walking. We didn't discuss that, but I do believe she's mine." The hours on the road had given him plenty of time to figure out all the possibilities of when Sophie had been conceived and born.

"She's yours all right." Dad's lip curved up slightly. "She's beautiful. What's her name?"

"Sophie. Can you believe I don't even know her middle name? I don't know if she goes by Williams or Harper. Here I am, her father, and I don't even know my own child's name." Trey's voice broke.

Reaching across the seat, Sam put his hand on Trey's shoulder. "Father God, be with my son right now. Let him feel Your presence and Your peace. Thank You for this beautiful little girl, my first grandchild. God, where there are things we do not understand, help us to simply trust You. Guide my son to make wise decisions, ones that will honor and glorify You. Amen." Dad released his shoulder. "How did you find out? Did Hailey tell you?" Sam pulled back on the street and headed out of town.

"No, if she'd had her way, I would have never known." The calm inside the truck flowed into the deepest parts of him. He had known coming to his dad would be a balm, helping him to sort out what he should do next. His dad never spoke without considering the facts.

"A few weeks ago, Hailey came to Washington to receive an award, and we ran into each other. I told her I wanted a divorce. The next day her aunt came and said there were things I didn't know. When Senator Bryant suggested filming a campaign ad at the pumpkin patch, I volunteered to do the leg work." Trey paused, replaying the early morning scene. "I actually met Sophie yesterday, but I thought she belonged to Todd. This morning I was talking to her when Hailey walked up. Sophie called her Mommy. So, no, Hailey wasn't the one who told me."

The rugged beauty of the mountains calmed him. He gave his dad time to digest the news. They pulled off the road beside a marked trail.

Trey glanced around. "Why did we stop here?"

Dad opened his door, glancing at him. "Let's walk for a bit. Mr. Patton isn't expecting me today. I seem to think better when I'm moving."

Trey followed along to a sign noting several trails and the distances.

"You up for a bit of a hike? There's something I'd like to show you."

The trail map indicated his dad chose the longer trail. Already behind, he hurried to catch up. No question about it, his father still maintained his good health. "Hey, are you sure you don't want that other trail? It might be more what I can handle."

"This one isn't bad." Dad kept up a steady stride, arms swinging. "I know what's at the end of both trails and I want you to see the end of this one. You'll make it—we'll take it slow."

Talking ceased as the two men hiked the weaving, uphill path, Dad always in the lead. Trey's head pounded with the exertion to keep up, and he stopped often to catch his breath. Once in a while, his dad turned around and smiled, encouraging Trey to catch up.

"Isn't Mom going to be concerned?" Talking depleted his breath.

"She'll be fine." The answer floated down the path.

"Are you trying to prevent me from coming back to visit?" He winced at the unfamiliar whine came from his mouth. This was hard work.

His dad smiled over his shoulder. "I want you to see this. You've been gone too long. This is the best place to get some perspective. We're almost there." The man disappeared around a corner.

Between the blood beating through his body and a growing irritation, Trey fought to keep going. How long would it take Dad to notice if he reversed direction and went back? He had come to talk, not hike. He rounded the corner and encountered a huge rock jutting into the sky. Trees surrounded the base.

Dad stood in a crag about six feet above the path. "It's about time you got here."

Trey leaned over and put his hands on his knees, fighting for a breath. "You brought me to a rock? What's at the end of the quarter-mile trail?"

"Oh, ye of little faith." His father quoted the familiar scripture. "Come around this way and you'll see where to climb up." Trey pulled his body up to where his dad stood and then followed him to the top.

Trey took a deep breath. This vantage point above the steep, rock strewn trail revealed a lush valley. Wildflowers danced at the edge of a small lake, its mirrored surface reflecting the peaks stretching lay beyond. A hush, like a cloak, fell around his shoulders.

"That's amazing." Trey spoke softly, not wanting to break the spell.

"Worth the climb?" Dad turned slightly and grinned.

He nodded. He needed this welcome respite to his day.

"Look over there." Trey followed the line from his father's finger and saw a lone elk walking towards the pool of water. "Most people stay on the shorter path. It's easier and quicker. But look what you'd have missed."

Trey shoved his hands into his pockets and studied the scene before him. What a contrast in his day. From the turmoil and deception of the morning to the calm, serene view before him.

"Trey, right now, you're standing at that sign at the base of the mountain. What you're facing is hard, and solid, and enormous. Most people would never attempt to climb it, choosing instead to take the shorter, easier route. The few who do decide to climb the path to the top are rewarded with something beautiful."

"They are also acclimated to the altitude and in better shape."

"That's true, but you can get in shape and overcome this."

"I didn't make this mountain, Dad. Hailey did."

"I disagree. You and Hailey did this together. It wasn't right for her to leave indefinitely, and I certainly don't condone her not telling you about the child. But what did you do?"

"I tried to be understanding for months. I wanted her to come back with me the summer after the accident." He'd made a mental list on the drive to Colorado of everything he'd done.

"Did you go back after that to offer her any support or try to work something out?"

"She accused me of being as controlling as her father." The memory of Hailey's harsh statement offended him as much today as it had three years ago. "My job took me to Brazil for several months."

"You knew better than anyone the pull Jim Harper has always had on that family. They'd just lost Jenny, and he was paralyzed. What options do you think Hailey thought she had?"

Trey paced to the end of the rock and turned to face his dad. The hurt he'd felt years ago came to the surface. "She chose him over me. I'm her husband."

"Why did she have to choose?"

"Because when she married me, she promised to leave Jim Harper and be my wife."

"Why didn't you go with her?"

"Back to Kansas? My job is in Washington. You can't move jobs like that around the country. She knew how important my job was to me, to our future."

"Trey, you have loved Hailey since you were kids in high school—even before that. You never doubted that you would marry her. You knew her better than anyone else. Did you really think she would leave her family at the most difficult time they'd ever faced?"

"She could have come back last year."

"Maybe she was scared how you'd react about the baby. What happened this morning?"

The angry threats played through his mind as he pictured Hailey kneeling on the ground in fear. "I—I told her I'd take Sophie away." He hung his head, ashamed of his words.

His dad nodded. "I want to encourage you to conquer this mountain. It will not be easy or quick. There will probably be times when quitting will seem like the best thing." He guided Trey to the edge. "When you and Hailey got married, you made a vow to God to love and cherish that woman until death."

"What if I don't think I love her anymore?" His stomach lurched as he voiced the thought he'd struggled with for hours.

"I believe you still love her. If you didn't, this wouldn't hurt you so much."

Trey tipped his head back and looked at clouds floating in the sky. "So I'm supposed to move back in with them?"

"I don't know. Your mom and I have been praying for you and Hailey, and we'll keep praying. If you are willing to climb this mountain, I believe God will reward you, but you have to decide what you're willing to do. Trey, you've got to be praying about this. What happened to the young man who planned to lead his family spiritually?"

"His wife left him." Trey picked up a rock and threw it. "I'm tired. What if I don't want to try?"

"Then you'll miss the view. And you'll be breaking the covenant you made with God." His dad turned and headed back the way they came.

Trey remained at the edge and scanned the valley. What had he expected when he drove here today? Had he thought his dad would agree to his divorce? He kicked at the loose stones then made his way down the mountain.

When they arrived at the trailhead, Trey stopped beside the sign and ran his fingers over the painted words. "What's at the end of the quarter-mile trail?"

"A lonely picnic table."

Trey laced his fingers behind his head and relaxed into the soft cushion covering the porch swing. A full moon illuminated the night, revealing the grandeur of the mountains. Would Hailey consider giving their marriage another chance? What would either choice cost him? He already lost the first two years of his daughter's life. He refused to miss any more.

His daughter... The thought brought the first real smile to his face. When he met her yesterday he'd been taken by her, and now she was his little girl.

The door slid open behind him. "Mind if I join you?" Mom held out a mug. "I figured coffee wouldn't make a difference in how you sleep tonight."

"Thanks."

"She's a beautiful little girl."

"How does it feel to be a grandma?" He took a drink, watching her over the rim.

"There are too many emotions at the moment to name just one." She turned the mug in her hand. "I'm amazed that I've suddenly got a granddaughter, but I'm sad about missing two years. It makes me furious with Hailey for keeping her from us, and I'm hurt she didn't want us to know."

"I tried to call my lawyer today but he's on vacation. When he gets back I'll find out what my options are."

Mom pulled her legs under her and faced him. The light shining through the window showed the concern on her face. "Are you sure that's what you should do?"

"Two hours ago you agreed about getting a divorce."

"I always think more clearly when I'm washing dishes, and tonight I cleaned out the cupboards and scrubbed every pan I own." She grinned sheepishly. "You're my baby, and it hasn't been easy to think of you being separated from Hailey the past two years. When you told me, my first reaction might have been a little harsh."

"Yes, but you are on my side, and I need that." He propped his feet on the deck railing.

"I always feel sorry for the parent who only sees their child every other weekend. You probably wouldn't get to see Sophie even that much. Are you sure you don't want to be more a part of her world?"

"Maybe I'll try for custody and she'd only visit Hailey." Memories of Hailey kneeling on the ground with their daughter assaulted him.

"Would that serve any purpose but revenge?" She took a drink of her coffee and watched him over the rim. "You'd have to put her in daycare or hire a nanny."

"I thought you were on my side."

Mom rubbed her forehead. "I want to be, but that would put me against Hailey, and I don't know that I can do that. A child needs her mom and her dad. I just think you'd better think through everything before you act. This can't be about revenge. It will only make you miserable."

"You're probably going to tell me I need to forgive Hailey, too." He swallowed a mouthful of lukewarm coffee.

"Probably."

"It took me two years to finally to end my marriage and send Hailey the papers. I want Sophie, but I don't know that I want her mom anymore. It's one thing to forgive, but I don't know if I'll ever be able to forget what she's done."

"Maybe that little girl will help you understand the choices her momma had to make."

CHAPTER NINE

Grass and dust flew as Hailey turned the mower around and headed back to the other end of the yard. She dreaded this endless job during the summer. If it weren't for the weddings, reunions, and corporate outings booked at the farm, she wasn't sure they'd keep the grass watered. It would save her hours each week if the grass was brown and dormant. Today, the monotony gave her ample opportunity to be tormented by questions.

Where was Trey? What happened to him after he left?

More than once in the last thirty-six hours, she'd been tempted to take Sophie and leave. Common sense always prevailed, but the thought lingered. She looked at the buildings and different attractions they'd added over the years. How could she leave all this? And more, where would she go?

Forcing her mind to focus on work, she considered what still needed to be done for the wedding scheduled for Saturday night. They had a general guideline to follow but weddings always made her nervous. There was no way to know what the bride or her mother would be like on the actual day. How many times had she met with both women to plan the event, only to encounter a completely different pair at the wedding, especially if weather dared defy the agenda? When a different shade of napkin could send the bride into tears, it did no good to remind the bride that windless days in Kansas were about as common as snow in July or that she had no control over the elements. Still, she always encouraged each bride to consider all her options before signing the contract with them. Luckily, this Saturday's forecast held no rain.

Hailey turned for another swath, and a newer model SUV stopped on the drive in front of the house. The driver's door opened and Trey stepped out. Swallowing the fear that rose in her throat, she adjusted the mower to a faster speed and approached him. Perhaps he'd leave his sunglasses on and spare her from seeing the pain and anger she had caused.

Turning the mower off, she faced him from the seat. Her legs might give out if she tried to stand. She was glad for her own sunglasses because she didn't want him to see the evidence of the tears she'd shed since yesterday.

"I'm glad you're back." She chewed on a piece of dried skin on her bottom lip.

"Are you?" His ash blond hair was disheveled and a scruffy beard covered his cheeks.

She nodded, biting her lip to keep it from quivering.

"I figured you'd hope I drove off the face of the earth."

"I'd like it if– We need to–" She paused to sort her jumbled thoughts. "Can we talk?"

"That's why I came back." Trey put his hands on his hips and looked at the ground. "I'd like those divorce papers."

Hailey forced down the lump blocking her throat. "I, um. . ." She took a deep breath. "They're in my room. Do you want to come in?"

The breath he'd been holding rushed out as soon as Hailey started up the steps. On the trip back from Colorado, he'd thought of his dad's challenge. Around Colby he remembered she still had the papers. If he could get those, it would give him more time to decide what path to take.

He trailed her into the familiar house.

"Who's here, Hailey? You're not finished mowing already, are you?" Jim's loud voice carried over the nightly news.

Hailey stopped at the door to the living room. Anxiety covered her face when she looked over her shoulder at Trey. "Not yet. I need to take care of some other things." She motioned for him to follow.

Trey glanced into the room as he walked past. Dark curtains covered the front window, casting the room in a somber light. Jim Harper sat in a wheelchair with his back to the door, facing a television. Trey stopped. He had never known Jim to watch TV. To the older man, sitting in front of the blaring box had always been a sign of laziness. Yet here he sat at six o'clock in the evening.

"That yard needs to be finished tonight so don't spend too much time talking."

"Come on." Hailey pulled on his arm. "You can wait in the kitchen while I get those papers from my room."

Jim looked over his shoulder. "Who did you say–" His eyes narrowed.

Trey freed his arm from Hailey's hand. "Hello, Jim." If he wanted to be a part of his daughter's life, he couldn't allow this man to intimidate him. He braced himself for battle and stepped into the room.

Hailey's gasp stole Trey's focus. The color drained from her face as she slumped against the door. She stared at him with swollen, red eyes. The sight stung, so he turned to her father again.

"What are you doing here?" The older man's hands gripped the arm rests on his wheelchair.

"I came to see my family." Trey kept his voice even.

"It's not your family anymore." Jim pointed to the door. "Get out of my house."

Trey choked back resentment and measured each word

carefully. "You should probably get used to seeing me because I'm going to be here a lot. Maybe you forgot that your granddaughter is my daughter? It's all news to me, but surely you knew who her father was. How convenient to not only manipulate your daughter into staying with you, but also mine." His courage rose with each spoken word. He should have stood up to this man years ago.

"I didn't manipulate anyone. Hailey's here because she wants to be. Now get out of my house." Jim pointed to the door, his hand shaking.

"Stop it." Hailey rushed between the two men and raised her palms. "Daddy, this doesn't concern you. Trey and I need to talk some things over."

The older man's face flushed red. "I'm your father and this is my house."

"Daddy, please."

The muscle in Jim's jaw twitched. "You shouldn't talk to him without our lawyer. He'll talk you into things that aren't right. Get him out of my house."

"Then we'll talk somewhere else." Hailey's voice quavered. She looked at Trey with pleading eyes. "Let's go."

Jim strained forward. "If you go with him, you might not be welcome back."

Hailey paused at the door and turned around. "How many times have you told me I can't leave because this place wouldn't make it without me?"

Trey held the door open and followed her onto the porch. "You okay?" He inhaled to stop the anger coursing through him.

She nodded. "What did you think he'd do? Welcome you back with open arms?"

"He needs to accept I'm back, and until we get things figured out, I'll be here plenty. Where's Sophie?" He needed to know before they went farther from the house. He would not leave his daughter with that man.

Hailey stepped off the porch. "She's with Ellen. Since you got us kicked out of the house, do you mind walking while we talk?"

"Will you be allowed back in?" He followed her on the path that led toward the collection of gray metal buildings used for the pumpkin patch.

"Do you think that's the first time I've ever left under those threats?" Her eyes clouded.

"Well..." A smile tugged at his lips. "I remember at least one other time. Seems to me that also had to do with you going with me."

"I was a senior in college. Surely I could decide if I wanted to visit your family over Christmas."

"I don't think visiting my family bothered him. He knew I intended to ask you to marry me on that trip." Trey thought back to that week. He had planned to make the time with Hailey perfect. They spent several days skiing with his family and after the last day, he arranged for the two of them to dine at a mountain lodge only accessible by sleigh. He asked her to marry him that night.

"This isn't the only time since I've been home, either."

Her words interrupted the playback of that evening. "Does he always talk to you like that?"

"He's really good with Sophie."

Resentment filled him again. Jim Harper had been there every day of Sophie's life while he'd only known about her for two days. He continued on with Hailey as she turned on another path that led to a field dotted with orange pumpkins.

"Do you mind talking down here? I can guarantee Dad won't interrupt."

An early evening breeze blew around them, offering the slightest refreshment from the hot wind that had blown all day.

"What does he do with all his time?" Trey shoved his hands into the pockets of his shorts and smiled when he realized Hailey had done the same. Could they pretend for a few more moments all was well between them?

"Just what you saw." She flashed a sad smile. "He watches lots of TV and stays inside most of the time. Once in a while he'll come out—usually to tell Todd or me what we're doing wrong."

"Does he drive or go anywhere?"

She shook her head. "We had a van remade for him, but he's never used it."

Trey squashed the flicker of sympathy. He refused to feel sorry for the man who had taken Hailey from him. The moments in Jim's house gave him a glimpse into Hailey's life. Unlike his feelings for the older man, he couldn't dismiss empathy for his wife so easily. But this was a business meeting.

He shook his head and pulled himself into work mode as they walked along the dusty tractor path that had been worn through the dried weeds. "You do have those papers, don't you?"

Hailey lowered her head, and her hair hid her face. "I put them in the mail on Tuesday, but Mr. Olson brought them back because I forgot to put a stamp on the envelope."

She couldn't have hit him harder with her fist. "You were going to let the divorce happen and never tell me about Sophie." Any compassion he might have been feeling vanished.

The path to Todd's house seemed miles long. Hailey's nerves were about to jump out of her. Since Trey had driven up she'd been on a roller coaster of emotion, not sure where each conversation would take them. More than anything else, she had to know what he expected with Sophie. What would he demand? If he wanted to take Sophie to Washington with him, even for vacations, could she let him? Would there be holidays when Sophie would be with him and she'd be left at home alone? The sickening chill of abandonment coiled inside her, heightened by the harsh reminder that she had done exactly what she feared to Trey. She couldn't blame him for the disgust he showed toward her.

"Would you have ever told me?" Trey stood in the path with

his fists clenched at his hips.

"You know now."

"That's not what I asked."

It was impossible to look at him and not see the hardness in his eyes. "I don't know." She shrugged, unable to meet his stare. "But now you know, so the other doesn't matter. We need to figure out what's going to happen. What are you thinking about Sophie?"

He stepped closer and lifted her chin so she had to look at him. "I'm going to be her dad."

"Washington's a long way away."

"I'll be here through Sunday afternoon. I want to spend as much time as possible with her and not have anyone interfere."

Hailey imagined her dad's reaction. She cringed. "You'd just keep her around here?"

"I don't know. I might want to take her someplace."

"She's got a schedule, Trey. You can't just run off with her whenever."

Trey's raised eyebrows challenged her. "You've made all the choices up until now. The way I see it, your days of single parenting are over, and you should probably accept it." The small muscle at the back of his jaw twitched. That had always been a sign of the depth of his anger. "I also want Sophie to be told that I'm her dad."

"Shouldn't we let her get use to you, first?" Hailey's protest sounded weak in her own ears.

"You tell her or I will. I want her to know who I am tomorrow."

Hailey backed away. "It will only confuse her when you leave in a day or two."

"I'm sure you probably don't want to hear this, but I will be back regularly until we get this figured out and have things in place for the future."

"Anything else?" His demands irritated her. If she didn't risk losing so much, she'd fight him.

"I want her to come and visit me."

"In D.C.?" Her voice rose in panic.

"Where else? That's our home."

"She's not even two. She can't get on a plane by herself. And who will watch her while you work? You have so much to learn about being a parent. You can't stick an address label on her and expect her to show up at your door. Once she's there, you're completely responsible for her care. You can't take her all the way to Washington and then put her in daycare while you run off to work."

Trey grabbed her arm and forced her to a stop. He moved in front of her and leaned down to meet her glare. "Then you bring her."

She stared back at him. Was he serious?

He ran his hand through his tousled hair. "You robbed me of learning how to be a parent. You didn't give me a chance to learn. So don't ever throw that at me again." His voice vibrated with fury. "I expect her to come and stay with me, and I will be welcome whenever I come back here."

"You should have called to make the arrangements for Senator Bryant." Hailey spun around to stomp away but was stopped by the pull of his hand on her arm. Why had he shown up now?

"I could have, but look what I'd have missed." The muscles in his jaw twitched. No matter how decent Trey had been, she had kept their daughter a secret from him and that would be unforgivable to anyone.

Hailey hurried down the path toward Todd's home with Trey following close behind. She needed to get to Sophie and somehow prepare the toddler for this enormous change in her little world. How did one go about introducing a child to her father?

The silence between them grew so heavy she struggled to breath. "Trey, Sophie isn't even two yet. If you just swoop in tomorrow and take her away for the day, she's not going to understand. It will scare her."

"Really? I'd have never thought of that. I figured she's been asking about me daily. After all, surely you've kept pictures of me around the house so she knows who I am."

Hailey squeezed her hands into fist. He didn't need to get sarcastic about it.

"I'm not planning on 'swooping in' and scaring her." He pierced her with a look. "You will be right there with us until she gets used to me. You're going to tell her who I am and do everything you can to make us seem like a family so she'll know exactly where I fit into her life."

"You want me to make us like a family? Are you going to continue treating me with such open contempt?"

"What else should I feel? You left me. You had our baby and never told me. Our daughter is almost two, and I'll never have those years with her. I don't feel anything but contempt."

Hailey swallowed tears. For as long as she could remember, Trey had loved her. His change didn't surprise her. What broke her heart was hearing the words.

CHAPTER TEN

Trey followed Hailey across the drive in front of Todd and Ellen's house, wishing he could take back his words. Somehow they had to get beyond the fighting and blame. They had to agree on some type of arrangement for Sophie.

The screen door on the garage opened and Todd came out holding Sophie. Wet hair trailed down her neck. Her pink nightgown had a picture of a cartoon princess on the front. She slid from Todd's arms and raced to Hailey. The door opened again and Joni stepped out.

"Aunt Joni..." Hailey exhaled while the two women hugged. "I forgot you were coming today."

"Do you remember Mom's sister, Joni?" Hailey stepped back and turned a questioning look on him.

What would Hailey's reaction be if he admitted that Joni had come to visit him? He met the older woman's gaze. He recognized the concern in Joni's face. "Of course I remember. It's good to see you again." He squeezed her hand, hoping she would know his gratitude. Their secret would always be safe with him—he owed her that.

"You seem to be doing well." She gave a slight nod, as though to acknowledge the silent pact.

Todd approached, his hand extended. "Trey, it's good to see

you." His eyes held no sign of duplicity, only genuine concern. "Hailey, I think Ellen wanted to talk to you."

She picked up Sophie and followed Joni into the house. When her shadow passed the kitchen window, Todd turned back to Trey.

"I need to go water the animals. Care to join me?"

Trey matched the other man's pace. "Hailey's already in trouble with your dad. I don't want to get you kicked out for associating with me, too."

"Yeah, he already called me." Todd shrugged. "You didn't think he'd kill the fatted calf for you, did you?"

"Not really."

"Don't worry about Hailey. She can stay here tonight if Dad is still upset." They reached the barn that housed several goats and a calf. Trey watched from the fence while Todd gave them grain and started the water. Todd leaned against the fence. "I'm glad you're back. Sophie needs her dad."

Todd's confession surprised him. "I don't understand why all of you kept her from me."

"No one else knew you hadn't been told. Until Ellen saw you with Sophie on Tuesday, we had no idea. I've thought about it a lot these past few days, and I guess we were led to believe that you didn't care. Not that you didn't know."

"You thought I wouldn't care about my own child? How much do you care about your child?"

"That's what didn't make sense. Once I knew Ellen and I were having a baby, I've hardly thought of anything else. It broke Ellen's heart when she realized who you were and that you couldn't even see the resemblance between you and Sophie."

Todd turned off the water and walked out the gate. He lowered himself on a hay bale and looked up. "It's not an excuse, but after the accident, we all lived in a fog for that first year. By the time Sophie was born, I never considered you hadn't been told. What are you going to do now?"

Trey wasn't ready to open up with Hailey's brother. He'd

always enjoyed a good friendship with him and his gut told him the other man was being honest. But how much could he risk? "For now, I just want to get to know her. I'll be back and forth between here and Washington."

Todd stood and they headed back to the house. "I don't know when the baby will be born or how much sleep we'll get, but you're welcome to stay with us anytime you're back here."

"I thought I might stay with Hailey."

Todd jerked around to look at him.

"That was supposed to be funny."

Todd raised one eyebrow and laughed. "You'd be sneaking around more now than when you two were dating."

Trey didn't want to remember those years. They had been good years, filled with fun and the excitement of first love. He would never have believed their love would come to this. "What's Jim able to do?"

"Well, he's almost perfected the way he criticizes."

"He had that down pretty well a few years ago. Does he do anything else?"

"Nope." Todd kicked a rock across the drive.

Trey stopped. "Why do you put up with his abuse? You could take your family and leave."

Todd stared over Trey's shoulder for several long seconds before meeting his gaze. "I ask myself that every day. Dad hasn't always been this bad, and he'd have lost the place by now. This farm and the pumpkin patch have a lot of potential to make it. I guess it comes down to being family and a love of the land. Compared to Hailey, I haven't made much of a sacrifice."

"Forgive me for not being impressed with her sacrifice." A dark blue truck drove down the lane. "Looks like you have more company."

"That's just Grant. He picked up some baling twine for me." Todd waved toward the pickup.

"Do you think there's anything going on between him and Hailey?"

Grant stepped out of the truck, but he didn't approach them.

"Grant and Hailey? Grant's like a brother to us."

Trey had seen the other man's interest at the café, and there was nothing brotherly about it.

"As long as you and Hailey are married, he won't be a threat." Todd spoke with confidence.

In a flash of pink, Sophie ran out the door and straight to Grant's arms. He tossed her into the air and caught her, then delivered a kiss on her cheek. "Hey, pumpkin pie. You smell good enough to eat." Grant hugged her to him.

Sophie leaned back and wrinkled her nose. "I not punkin pie." The two laughed.

Todd nudged Trey's arm. "That's the one I'd be concerned about. He's the closest thing to a daddy she knows."

Hailey stood inside the garage door. The scene on the drive could have come from a bad movie. They owned hundreds of acres of land, but things were beginning to feel crowded. Trey's face resembled stone as he watched Sophie's antics with Grant. Grant's stilted actions showed he wasn't comfortable with Trey standing behind him. The headache that plagued her the last two days throbbed.

"Evening, Grant." She joined the men and held her arms to her daughter. "It's time to go home, Sophie. I have lots to do."

"'Night." Sophie kissed Grant's stubbly cheek.

"Goodnight, sweetie." He released her to Hailey's arms. "Need help with anything?"

Trey stepped up next to her, meeting Grant's stare. "I'll help her."

Hailey forced a smile. "No, but thanks for asking."

"Let me know if you need anything." Grant never took his eyes off of Trey.

Trey's hand burned on her lower back as he gently pushed her off the concrete drive. Even Sophie remained silent as they walked around the house and out of view. Trey's hand dropped away, and once again she felt exposed.

He opened his arms. "Would she let me carry her so you don't have to?"

Hailey shrugged. "Sophie, do you want Trey to carry you or are you going to walk?"

Sophie looked at the unfamiliar man and smiled before pushing her head into Hailey's shoulder.

"Okay, I'm putting you down to walk." Hailey set the child on her feet and took her hand. The three walked slowly up the hill with Sophie in the middle.

"What do you have to do tonight?"

"We have a wedding scheduled for Saturday. I need to make cream puffs and mini cheese cakes. There's also the lawn to finish." Hailey's eyes darted between Sophie and Trey.

Sophie stopped and lifted her arms. "Up."

Hailey bent over to pick her up but changed her mind. "Would you like Trey to carry you the rest of the way?"

Sophie turned and scrutinized him. Hailey sighed in relief when the small arms stretched toward him. In one swoop, Trey positioned her on his hip. For a few moments, Hailey wanted to pretend they were a normal family. The tension of the past two days would probably remain until Trey left on Sunday.

She searched for a safe topic. "Things look good for Senator Bryant's reelection."

"It does. With this win and several other key victories, he'll become one of the most powerful politicians in Washington."

"He seems like a good man." She slowed her steps as they neared the house. "We'll go in the basement patio door."

"Avoiding your dad?" He touched her shoulder.

They crossed the grassy slope behind the house. "Sophie and I live down here, so we come in this way a lot. Dad's probably already in his room."

"He can take care of himself?"

"His physical needs, but I make his meals and do the laundry. Sophie, thank Trey for carrying you home."

Sophie gave him a shy smile. "Tanks you."

Trey's gaze never left the child's face. "You're welcome. I'll see you tomorrow?"

She wiggled in his arms. He set her down and watched as she toddled away. When he straightened, a veil had once again fallen, leaving his eyes unreadable. "You won't have to be with us all day tomorrow, just until Sophie feels comfortable with me."

Irritation rose. "I'll decide when I'm going to leave. I have too many things to do to wait for your permission." She turned to follow Sophie but his hand on her arm stopped her.

"I'm trying to keep this from getting ugly. Maybe you could try, too?" He let go. "I'll stay out here while you get those papers."

Hailey nodded and hurried inside. She'd left them on her dresser, knowing no one would see them there. The knot in her stomach tightened as she went back outside. Joni stood close to Trey, talking. When she approached, both looked at her.

"I was just explaining to Trey that I'll be staying with you and Sophie through October." Joni moved toward the house. "I'll get Sophie to bed." She closed herself inside.

Hailey held out the envelope.

Trey took it, slid his finger under the sealed flap, and pulled the papers out. Shuffling through them, he stopped on the last one and looked up. "I'll keep these until we decide what we're going to do."

"Don't you mean what you decide?" The thought of him having all the control scared her.

"Do you need to be reminded that I haven't had any say so far?"

She didn't. "What are we deciding?"

He matched her sarcasm with his own. "Nothing major–how we're going to share our daughter and if there's any way to save this marriage."

"You'd actually consider that?"

"Only because my dad reminded me I'd be breaking my vow to God. I'll see you in the morning."

Hailey collapsed on the patio chair and covered her face with her hands. How had she thought this would end?

Joni squeaked open the door. "Hailey? Are you okay?"

She rose and walked to the house. "I don't know if I'll ever be okay again." She tried to smile, but a sob escaped as Joni drew her into her arms.

"When we're our weakest, God can work best." Aunt Joni whispered against her hair. "Trust Him, Hailey."

"It's been so long. I'm not even sure He knows me anymore." She stepped back.

"You're His child. A father never forgets his child."

"I'm glad you're here." Hailey gave her another quick hug. "I'm really going to need you." The roar of an engine cut through the quiet evening. "That's the lawn mower."

Joni grinned and pulled her into the house. "You can thank Trey tomorrow. Let's get busy on those desserts."

CHAPTER ELEVEN

The brown, hardback motel Bible slid to the center of the scratched table. Trey leaned back in the old chair and ran his hand down his unshaved face. Since four o'clock, he'd been trying to find a verse, any verse, that would give him direction. He found many verses, just none he liked. Hailey wouldn't move back to Washington, so what choice did they have? Even if she was willing, he didn't know if he had it in him to try again.

His emotions went beyond the physical attraction he still felt towards her. Any man would find it easy to appreciate her pretty face and toned body, and he was no different. But she had walked away from him and stole the first two years of his daughter's life.

"God, I don't know if I can change how I feel about Hailey."

I can change how you feel, if you give her to Me.

"The obstacles are huge."

I created everything from nothing. Give them to Me.

A knock on the door startled him. Housekeeping arrived earlier than usual. "I'll be leaving in about an hour."

Another knock.

"Just a minute." He pulled a t-shirt over his head and opened the door. Hailey. No doubt about it, he still found her attractive. "You're up early." Trey leaned against the doorframe. He bit back a sense of satisfaction when her gaze traveled the length of his frame.

The interest in her dark eyes warmed him. At least something hadn't changed between them.

"I thought we'd take you out for breakfast." She crossed her arms.

"You know you're in a small town when they give out room numbers to anyone."

Hailey snorted. "Like I would ask for your room number. That would ruin my reputation. You're the only vehicle parked on this side of the motel. It wasn't hard to find you."

Trey stepped out the door looking both directions. Hailey was right—only his rental sat in the empty lot beside Hailey's truck with Sophie inside. "Do I need to clean up?"

"It's Windsor. You look fine. I'll wait in the truck."

He hurried to change into clothes that hadn't been slept in. On the way out the door, he grabbed the large pink gift bag he'd packed the night before.

Sophie's car seat sat between them on the bench seat. "Hi, Sophie. Are we going to spend the day together?"

She twisted her head into the side of her seat.

"She'll warm up before long." Hailey pulled in front of the café. "Marybeth should have our order ready to go. I'll be right back."

Relief filled him. It had been one thing to eat breakfast there as a stranger, but he wasn't sure how the early morning diners would take it if he showed up with Hailey and Sophie. Besides, Grant's truck parked across the street took away any remaining desire to eat inside. Trey reached into the bag and pulled out the first box. "I got you something."

The child kept her face hidden, but turned enough to expose one eye and looked at the wrapped box in his hand.

"Would you like to unwrap it? It's for you." He held the gift towards her and waited.

Her face peeked farther around the edge of the seat.

"Maybe I should see what's in it." He slid one finger under the tape while she leaned forward. "Want to help?"

Sophie tore a narrow piece of paper off and grinned. Together they unwrapped the box. She giggled at the stuffed bunny inside.

"This bunny can stay in your room." He pushed the toy to the curve of her neck. "What's her name?"

"Puppy." She wrapped it in her arms and squeezed.

Hailey opened the door and set the bags down. "What have you got there?" She climbed into the cab and started the pickup.

Sophie held the bunny to Hailey's face. "Arf-arf."

"Wow! Did Daddy– Trey get you that?"

"Arf-arf."

"What's this all about?" Trey rested his arm on the back of Sophie's car seat and nodded at the bags.

Hailey chewed on her bottom lip before answering. "It's breakfast at the park. What's wrong with that?"

"Maybe you don't want me at the farm?"

"You've been in politics too long. Most of us don't live with ulterior motives." She pulled into the park. "I just thought it would be nice for both of us to be on neutral ground." She opened her door. Turning back to release Sophie from her seat, she speared him with a look. "See? No ulterior motives. I'm just trying to give you some time with your daughter." She placed Sophie on the ground and grabbed the café bag. Sophie ran to the merry-go-round a few yards away.

He followed Hailey to the concrete table and picked up one end of the blue vinyl table cloth she shook. "Before we go any further I need to know what's going on between you and Grant." Asking caused his stomach to churn.

Her head jerked up, eyes flashing. "Looking for a biblical reason to justify divorcing me?"

"I need to know where things stand." He caught the Styrofoam box she pushed across the table before it fell to the ground.

"You know what, Trey?" She threw a fork onto the table. "I'm the same girl I've always been. I never ran around on you–and I still haven't. There have been some tough choices that I've had to make, and maybe I haven't made the right ones. But I have been faithful to you." Her voice shook. "Sophie, let's eat."

Sophie ran to the table. "Swing."

"Eat your pancake and then you and Trey can play." She pulled Sophie onto her lap and opened a carton of food.

He eyed the container she'd tossed his way. Part of the contents spilled over the edge and he swiped it off with his finger. At least she still remembered his favorite—biscuits and gravy.

"Think this will taste as good as it did in high school?" He'd not mention he didn't usually order them over easy.

"Nothing's as good as it seemed in high school." Bitterness spilled from her mouth like the gravy over the side of the box.

He stirred the broken chunks of biscuits around with his plastic fork. She was right. Even his breakfast resembled their marriage— artificial, torn in bits and pieces and no longer resembling what it started out to be. He closed the lid and pushed away the box.

"Swing." Sophie spoke with a mouthful of pancake.

"As soon as you eat a few more bites." Hailey continued to help Sophie, never opening her own meal. A tense silence settled around them.

"Go?" Sophie wiped her sticky mouth on her purple shirt sleeve.

Hailey closed the carton and pushed it to the center of the table. Trey waited, leaning forward with his hands on his knees. Waiting for Sophie. Waiting for Hailey to tell Sophie who he was. He gulped. How would she explain this for a two-year-old to understand and accept?

She cradled Sophie close and took a breath. "Sophie, do you remember what Uncle Todd is going to be when the baby comes?"

Sophie nodded.

"He's pretty excited, isn't he?" She bit her bottom lip. "Did you know... Um, you have a daddy, too. Your daddy is Trey. He's come a long way to meet you and play with you."

His daughter's clear blue eyes stared at him from across the table. He tried to swallow the knot lodged in his throat. This beautiful child was his daughter. The love swelling his heart overwhelmed him. She wiggled off Hailey's lap and marched around the table and stood at his side.

She cocked her head to the side. "Swing?"

Trey tried to clear his constricted throat. "Sure." He glanced at Hailey. "Thank you."

Her smile quivered as she gave a slight nod before looking away.

Sophie pulled him towards the swing. The softness and warmth of her hand covered the ache in his heart. His child. Some how, this little two-year-old had just wrapped him around every one of her tiny little fingers.

CHAPTER TWELVE

"Need any help?" Grant stepped into the covered pavilion. "How'd you know?" Hailey moved to another round table and lit the lantern at the center of the sunflower and daisy arrangement. "Todd took Ellen to the hospital so it's just Aunt Joni and me."

Grant took the lighter from her hand. "I wish I could say male intuition, but I passed Todd and Ellen on the road and, judging by their faces, I figured I should come and see how you're getting along."

"Do you mind staying for a bit? Once we get the food put out and everyone started, I think we'll be okay. The ceremony should be finished in about fifteen minutes and then they'll be ready to eat." She rushed to the kitchen door and turned around. "Thank you for coming. With both Todd and Ellen gone, I was getting nervous."

"Just tell me what to do." He continued weaving his way through the maze of tables. "How many are you serving tonight?"

"They have RSVPs for three hundred. Come in the kitchen after you get those lit." She pushed through the door where cool air greeted her. "It feels better in here than out there." At the oven she grabbed a pair of hot pads. "Are the salads ready to be taken out?"

"Right here." Joni emerged from the cooler, pushing a cart loaded with large bowls. Potato and pasta salad, a vegetable platter, and an assortment of fresh fruits would complement the pork loin and brisket waiting in large roasters.

Hailey opened the oven door and reached for pans of fresh rolls. "What would I do without you?"

"You'd probably have to shut down." The older lady gave the same reply every time. The kitchen door opened behind her. "Or, you'd have to pay Grant to stop farming and selling seed to help you full time."

"Wait a minute." Grant gaped at them. "You mean, someone gets paid for doing this?" He took the cart from Joni and pushed it to the door. "All I ever get is leftovers."

Joni followed behind him, shaking the serving spoons at this back. "I'd think Hailey's leftovers would be real good pay for a bachelor." She paused at the door. "We'll put these on ice."

Hailey glanced up from where she buttered the tops of the rolls. "That's fine, but leave them covered until we have people up here." Alone in the kitchen, she ran through the list she'd printed off last night. After nine weddings in two years, she knew what needed to be done, but her mind had struggled to stay on task.

She transferred the hot rolls into baskets. She'd been behind all day, due to Trey's demand that she spend yesterday with him and Sophie.

"You want the meat out next?" Grant interrupted her thoughts.

"That would be fine."

He frowned. "Everything okay?"

"Just a lot to get done." She gave him a weak smile. He left with the first roaster, and she continued filling breadbaskets. Her mind played back yesterday. Trey played with Sophie all morning. Clearly their daughter had thoroughly enchanted him. Hailey sat on the bench most of the time, not wanting to intrude. Not that she hadn't wanted to be part of their time, but Trey hadn't welcomed her to be any more than a bystander. It was bittersweet to watch

Sophie's antics and Trey's responses. The lost years couldn't be made up in a few hours, but when Hailey had left after lunch, the two were becoming friends.

"Anything else? The guests are starting to come up the path." Grant reached for the second tray of roll baskets. "Where's Sophie?"

Hailey refused to meet his eyes. "She's with her father."

He slammed the tray on the table. "He's still around?"

She nodded.

"For how long?"

"He leaves tomorrow."

The door opened and Joni hustled in. "The place is filling up. I'm going out to serve tea and water. Grant, would you watch for any dishes that need to be refilled? There's extra bowls of everything in the cooler." She retreated from the room.

"I think when she quits coming I will have to shut down." Hailey removed her stained apron and replaced it with a clean one. "I'll go out and make sure everything's okay." She didn't want to continue the conversation with Grant. Her feelings and thoughts about Trey, the pain she'd caused, and Sophie's welcoming response to him... She wasn't ready to share that rawness with anyone.

Trey drove through the parking lot filled with cars. White lights twinkled from the trees surrounding the pavilion area, and tiki torches glowed around the dance floor he'd helped Todd set up yesterday. At the bottom of the hill, kids bounced on the air pillow. To his right, a line snaked down the hill where tubes had been buried, ingeniously creating slides that could be ridden down using saucer sleds. He fought against being impressed...and lost the battle. Hailey had added some nice touches to the pumpkin patch. Judging by the number of cars, this had become a popular wedding destination. Trey parked in the only available spot near the house. He'd seen Jim yesterday when he'd taken Sophie back home. He figured Hailey must have talked to him because the man had ignored him. Trey still didn't feel welcome, but as long as he had his daughter, he didn't care.

"It looks like everyone's busy." Trey lifted Sophie from her car seat and kissed her forehead. "Do you know this has been the best day ever for your daddy?"

Sophie put her hands on each side of his face and rubbed her nose to his.

"What should we do until Mommy is done?" He experienced a oneness to Hailey when he used that word. Together they had formed this little miracle of a daughter. No amount of deceit or anger could diminish that fact.

Sophie wiggled out of his arms and grabbed his finger. "Tree." She pulled him down the drive.

He followed her. "Which tree?"

"House."

"Honey, I'm not going to take you into the house. We'd better wait for Mommy." Sophie continued to tug him toward the house. When they got near, she let go and ran past the front door and around the side. He jogged to keep up with her in the evening twilight. He stopped when Sophie pointed up into the old cottonwood that stood taller than all the others. She waddled to the base of the ladder and, with a giggle, climbed the first step.

"Whoa." Trey took quick strides to the ladder and grabbed her waist. "I don't think you're big enough to go up there." Memories flashed in his mind.

"Go." His daughter strained against him, reaching for the rung.

"How about I go up with you?"

"Me cwimb." She pulled herself to the rung and found her footing.

"All right, but I'll be right behind you if you get scared."

"Me big." She reached for the next rung.

Obviously she'd done this before. He couldn't believe a child her age could be allowed to climb this high. How well was she supervised during the day?

Trey pulled himself onto the deck and reached for the railing to give it a hard shake. To his surprise, it still held firm.

"No-no." Sophie's head poked out of the door. Trey bent down and followed her through. He squeezed his eyes shut against the memories. How many hours had he spent in this little wooden shack, hidden among the leaves? The table he and Hailey had lifted up here to do homework sat in the corner. He smiled at faded paint stain in the center of the top. The green paint had spilled when they were creating a scene from the Revolutionary War their sophomore year.

Sophie tugged him towards the window. Her blue eyes rounded with conviction. "No-no." She pointed to the scratched writing.

Trey studied the words. "We shouldn't write on the walls, should we Sophie?"

"Mommy."

"Your mommy wrote these words."

"She cry." Sophie ran her finger over the letters.

The realization of her simple words dawned on him. "These words make her cry?" Funny how much that affected him.

The sun dipped behind the horizon and darkness invaded the wooden shack. Trey led Sophie onto the deck. He sat at the top of the ladder and pulled Sophie onto his lap. The feel of her leaning back warmed him and brought a smile to his face.

"Honey, those words in there are good words. Did Mommy tell you she built this treehouse?"

Her head shook against his chest.

"She did, so those walls are hers. It's okay that she wrote on them. But you'd better never write on your walls, right? Only on paper." He tickled her.

She giggled and turned to her side. She laid her head on his arm. Through tired eyes she gazed up at him as she lifted her left hand and stuck two fingers into her mouth.

Trey pulled her closer and kissed her cheek. "I love you, Sophie. Daddy's so glad he found you."

Her eyes drifted shut.

In the stillness of the darkening evening, the celebration reverberated across the acres. Children yelled and laughed as they played among the trees, competing with the voices of the adults and the music from the dance floor. The mingled sounds floated around him. He gazed at Sophie's cherub face and let his mind fill with the past.

He and Hailey had been friends since he'd moved to Windsor in sixth grade. He'd been with her through Brandon's accident and had spent hours weeding the pumpkin patches. She pushed him to excel and challenged him like no one else. Too scared to risk the friendship, he'd waited until their senior prom to tell her his feelings.

Sophie moved in his arms, dragging him to the present. He put her over his shoulder, held her back with his left hand, and carefully started down the ladder. At the bottom he looked back to where he had sat with Hailey the morning after prom. He remembered nothing about the sunrise, but everything about their first kiss.

"The good thing about helping you out once in a while is I get my hands real clean." Grant rinsed another pot in the bleach water and set it on the rack.

"I'm not sure if that's a compliment or not." Hailey answered from across the room where she put other serving dishes away. "Thanks for staying. Aunt Joni has been here since this morning and looked worn out."

"How much longer do you expect this party to go on?" A glance at the clock above the door showed twenty after nine.

"The bride and groom are planning to leave at nine thirty. It usually wraps up pretty quickly after that."

"I'm surprised you haven't heard from Todd yet." He checked his phone again, but no new numbers showed.

"You know it can take a while."

The noise from outside filtered into the kitchen. Grant looked up just as Trey walked in carrying a sleeping Sophie in his arms. He and Trey locked gazes.

Grant stole a glance at Hailey.

With her back to the door, she tossed clean utensils into a drawer. "Remember how it was when I had Sophie? I never thought that night would end."

Trey's narrowed gaze darted between Grant and Hailey. Envy and bitterness filled Trey features. Somewhere deep inside Grant, empathy stirred. He stepped away from the sink and reached for the towel to dry his hands.

Hailey closed the drawer. "As soon as I'm finished here, I'm going to run in to the hospital. You want to go?"

Grant grimaced. "No." He laid the towel back on the counter. "I think I'd better get home. Let me know when the baby comes."

"I will." Hailey placed the last stack of dishes in the cupboard and turned. The smile on her face fell when she looked past him to Trey. Defeat filled her eyes. "Thanks for helping tonight. Don't forget the food Joni set aside for you."

Grant tried to give her an encouraging smile but the heaviness of his own heart stole his ability. He took the plastic grocery bag from the fridge and headed for the door. As he went, he let his eyes linger on the sleeping child. He'd hoped that one day Sophie would be his. Clearly Sophie's daddy would put up a strong fight before any other man would get that privilege. Trey and Hailey were gearing up for a long battle—a battle in which he had no part.

CHAPTER THIRTEEN

Hailey moved around the stainless steel island to get to the sink Grant just abandoned. She would not feel guilty about Grant being here tonight. He was a friend who helped out when she need more man-power. She didn't need to explain anything to Trey. Her comments about Sophie's birth echoed in her mind. Maybe Trey hadn't heard them—but his scowl assured her otherwise.

Plunging her hands into the warm water, she started scrubbing another pan. "You must have worn her out. You can put her in the play pen over there." Hailey motioned with a wet dripping hand but her gaze never left the sink.

Trey's footsteps reverberated across the floor.

Would they ever get beyond these uncomfortable moments? She immersed the pan into the other sink of bleach water. From the corner of her eyes, she noticed Trey moving up beside her. With her hand covered in suds, she pushed a piece of hair behind her ear. A trail of cold bubbles tingled against her cheek. Heat burned in her face when Trey wiped it dry. She kept her eyes fixed on another pan, but could not escape the weight of his gaze.

"You look as tired as Sophie."

"It's been a long day." Longer because she'd gotten so little done yesterday.

"The lights and decorations outside look great." He leaned his hip against the edge of the sink and waited for her to finish. "How many were here tonight?"

"We served almost three hundred." She glanced at him when she handed him the next pan.

"Senator Bryant would like a simple meal served when he's here. Hamburgers and hot dogs maybe."

"How many are you thinking?"

"The meal would be by invitation. I'd guess about fifty."

"You can let me know the week before." Her hair came loose and fell back onto her cheek. She blew out the corner of her mouth to try and move it off her face. When Trey's finger brushed against her skin she turned and met his unbending gaze.

"I don't want Grant helping that day."

"It will depend if I'm short-handed. With Todd and Ellen gone tonight—"

"I don't want him here." He tucked the strand of hair behind her ear. "If you need help, hire someone for the day."

She plunged her shaking hands deep into the now dirty water. "You won't be here. Grant's a friend, helping out. That's all."

The outside door opened, and the mother of the bride walked in. Hailey breathed a sigh of relief as she wiped her hands on her apron and greeted the woman.

"I think we're almost ready to leave." The woman's smile filled her face. "Thank you for all your work. This was lovely."

"I'm so glad you and Kelly chose to have it here." Hailey gave her a quick hug. "It looked like everyone had a good time."

"I've only heard the most positive remarks. I can't believe how much easier this wedding seemed compared to her sister's two years ago." She rolled her eyes toward the ceiling. "The food and decorations were perfect. This is a little something to thank you."

Hailey took the offered envelope and smiled. "I loved working with you both. Let me know if we can ever host anything else."

"No more weddings, but I heard several of my siblings suggest we come here for our family reunion."

"Just let me know." Hailey crossed to the desk beside the playpen and put the envelope into the deposit bag. She gazed down at Sophie's sleeping form. Chocolate outlined Sophie's lips and her curls drooped, attesting to the long, hot day she'd shared with her dad.

She turned to find Trey wiping the counter around the sink with a rag. "Where'd you two go?"

"The zoo."

"All day? Was she grumpy without a nap?" Hailey grabbed the last few dishes and stacked them in a cupboard.

"She fell asleep on the way to the gorilla house, so we just camped out in there until she woke up."

"The gorilla house?" Hailey scrunched her nose up at the thought of the smell.

"It was more bearable than the reptile building." He grinned. "And a whole lot more entertaining. You wouldn't believe what people will do to get those gorillas on the other side of the glass to notice them. But the gorilla rarely did more than stare."

Hailey's phone vibrated in her apron pocket. Her heart jolted when she saw the number. "Do we have a baby?"

Todd's laughter rang. "A little boy."

"Wonderful. How's Ellen?"

"The doctor's finishing things up, but she's doing great. How about you?"

"I'm almost done with clean-up. Do you care if I come and see my new nephew?"

Trey tossed the dish cloth into the sink and walked to where Sophie slept.

"We were hoping you would. Dad said he'd see him when we bring him home. Come in the emergency room doors."

Hailey closed the phone as Trey picked up Sophie. Remembering her promise to let Grant know, she sent him a text.

"I'm serious, Hailey. I don't want Grant around."

The heat of guilt rose on her face as she flipped the different switches to turn off the outside lights. "He's a friend—you know that."

Trey held the door open for her and then walked beside her in the dark. "You and Todd might be the only ones who don't see his feelings run deeper than that."

Hailey looked at the ground as they walked toward the house. She could make any number of excuses, but she knew Trey was right.

"Hailey..." He stopped, careful not to jostle Sophie. "You're still my wife. I'd like you to remember that."

"You mean that promise to honor and obey?" She kept her voice low.

He nodded slightly.

"And you'll remember to love and cherish, right?"

He winced before she turned on her heel and marched to the front door.

Hailey had already disappeared inside the house when Trey reached the porch. The door stood open, making the exchange between her and Jim impossible to ignore.

"Do you want to go to the hospital?" Hopefulness carried in Hailey's bright voice. "It would mean a lot to Todd if you came."

"I'll see him when they get home." The terse reply competed with the commercial jingle. "It's too late to be running all over the place."

"It's their first baby. They want us to come see him."

"If you want to run around this late at night you can, but I'll see the baby when they get home. Stop nagging me about it."

"I'll leave Sophie with Aunt Joni." Defeat laced her tone. "Good night." Hailey entered the foyer. "Why are you still standing out there?"

"I'm not sure how welcome I am in this house." He followed

her down the steps and into her old bedroom. "This isn't your room anymore?"

"It's always been a little girl's room. I took the guest room." She pulled back the sheets and waited for him to lay the sleeping child on the mattress. "It gives us our own space." She pulled off Sophie's shoe and groaned when sand sprinkled over the sheet.

"Sorry. I forgot about that."

She wiped the sheet clean and pulled the blankets around Sophie's shoulders. After a quick kiss on the child's cheek Hailey stood up.

He leaned over and kissed his child before whispering against her ear, "I love you, Sophie."

Hailey tiptoed from the room and then jogged up the steps. Trey took two treads at a time to catch up and followed her onto the porch. She closed the door behind them and headed to the garage. Trey trailed her, debating whether he should follow her all the way to the hospital. She opened the garage door, and to his shock the brown Explorer they drove in college waited inside.

"You still have that thing?" He walked around it, taking note of the dents, rust spots, and a missing back door handle.

"It's been a good vehicle." Hailey's scowl dared him to disagree.

"How many miles does it have on it by now?" He opened the front door and leaned in to look at the odometer. A low whistle escaped his mouth. "Maybe I should ask, how many times has the odometer rolled over?"

Hailey squeezed around him and slid into the driver's seat. "Do you mind? I want to get to the hospital while the baby is still a newborn."

Trey stepped back and slammed the door shut. He rested an arm above the opened window. "I'll be by in the morning to go with you and Sophie to church."

The vehicle chugged when she turned the key. "I don't know if we'll go." She chewed on her bottom lip when the chugging died. She twisted the key twice more, but nothing happened. She hit the steering wheel with her palm.

"I'll take you." He stepped back so she could open the door.

She glared out the windshield.

"I said I'd take you, Hailey. We'll look at this heap tomorrow."

She sat unmoving.

Trey pulled the door open. "Come on."

Hailey jumped out and hastened up the hill to his rental car parked on the drive.

Glancing down, he chuckled at the sight of an empty space where the door handle should have been. He left the relic behind and joined Hailey in the rental.

"Why are you still driving that junker?" He pulled onto the highway. He didn't mention the door handle.

She gazed out the passenger side window. "I like driving it."

"Surely you could afford something with fewer miles."

"It's fine. When I'm ready for something else, I'll buy it. For now I want to drive the Explorer."

Trey swallowed his reply. He remembered their excitement when he bought it used, eight years ago. They'd driven it from their wedding with cans rattling from the back. It had been their only vehicle until they moved back east and decided to get a smaller car that would be easier for her to park in the busy city.

"Do you know what's wrong with it?" He hoped she wouldn't get angry with his probing. He bit back a smile when she sighed.

"The biggest thing is probably that the transmission might be going out."

He coughed. "Oh, only the transmission? What are some of the smaller things?"

Hailey crossed her arms and glared at him. "What does it matter to you? I'll get it fixed and it will be fine."

"It's not worth fixing, Hailey."

"How do you know? Are you a car repairman, too?"

"Who told you it was the transmission?"

"It will only make you mad if I tell you."

Trey almost laughed. Her answer told him everything he needed to know. "Did he think you should get it fixed?"

She sat in silence.

"Did he?"

"No." She spit the single word out.

"We need to get you a new car."

"I'll get it fixed so that won't be necessary."

"I want to get you a new car, Hailey. I don't like the idea of you and Sophie being stuck in the middle of nowhere."

Guilt flashed across her face.

"Has it broken down when you had Sophie with you?" When she didn't answer he continued. "Either tomorrow or the next time I come we'll go car shopping. Think of it as a gift to Sophie."

"A car isn't a gift for a two-year-old. Don't you think you've given her enough things? You don't have to keep buying her stuff."

Trey drummed his fingers on the steering wheel. "I missed the day she made her entrance into the world, and I didn't receive any invitations to her first birthday party. There've also been two Christmases without any gifts from her daddy under the tree. No, I don't think I've given her enough gifts."

Her sigh told him plenty. "What time does your plane leave tomorrow?"

"Late afternoon." They needed to discuss Sophie visiting him, but he now wasn't the best time. He should have considered that before he brought up the missed celebrations. "I'm not going to be able to get back here for a few weeks. I want you–" He tamped down the demand. "Would you please consider bringing Sophie to visit?"

"We're so busy right now getting ready for opening weekend."

"Just for Labor Day weekend. We're getting to know each other, and I don't want to lose what we've started. You could fly in Friday evening and leave Monday morning." He held his breath, waiting for her to answer.

"It would only be for the weekend, because next week is

busy and then we open. But since you're talking about a holiday weekend, I doubt I'd even be able to get tickets."

"I'll take care of that." Anticipation replaced the dread about leaving. His daughter would be coming home.

CHAPTER FOURTEEN

Who did he think he was? To have Trey so suddenly back in her life—and for good—left her feeling raw. The change had been too fast, too unexpected for her to fully process. He didn't want Grant to help at the pumpkin patch, and now he was going to buy her a new car? She wanted to scream. Or cry. Why had she agreed to take Sophie to visit next weekend? Any ability to refuse him had disappeared. Trey wasn't asking too much for Sophie to visit, but the idea terrified her.

Hailey stopped at the main desk in the maternity ward to ask for Ellen's room number. The nurse pointed toward the door at the end of the dark hall. She started off.

"Which room was Sophie born in?" Trey's whisper carried from behind her.

Hailey swallowed. "I didn't have her here."

He stopped her with a hand on her arm and stepped in front of her. "Why not?" Confusion clouded his face, then as awareness dawned, his jaw tightened. "Are you going to tell me?"

"I wanted a more natural environment."

"Really?"

"It's a very good place. They work with you so you don't need pain meds."

"How long did you stay after Sophie was born?"

When would he run out of questions? "Just a few hours."

A tight smile crossed his lips. "I assume it wasn't as expensive as a hospital? You could probably pay for it out of pocket—no need to use your insurance." The muscle in his jaw ticked.

Hailey focused on the top button of his shirt, not willing to see betrayal in his eyes. "That wasn't the reason. I—"

"It wasn't? Quit lying to both of us, Hailey. You know the main, if not only, reason you went there was to prevent me from seeing the insurance papers."

Angry tears clouded her eyes. She tried to keep her voice quiet, not wanting everyone else in the ward to hear them. "It's a very good place, and I'd have another baby there."

His eyes glistened. "Well, it won't be my insurance you'll be trying to avoid when that day comes."

The harsh truth stung. She had lost her husband and there wouldn't be another baby. How long would she pay the price for her actions? A lifetime... She scurried up the hall. "This is their room."

"I'll wait over there." He motioned to the waiting area at the end of the hall.

"Are you sure? Todd and Ellen won't mind if you come in." She forced herself to look him in the eye. His words had hurt, but no less than her deceit had cut him.

"I'm sure. Come get me when you're ready to leave." She watched as he moved across the hall to the window of the nursery and stopped. The stony fury in his face pierced her. She'd done this to them, and the realization left her empty as she pushed the door open.

Todd and Ellen looked up with excitement dancing in their eyes. Her brother sat in the chair, holding the swaddled baby, while Ellen ate a sandwich.

Hailey put her finger under the baby's tiny hand. "What a beautiful little boy. Congratulations."

"Dad and Sophie didn't come with you?" Todd studied her

face. "You okay?"

"Trey brought me. The Explorer wouldn't start."

"Where is he?"

She gestured to the hallway, afraid she would cry if she spoke.

"Let Aunt Hailey hold you for a while." He nestled the bundle in her arms, then he went out the door.

"He's really beautiful, Ellen." Hailey pulled the knit cap up, revealing dark hair. "What's his name? Todd didn't tell me on the phone."

The new mother smiled. "Jacob Michael."

"Are your folks on their way?"

"They left as soon as we called them this afternoon. When Todd called after Jacob was born, they were almost to Tulsa. They'll be here in the morning."

Both women looked up when Todd walked in with Trey following.

"Congratulations." Trey's smile didn't mask the sadness in his eyes.

"Thank you." Ellen bit her lip and blinked back tears. "Would you like to hold him?"

Hailey stood and held out the blue-wrapped bundle. "Go ahead. It's easier than keeping hold of Sophie."

Trey looked from the newborn to her.

"And a lot lighter." Todd sat down on the edge of the bed and picked up Ellen's hand.

Trey finally held out his arms, and Hailey laid the baby in the crook of his elbow. He cleared his throat, never lifting his eyes from the infant. He ran his finger down the baby's cheek. "Was Sophie this tiny?"

"Who are you calling tiny?" Todd defended his son. "This young man weighed eight pounds, six ounces, I'll have you know."

Trey raised his eyes to Hailey's. "How big was Sophie?"

"She came a little early. She weighed five pounds, two ounces."

Concern filled his face. "Was she okay?"

"Perfect." Hailey fought down the enormous guilt that threatened to consume her. Her choices had prevented Trey from experiencing this miracle with his own child. Why had she never considered all she'd cheated him out of? She battled shame for the pain she'd inflicted on him.

But she hadn't had a choice. Her list of options had been short and she'd chosen the only one that came close to being right. Trey would be fine and move on without her, but her dad would never be able to move on alone.

"Knock, knock." The door opened and a nurse breezed in. "Are you both doing all right?" She touched Jacob's head before moving to Ellen. "Do you need something to help you sleep?"

"I don't know if I can sleep." Ellen grinned. "I can't believe Jacob's finally here."

"I know, but you've had a tough day, and when you leave here it will just be you and Dad." The nurse handed her a cup with a white pill in it. "This will let you relax."

Trey never took his eyes from Jacob's face. "We'd better go. Are you ready, Hailey?"

"I'll bring Sophie tomorrow. She'll be so excited." Hailey hugged Ellen and then turned to hug Todd. "Thanks for letting us come."

Her brother wrapped her in his embrace. "Forgive yourself, Hailey," he whispered in her ear. "You two can get through this."

Hailey blinked against tears and nodded.

"Thanks for bringing Hailey." Todd took the baby from Trey. "You're welcome to come and see Jacob anytime. In fact, we'd be happy to reserve midnight to six as your designated time."

"I might take you up on that." Trey smiled at Ellen. "Thank you."

In silence, Trey escorted Hailey from the hospital. Outside, he took her arm and pulled her to a bench. "Tell me about the day Sophie was born, please?" His shoulders slumped as he pinched his lips tight to stop their trembling. He needed to know the details—to somehow be a part of the day.

Hailey sighed and nodded. "She came almost two weeks early on January 18. It was cold and icy. It took Todd a couple of hours to get to the clinic. I was in labor for about twelve hours before she finally came. She was small but healthy and so beautiful. They put a silly pink hat on her and I kept taking it off so I could see her hair—it was a little darker than it is now, and she had lots of it. The first time she looked at me, I thought she looked just like you."

He laid his hand on her arm, needing the connection. "Who brought you?"

"Dad stayed home, so just Todd. He drove everyone in the waiting room crazy."

"Was Grant with you?"

"I'd never ask another man to be there."

"So you were alone?"

Hailey gave a small laugh. "The clinic staff were amazing."

"Why did you have her all by yourself?" He coiled his fingers around her arm. "I would have been there even if you'd called on your way to the hospital. Why didn't you call?"

She shrugged. "I don't know anymore." She closed her eyes. "I'm sorry, Trey. I shouldn't have kept her from you, but there weren't other options. There still aren't. I can't leave here. I don't expect you to forgive me, but I hope you can believe that I am sorry.". She pulled her arm away from him and stood. "I'll wait for you in the car."

"Someone left the light on in the shed." Hailey's voice filled the dark car when he turned into the drive, her first words since they left the hospital.

He didn't care about a light on in the shed. And he didn't care that Sophie hadn't been born in a hospital—there were other good options. But fury still filled him. Such lengths to which Hailey had gone to prevent him from knowing.

She sighed. "Thanks for taking me."

He turned a glare on her. "We could have figured things out." His voice emerged hoarse. "I don't understand why you made these choices without me."

"You didn't want me to stay in Kansas any longer." She crossed her arms over her chest and glared out the window. "Dad still needed my help, and I knew you were going to South America. I didn't want to be left in that city alone."

He gripped the steering wheel and stared out the window. "If you would have been honest with me, I would have understood." His stomach twisted, knowing that might not be the whole truth. "What did I do to make you think I wouldn't help you?" He braced himself for the answer that had eluded him for almost three years.

"You wanted to control me just like my father does."

The words struck like a punch. "That's not— I'm not—" He put the car in PARK and searched for a defense. "I would have helped you, if you would have asked."

"I couldn't take that risk. I had to be here for Dad."

He would never understand her. "Go on to the house. I'll get the light in the shed on my way out."

She opened the door and stepped out. "Thanks again." She strode away, her frame disappearing in the shadows.

Backing up to the corner, Trey parked the car and got out. Croaking frogs along the creek and the buzz of mosquitoes broke the stillness of the night. A light shone between the three foot opening in the tall sliding door. Trey ducked into the building and stopped. He backed into the shadows, hoping he hadn't been heard. Jim sat in his wheelchair behind the tall front tires of the John Deere combine. Several tools lay across his lap. His extended arms reached inside the machine.

Trey hadn't expected the surge of empathy. Could he get out of the shed without being noticed? The clatter of a metal tool hitting concrete and the expletive that echoed off the aluminum walls jolted Trey from his thoughts.

Jim maneuvered his chair to the back of the combine. Using another tool, he leaned forward and swiped at the wrench that was just out of reach. Unsuccessful, he looked around the building. "You can quit hiding. Nothing like watching a lame man struggle."

Trey pushed away from the door and ambled toward him. "I came in to turn off the lights. I didn't realize you were in here." He picked up the dropped crescent wrench and held it out.

"You must enjoy seeing me like this." Jim spit the bitter words.

"Not really." Trey leaned against the combine tire and forced himself to relax. "If you weren't like this, I wouldn't be dealing with the mess concerning my wife and daughter."

Jim gave him a shrewd look. "Your marriage wouldn't have made it anyway. Hailey wasn't happy in Washington, and you were too busy to notice."

Trey bit the side of his cheek. Why did he try to reason with this man? No one ever won. "I didn't think you handled any of the farming anymore."

"Fixing something isn't farming."

"Why don't you find a way to do more?"

Jim's grip on the wrench turned white. "I'm not a politician with unlimited money."

"There are ways."

"It's noble of you to be so concerned about me. But Hailey's right where she belongs and she's not going back." Jim moved the chair back to the side of the implement.

"She belongs with her husband." Trey balled his fists. "Why would you want her to break the marriage vows she made before God?"

Jim clamped the wrench on a bolt and began tightening it. "God and Hailey are the reason I'm like this."

Had he heard the man correctly? Jim blamed Hailey for the accident? "The other driver ran the stop sign. Hailey couldn't have ything to stop it."

here's no such thing as an accident—just carelessness."

he same thing would have happened if you'd have been driving." Trey's voice grew louder.

"Then I'd be the one walking." Jim looked over his shoulder at Trey. "This place needs Hailey, and she understands we're all paying a price for that night."

A sick feeling threatened to overwhelm him. He needed to get out of there before he said too much. Without another word, he turned and stomped to the doors.

"She's accepted things for how they are. Don't mess everything up." Jim's final remark followed him into the night.

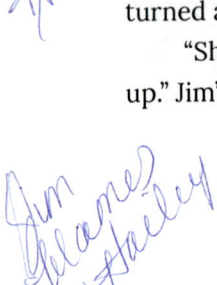

CHAPTER FIFTEEN

Hailey tucked her legs under her and took a drink from the mug warming her hands. The stillness of the morning conflicted with the thoughts warring within her. A week ago she'd sat here on the porch swing, marking off all she'd accomplished the previous week and creating a new list for the coming one. Her days had been predictable. She took another sip and leaned her head back. Two weeks until the pumpkin patch opened, and now she'd committed to a trip to Washington. It didn't take much thought to know what her dad's reaction would be.

A branch snapped behind her. Startled, she looked over her shoulder to see Trey strolling toward her.

"Morning."

Hailey faced forward but not before she noticed how good he looked. Here she sat an old pair of pajama pants and sweatshirt, her hair sticking out in every direction from an elastic band. She hadn't even brushed her teeth. But he could have stepped off a magazine page. "What are you doing here so early?"

He stopped beside the swing. A smile played at the corners of his mouth. "I see you were expecting me." He glanced at his watch. "It's not really that early, either."

"There's coffee in the kitchen if you want some." She took another drink, annoyed to see her hand shake.

Trey nodded his thanks before disappearing into the house. Within minutes he returned and sat in the chair beside her.

"I can't believe Sophie is still asleep." He stretched his legs, crossing them at his ankles. "What time does church start?"

She raised her cup to her lips, looking at him from over the rim. "Same time as it always does, I suppose."

Trey nodded slowly. "You're not going this morning?"

"Wasn't planning on it." She refused to look away.

"Is that just this morning or a regular occurrence?"

"I don't see that as any of your business."

Trey motioned at the treehouse. "Sophie took me up there last night while we waited for your party to end. I can't believe it's still there."

"Not too bad for twelve-year-old builders." She smiled at the memory. "You thought the railing would fall off the first time anyone touched it."

"And you had to prove it wouldn't by leaning over it." He chuckled. "Think Sophie will ever know how special that place was to us?"

Hailey shook her head. "There's plenty she doesn't need to know."

"Sophie climbs that ladder pretty fast." The change in his tone sounded strangely parental.

"She's not scared of much."

"It might be good if that ladder came down until she's older."

She sighed. "Is there anything you think I'm doing right?"

He held up his hand. "I'm not accusing you of anything. She got away from me yesterday and scooted right up that ladder. It's not safe until she's old enough to get back down and she can understand the danger of being that high."

Hailey ran a hand over her hair. "Is this why you came out here so early? Just to tell me everything I'm doing wrong?"

Trey leaned forward and set his coffee mug on the table. Resting his elbows on his knees he tented his fingers in front of him before looking at her. "I thought I'd go to church with you and Sophie this morning. I didn't realize you didn't go anymore."

A finger of shame curled through her. She shrugged, hoping to dislodge her guilt. "It's really not your business."

"Because of Sophie, it is my business. I want her to be raised in church. We were raised in church. Why wouldn't you want Sophie to have faith?"

"It's hard to go to my old church. No one understands why I'm raising Sophie without you. They all thought we were the perfect couple. I got tired of their sympathy."

"They all think I left you?"

She bit her lip. What was the verse about the truth always setting you free? Freedom was not what she felt right now.

"It's good to know you feel a little guilt at making me into the bad guy when I never had a clue." He picked up his mug and stood. "I'll go wake Sophie while you get ready. We'll visit a church in town. One with a big congregation so no one will know anything about us."

"Why is this so important to you? After we moved to Washington church wasn't very high on your list."

"I know. If it would have been we probably wouldn't be here now."

"That wasn't so bad, was it?" Trey glanced at her before pulling out of the busy parking lot.

She shrugged. "I guess not. It's certainly a big church–lots going on." If she were honest, she'd admit it had been like a glass of water at the end of a hot day. Whether from guilt or conviction, her stomach pinched, knowing she'd been the one who had walked away from her faith. There would be plenty to think about once Trey left.

"Are you okay, Sophie?" She looked into the backseat.

Sophie's smile showed off her dimples.

Hailey turned forward. The car rolled past their turn. "You missed the corner."

"Guess I did." He lifted and eyebrow and grinned.

"You could pull in here and go back."

"I could." He continued to drive down the street. "What do you think of this car?"

"This rental? It's nice." She watched his face, trying to figure out this change in the conversation.

"What about you, Sophie? Do you like this car?" He studied her in the rear view mirror.

"Yes. Car." Her giggle rang inside the vehicle.

"Really? You like this one?" His smile widened as if sharing a private joke with his daughter. "Should Daddy buy you one?"

Hailey twisted sideways in her seat and gaped as Trey turned into the car dealership. "Trey, you can't be serious. You can't buy your two-year-old a car."

"Sophie, can I buy you a car?" He pulled into the parking space and looked over his shoulder at the small girl.

"Car." She pointed out the window.

Trey smiled at Hailey. "Are you jealous I'm not buying one for you?" The dimple that matched Sophie's deepened.

"No, I don't need one—and neither does Sophie." The words stumbled from her confused mouth. Why was she arguing with him over buying a car for their toddler? "Trey, she's two. Wait fifteen years and then we'll both be glad for you to buy her a car."

"Honey, if I buy you a car, who would you let drive it?"

Hailey faced her daughter. Shaking her head she pointed to herself and mouthed no.

"Mommy."

The little traitor.

"That's just what I was thinking. If I buy you the car, Mommy will have to drive it for you. Then when Daddy is away he'll know you are safe and not broken down on the side of the road." The sing-song tone of his voice belied his concern.

Hailey looked out the windshield and crossed her arms. "This is absolutely silly. You cannot buy a car for a two-year-old. There is nothing wrong—"

Trey raised his eyebrows.

"Okay. There is almost nothing wrong with the Explorer. It just needs a few things."

He pointed a direct look at her. "I've already talked to Todd about this so I know the 'few things' that need fixed. It's time for a new car."

"Then I'll buy it." She winced. He'd call her bluff. The pumpkin patch did well, but all the money went into the farm account. She'd have to get her Dad's approval to make a major purchase of a new vehicle. He wouldn't be against it. In fact, he'd encouraged her for two years to get rid of the Explore. She'd always figured it was more about breaking all ties to Trey than anything else, and that was why she kept driving it.

Trey's touch on her knee burned through the skirt fabric. "You're welcome to help pay for it. Sophie is my daughter, and I want to know that she is safe. I can't be here every day with her, but I can make sure the vehicle you are driving is reliable." He motioned toward the building. "The salesmen in there are waiting for us, and we're not going to fight about this in front of them. If you like this car all you have to do is pick out the color. If you want something else, say so and we'll look at it."

His serious gaze seared her. A reliable vehicle meant a lot to him. Resigned, she nodded. "Okay. Let's go pick out a car for Sophie."

With a wink, Trey got out and carefully lifted Sophie into his arms. "What color do you want, sweetheart?"

"Pink."

Hailey laughed at the grimace on his face.

He placed his hand on Hailey's back. "You pick the color, Mom. I'm not buying a pink car."

Warmth flooded over her at the intimate gesture. Even though

Trey dropped his hand to open the door to the dealership, Her flesh tingled from his touch.

An older salesman hurried towards them. "How can I help you folks today?"

Sophie cupped Trey's face in her small hands and pulled him down until his nose rubbed against hers. "Pink car."

CHAPTER SIXTEEN

A 727 taxied across the tarmac and into position alongside the covered walkway awaiting its approach. Trey slid his laptop into the leather bag and leaned back in the vinyl chair in the crowded waiting area. In a few minutes the big metal doors opened and the clamor of disembarking passengers filled the air. Normally he enjoyed watching this ritual of homecoming—the embraces, well wishes, shy smiles of hello. But today it only served to remind him of what he had missed the last two years. He'd not only left his wife and daughter at Harper Farms—he'd left his heart.

Above the growing cacophony of voices his phone rang, and he frowned as he recognized the caller ID. He wasn't ready to answer the questions he knew were forthcoming. "Hey, Dad."

"I'm just heading back to church for a meeting. You keep coming to mind. How are things going?"

"I'm getting on a plane in a few minutes." He rolled his shoulders to release the built up tension.

"It's too bad you can't take a few more days of vacation."

Trey stepped to the window overlooking the busy tarmac. "The election is nine weeks away. I have to get back."

"You're planning to stay in D.C.?"

"We've been over this. I've worked too hard to get to this point. Rob Bryant will become the Majority Leader after the election. I'll be his Chief-of-Staff."

"What about Hailey and Sophie? Has anything changed there?"

Trey squeezed the bridge of his nose. "Hailey's as stubborn as ever. I asked her to bring Sophie for a visit, but I'll be surprised if she doesn't find an excuse to cancel. I'm hoping she'll bring her for my birthday."

"Labor Day Weekend? That's right around the time they open the pumpkin patch, isn't it?"

"She can leave if she considers our marriage worth fighting for."

Silence fell on the other end of the connection.

"Dad? Still there?"

"You think Hailey should pack up and go back to Washington?"

"We can't figure anything out with us in two places. How long can we keep up this long distance? Bryant isn't going to be interested in a C.O.S. that's always running back to Kansas."

"You're willing to give up nothing for your job, but you think Hailey should give up everything for your marriage."

"No, I've–" He fought to find the words to explain.

"In the seven years since your wedding, how much energy would you say you've given to building your career? You don't get to be Chief-of-Staff for the Majority Leader by working nine to five, Monday through Friday."

The announcement for his flight sounded over the speakers. "Dad, I have to go."

"Let me ask one more thing."

Irritated with the direction of the conversation and the time crunch, Trey sighed. "Fine, but make it quick."

"In the three years Hailey lived in D.C. with you, did she like it there? Was she happy?"

"Of course she was happy. We had three good years there. I've got to go, Dad. Thanks for calling. Tell Mom hello for me." Trey pushed the button to disconnect.

Leaning forward during takeoff, Trey looked down to see the

patchwork of farmland below. As the plane climbed in altitude, he searched for familiar landmarks. Maybe if he could pick out the Windsor CO-OP, he'd be able to see Harper Farms. That might make it seem he was closer to Sophie and Hailey. After a few minutes, he pulled the shade and sat back. His dad's last question ran through his mind. Trey had lied, and he figured his dad knew it too.

The first year in Washington had been exciting. Sometime during the second year he sensed a growing frustration in Hailey. Advancing his career as quickly as possible meant more of his time. His hours away from home blurred between the hours spent at the office and going to high-powered receptions in the evenings.

"Something to drink, sir?" The smiling attendance handed him a napkin.

"Coffee."

"Regular or decaf?" She pulled the Styrofoam cup from the stack.

"Regular. Black, please." Setting the cup on the tray in front of him, he watched the steam rise, and with it came a memory. The first Friday in May, and Hailey had asked him several times as he dressed for work if he had plans for dinner that evening.

"Nothing I can think of." He shrugged into his jacket and straightened his tie.

She turned her coffee mug around in her hands. "So, I should make dinner tonight? Or were you thinking we'd go out?"

"It would be great if you fixed something. I eat out so much." He opened the door and turned back. "I'll come home early. Maybe we can watch a movie or something."

By the time he got off the Green Line at L'Enfant Plaza and caught the Red Line to Capitol South, he'd forgotten all about their evening plans.

When Senator Bryant asked Trey to attend a reception, he willingly agreed to go. To be asked to represent the senator after only a month on staff! Adrenaline surged through his body as he envisioned networking with one of the most influential special interest groups.

The night had been everything he'd imagined and more.

When he opened the door to their dark apartment, he felt drunk with power. He could hardly wait to share the excitement with Hailey. But the candle-perfumed air stopped him short. Candle stubs studded the table, and wax had hardened into mountains on the tablecloth Hailey's grandmother crocheted for their wedding present.

Dread replaced elation as he set his computer bag down. Two place settings of china—one clean, the other filled with uneaten food—sat on the table. A platter held some type of Chinese dish. He recognized the rice, but the meat mixture on top had become congealed and gray. The rolls in the basket were dried out.

A cake box from the bakery on the corner sat at the end of the table. With trepidation he lifted the lid to peek inside, then quickly closed it again.

May seventh. Hailey's birthday.

"Did you have a good evening?" Hailey's voice broke the silence.

He searched the dark room. She sat in her grandmother's rocking chair.

"Something came up." A lame excuse. "I'm sorry, honey. I'll call in tomorrow and we'll spend the whole day celebrating."

Her smile never reached her eyes. "That won't be necessary. While I waited for you, I bought myself a ticket home."

Those words knocked the air from him. Numerous thoughts flashed through his mind, none of them sticking long enough for him to say anything.

"Todd graduates next week from college. I'd like to be there."

He finally found words. "I thought we were going back for the Fourth of July."

"There's really no reason for me to miss his big day. You'll be fine while I'm gone. In fact, I doubt you'll even notice." She stood and marched toward the bedroom.

"Hailey."

She stopped.

"I'm sorry I didn't come home for dinner."

"I'm going to bed now." Her voice trembled. "My flight leaves early in the morning."

"Tomorrow?" He stood behind her and slid his hands onto her hips.

She stiffened.

"Please. Give me a chance to make this up to you. We'll spend the day—"

"My birthday ended twenty minutes ago. There's nothing to celebrate." She wrenched away.

His eyes locked on the single suitcase beside the door, waiting for morning. He breathed a sigh of relief. One small suitcase meant she wasn't leaving for good, only going home for a short visit.

That one small suitcase had been very deceiving.

Balancing a bag of groceries and his computer case, Trey pushed the apartment door open and flipped on the light. He set everything on the kitchen counter and reached for the manila envelope with his daughter's name in the left corner. Hailey had handed it to him before he left on Sunday. Without thinking, he'd pushed it into the front pocket of his bag and only remembered it on the way home from work today. It had been a long day and he missed Sophie. He pulled out a torn page from a coloring book. The multicolored flowers and butterflies displayed the talent of a twenty-month-old. The fridge would be a good place to display the piece of art. He secured it with two magnets that advertised neighborhood restaurants. He turned back to the counter and shook the envelope again. A photo with Sophie and him and a folded paper slid into view. Hailey had scribbled a note to explain Sophie made the picture for him. She'd taken the photo on Friday and thought he might like it.

Trey glanced at his watch and reached for the phone. Sophie would be in bed soon. He'd called her each night since coming back to D.C., not wanting her to forget him before they arrived Thursday evening. Holding the photo, he crossed to the only window in the living room and waited for Hailey to answer her phone.

"Sorry I'm calling so late." He looked at the photo.

"I wondered if I should even answer because Sophie fell asleep on the way home from town tonight. She's already in bed." Hailey's words were rushed.

Trey had noticed how quickly she'd passed the phone to Sophie every night when he called. Now he understood—she thought he didn't want to talk with her.

"I wanted to thank you for the package you sent home with me."

"Sophie wanted you to have it."

"It looks great on the fridge. Right under the China Garden magnet."

"Are they still there? I'd love some of their General Tao." Hailey stopped and silence hung between the miles that separated them. Before Trey could respond Hailey spoke again. "When Sophie wakes up, I'll tell her you called."

"We'll take Sophie there on Saturday."

"Trey, I'm not sure how that's going to work out."

"She either comes with you or without you, Hailey. It's your choice." He propped the photo on the book shelf.

"It really would work better in November. Things are getting so busy here."

"That's great if you can bring her then. But it doesn't change the plans for this weekend."

"Trey—"

"If Sophie isn't here on Thursday night, I'll get my lawyer involved."

She gasped "You'd do that?"

Trey closed his eyes against the hurt in her voice. "Yes, I would. You agreed to bring her."

"Then I guess there isn't a choice. But I'll stay in a hotel."

The request surprised him. He hadn't considered her staying

elsewhere. This was her home. "You don't want to stay in your own home?"

"I'll get a room."

Annoyance spread through him. "I don't want to visit Sophie in some hotel. Are you willing to let her stay here?"

"I think so." Hailey paused. "I'm sorry. It will just be easier if I stay someplace else."

"What are you so afraid of?"

Her silence spoke volumes.

"I promise I'll keep my distance." He tried to lighten the conversation.

"It's a small apartment—distance would be hard to find."

"Maybe that's what we need." He ran his finger over the picture and wished he had a picture with all of them in it.

"Sophie misses you. She'll be glad to see you."

"And you? Will you be glad?" The questions came out before he could stop them.

A pause fell. "I think I gave that right up three years ago."

"Look how far we've come in less than a week. We're actually carrying on a civil conversation."

She laughed softly. "Only because the one you really wanted to talk to is sleeping."

"You're the one who gives the phone away quickly each night."

"I'll tell her you called." Her tone turned crisp. "Tomorrow is Todd's birthday, so we're getting together for cake and ice cream. She'll be up later."

"I'm going to join a Bible study that meets on Wednesday nights. I'll try to call around supper."

"Is it with a church?" Disbelief laced the words.

"No, it's a group of men I work with. You'd be surprised at the number of congressmen and senators who are Christians. They really do want to do the right thing. I'll tell you about it when you get here."

"You understand about the hotel room?"

"No, but I'll find you one. It's good talking to you, Hailey." Trey set the phone on the table and looked around. How much was he willing to sacrifice for his life to stay this way? He lived alone. Work consumed all of his energy. His peers considered him successful, but he wondered what his own desire for success would cost.

A bottle of water from the fridge and a half eaten sandwich from last night made up his meal. Sitting at the table, he opened the box he received in the mail. The manual inside was filled with photos and diagrams of altered farm equipment. He dialed Todd's number.

"Getting any sleep?" The cry of a newborn echoed in the background. He clenched his jaw, fighting against jealousy.

"Nope."

He cleared his throat. "Have you looked at that site I told you about?"

"Yes, and I got the manual you ordered for me." He paused. "Do you think this would work?"

"I'm looking at the flatbed pickup with the chairlift on it. Did you watch the video? Why couldn't we do that? With a few changes to the combine, he could drive it again." Excitement built as Trey looked at the drawing. "It's worth trying."

"What if he doesn't accept it? Dad doesn't seem to like anything."

"I don't know, but I have to try. I want my wife back." He'd thought those words, but hadn't spoken them before now.

"Okay, we'll try it. I'll talk to a man in town who has a welding business. I think he'd help us figure it out. You'll be back in a couple of weeks?"

"I'm planning on it. Has Hailey said anything about this weekend?"

"Not to me." Todd's voice became muffled. "Ellen, has Hailey said anything about this weekend? ... No. Trey, not a thing."

What was she thinking? She would tell them, wouldn't she? "All right, I'm sure she will." He hurried on. "I've been checking, and

I think I can get some grants to help with the funding for the new equipment."

"You realize Dad may never thank you."

"I know, but it might be what makes a difference for all of us. Let me know what you find out."

"Anyone want more ice cream?" Hailey fidgeted with the handle of the metal spoon. "Dad, do you want anything else?"

"I'm fine." He looked back at the matching game he and Sophie were playing.

"Grant?"

"I need to get home." He stood and pushed his chair under the table. "Happy birthday, Todd."

Todd shook the offered hand. "Thanks for helping me celebrate."

Grant moved beside her at the counter and took the spoon from her hand. "Walk me out?"

A chorus of good-nights sounded around the room as chairs scrapped the floor. Aunt Joni moved to the sink while Ellen collected the dishes.

"What's going on with you tonight?" Grant muttered once they were in the hall.

"Nothing."

"Something's going on. You jumped every time someone talked to you, and you're as scattered as an old hen."

"That's a compliment." Maybe Grant would be the ally she needed to help tell her dad about the coming weekend. She took a deep breath. "I'm taking Sophie to see Trey this weekend."

"You have got to be kidding." His voice rose with each word. "What are you thinking?"

"Is everything okay out here?" Todd stood in the kitchen doorway with Jacob cradled in his arm.

Grant guided her back to the kitchen. "Do you know what she's got planned?"

Todd raised his eyebrows. "I've heard she had something going on, but don't know what it is."

Grant let go, and she hurried to stand by Ellen, who continued to scoop ice cream into plastic containers. Jim looked up from the game.

"I'm— Well, I'm—" This wasn't how she'd planned to tell. She almost giggled at the thought. She hadn't planned how she'd tell. That's why it was Wednesday night, and she still hadn't come up with a way to break the news. She filled her lungs and let her answer rush out. "I'm taking Sophie to visit Trey this weekend."

Jim's eyes glinted. "No, you're not."

"That's crazy." Grant's hand hit the counter. "Why would you even consider that?"

"You are not leaving right now. This is our busiest time of the year. Leaving would be completely irresponsible, and you're not irresponsible." Her dad spoke with measured words, his eyes wide with disbelief.

Hailey looked around the room. Only Grant and her dad were angry. Todd gave her an encouraging smile.

"I will not allow you to go." Jim's face grew mottled.

"She's an adult." Aunt Joni turned from the sink. "Let her make her own—"

"You stay out of this." He shot the older woman and angry glare. "It doesn't concern you."

Aunt Joni leaned against the cabinet with her arms crossed.

Hailey squeezed her hands together to keep them from shaking. "I don't have a choice. Trey will get his lawyer involved if I don't take her."

"We'll get our own lawyer."

"We're not getting a lawyer. Trey deserves to know Sophie. I don't want things to get any worse."

Her dad pointed at her. "He's trying to manipulate you. You

can't even see it."

Anger replaced her nervousness. She stared at her dad. "I know what manipulation is better than anyone. You have taught me well."

Jim threw the cards across the table and pushed his chair back. "You won't use a dime of my money to pay for this."

"Trey is taking care of things."

"You're going to stay with him for the weekend?" Grant raised his eyebrows.

Hailey grabbed the dishcloth from Aunt Joni's hand and wiped the counter. "I'll stay at a hotel."

Grant gave her a look of disgust. "At least you've thought that through."

"If I chose to stay at Trey's, I'd be fine. He only wants to see Sophie." Speaking the truth aloud only made the reality bitter.

"And don't forget"–Todd's stare never wavered from Grant's face–"she's married to the man. She should stay with him."

Jim smacked the table with his open palm. "We don't need your input. Hailey, you'll put us behind, and we probably won't be ready for opening weekend. You're being irresponsible."

"I'll do her work." Aunt Joni's expression dared him to say anything.

He swore. "You're not a part of this."

Aunt Joni stomped to the table and bent forward to meet Jim's gaze. "If she wants to go, she'll go. I said I'd do her jobs–everything except take care of you. If you don't want my help, you don't need to eat for a few days. That might teach you a lesson."

Todd cleared his throat. "I agree that she needs to go. We'll be fine for a few days without her."

"You are all a bunch of fools." Jim shoved the table aside before maneuvering out of the kitchen.

Grant's fists rested on his hips. "You're really going?"

Hailey took one step close to him. "I have to try to make things right where I can. Please understand."

"I think he's only going to make things worse for you."

Todd stepped between the two. "I think it's time for you to leave. Hailey is trying to correct some of the wrongs. She doesn't need you to be against her."

Grant shook his head before turning and stomping out the front door.

An eerie calm settled over the kitchen—the kind of calm that followed a tornado. Hailey looked around at her small group of supporters and smiled. "I think that went quite well."

CHAPTER SEVENTEEN

Hailey's stomach still churned from the rough landing. The florescent lighting of the terminal magnified the ache behind her eyes. Nerves, she told herself—tomorrow would be better.

She clutched the handles of the stroller as she pushed Sophie through the flow of passengers toward the luggage claim area. She found the elevator that would take them down a level, and she ran to get in before the doors closed. When they opened a few seconds later, Sophie stretched her hands to Trey and squealed. "Daddy!"

"Hey, little lady. Look who wanted to come and meet you." He knelt in front of the eager toddler and offered her a stuffed panda sporting a hot pink bowtie.

Hailey's stomach knotted tighter. If they couldn't get things worked out, would she be able to share Sophie with this man? The thought of standing on the sidelines while he spent time with their daughter left her empty.

Trey stood and smiled at Hailey. "Thanks for bringing her."

"I wasn't sure we'd ever get out of Chicago." She pressed her lips tight as the greasy smell from a food vendor drifted past.

"Are you okay?" His forehead wrinkled in concern. He took control of Sophie's stroller and pushed it through the throng waiting for their luggage to be brought out.

"I'll be fine." Hailey swallowed hard and searched her purse for the luggage claim ticket. Maybe he wouldn't see how miserable she felt. "I'll go grab our bags."

Trey slid the tickets from her fingers. "Only two? Tell me what I'm looking for and I'll get them."

"You'll recognize mine. You probably still have the matching one." Hailey regretted the words as soon as she spoke them. She hurried to add, "Sophie's has frogs all over it."

"Frogs?" He raised one eyebrow.

"It's easy to spot." She looked around at the people wearing business clothing. "I doubt too many of these people pack their suits in a bag covered with pink and green ballerina frogs."

His laugh sounded forced. "I bet you're right. I'll be right back."

When Trey had their luggage, he motioned them toward the exit. Hailey followed with Sophie. Her body felt so heavy, causing her to lag behind. By the time she and Sophie got outside, Trey was loading their bags into a dark car at the curb. Hailey shivered and wrapped the sweater around her more tightly.

"It's easier to use the car service than find parking." Trey took Sophie and collapsed the stroller. As soon as everything had been loaded, they slid into the back with Sophie's car seat between them. Sophie jabbered to Trey, and Hailey leaned her throbbing head against the side window and let her eyes close.

If she could get a decent night's sleep things would be better. It was good she was staying at a hotel. At Trey's she would never rest. It would be nice if she had some idea of what to expect—knew what he expected of her.

"Your mom must be tired."

Hailey opened her eyes.

Sophie patted Hailey's leg and grinned. "Mommy sleep."

He looked at Hailey, concern written on his face. "Are you sure you're okay? I don't know that I should leave you at the hotel alone."

"I'm just tired." She hadn't slept well since he invited them to come. "Do you have to work tomorrow, or are you taking the day off for your birthday?"

"It's Labor Day weekend. I won't go in. Will you spend the day with us?"

She leaned her head back on the seat and closed her eyes. If she could shut out the motion and the light she might feel better. "Am I welcome? I can stay at the hotel if you want to be with Sophie."

"You're more than welcome to come with us." His voice was warm. "I thought since the weather's nice, we might go to the zoo and then out for dinner."

"You want to spend your thirtieth birthday at the zoo?" Hailey opened her eyes again.

"Go zoo." Sophie grinned up at her dad.

"That's right, Sophie. Do you remember the different animals we saw the last time we went?"

"Elfint, raff, hip-bow." She continued to list off the animals using her fingers to count.

"This zoo has something very special. Can you guess?" He shook Sophie's new panda sitting on her lap. "Giant pandas from China. Would you like to see those?"

"Panna! Panna!"

His gaze shifted to Hailey. "Are you sure you're okay?"

Nausea rolled through her middle. "I think I will be. When I'm out of this moving car."

"You probably don't want to stop for dinner?"

"Maybe you and Sophie could go out tonight without me." She put her hand over her mouth and took deep breaths.

Trey touched her forehead. "I don't feel right about leaving you at the hotel. Come home with me until you're better."

What was worse? Being in a hotel room sick or in an apartment filled with memories? "You weren't planning on me. I'll be fine at the hotel."

"As soon as you're feeling better you can go to the hotel, okay?"

She nodded. Right now she needed everything to hold still.

"Hailey we're home." Trey reached over and touched her jean-clad leg.

She shuddered and drew her hands to her mouth. "I'm going to be sick."

The driver shoved a bag towards him. He held it open while she fulfilled her prediction. Not the homecoming he'd planned.

She laid her head against the seat, her eyes closed. "I'm so sorry, Trey. You really should have taken me to the hotel. The driver still can."

He handed her a tissue. "Nonsense. Who could help you there? Will you be okay while I get Sophie out of her seat? Then I'll help you down the steps."

She nodded.

Holding Sophie on his hip, he wrapped his other arm around Hailey and half carried them down the steps. As soon as Sophie's little feet touched the ground she began exploring the living room. Hailey pulled out a chair from the table and slumped into it, laying her head on the table. He jogged back outside to the waiting taxi. By the time he brought in the luggage and stroller Sophie had settled herself with crayons and paper at the coffee table and Hailey sat on the edge of the couch. Tears rolled down her pale cheeks.

He knelt in front of her. "Are you all right?"

"Everything's the way I remember."

He shrugged, surprised by the emotion he felt. "No reason to change anything since it's just me." Would he ever get past the bitterness? Hopefully she didn't hear it.

"It looks...good." Her smile didn't reach her eyes. "Would it be okay if I just laid here on the couch for a while?"

"I'll grab some blankets." He hurried to the linen closet. Why was he suddenly so unsure about having Hailey here? He'd dreamed of what this moment would be like—perhaps that was the difference. In his dreams, she came back to live. In reality she'd only come to visit. On Monday night, the apartment would be empty and he would be alone.

"I can make my bed here." Hailey stood up, arms tight around her stomach. Her face blanched white again as she looked frantically at him. "I'll be right back."

Trey winced as he heard her in the bathroom. "It sounds like Mommy's pretty sick." He scrunched his nose up at Sophie. She nodded and went back to playing with the doll he'd propped up on the toddler bed he had set up in the corner of the living room.

Hailey staggered back to the couch and fell in a heap on the blankets. Moaning, she rolled onto her side and pulled her legs up.

Kneeling beside her, Trey pulled a blanket over her shoulder then brushed a matted strand of hair off her face. "You'd better drink something." He picked up the glass he'd set on the end table.

"I won't keep it down."

He pressed his palm against her forehead, surprised to find she wasn't feverish. "Any chance this is food poisoning?"

She lay so still he thought she'd gone to sleep. "We ate lunch before getting on the plane."

"What did you have?"

"A chicken sandwich with mayo." She swallowed hard. "I wonder..."

"Probably."

Opening her eyes, she sighed. "I've apologized to you so much in the past two weeks, but I'm sorry you have to deal with this."

The bitterness from earlier disappeared, leaving sympathy for this woman who felt so sick. He leaned over and kissed her on the forehead. "You didn't plan for this to happen."

"I'll be better tomorrow." She closed her eyes.

"You think so?" He had his doubts.

"Eat, Daddy?" Sophie hugged the doll he'd left on her bed and came to stand beside the couch. "See baby, Mommy?" She held the doll inches from Hailey's face.

"How about you show Mommy your new doll later." He slid his

arm around her tiny frame and pulled her and the doll back. "Are you hungry?"

"Baby Jake hung'y."

"You want to take the doll with us?" He had a lot to learn.

Her cheeks dimpled with a smile. "He hung'y."

"Of course he is."

"I'll be okay," Hailey murmured.

"We'll just run and get something from down the street. Do you need anything?"

She shook her head.

"We'll be back in less than an hour."

"Okay."

Trey bent over Hailey and whispered, "Do you know where that doll can eat?"

Hailey smiled with her eyes closed. "Any place that serves spaghetti or chicken nuggets."

Trey touched her cheek again. It felt right having them here.

CHAPTER EIGHTEEN

Trey stared at the red numbers—6:13—on the nightstand clock. He hadn't heard Hailey since he'd been up with her three hours earlier. Throwing the covers off, he stumbled out of bed. The hallway's dim light illuminated the living room enough for him to see the empty couch. Sophie's little foot stuck out from the pale green daisy quilt the senator's wife, Amanda, had given him last week for Sophie's visit.

Light seeped under the closed bathroom door. He listened for a moment before knocking softly. "Hailey, are you okay?"

Silence.

"Hailey?" He spoke louder and knocked again.

Still silence.

"I'm coming in." He pushed the door open. Hailey lay curled up on the floor between the stool and the sink. Evidence of her last few hours gave proof to how miserable she was. Blood pounded in his head as he fell to his knees beside her. "Hailey?" He pushed his hand under her neck and gently lifted her head.

"I . . . feel . . . terrible." The hoarse words escaped between dry lips.

"Let's get you back to the couch. You'll be more comfortable." And he'd be able to to figure out what to do with her. He put his other arm under her knees and started to stand up.

"No," she whimpered. "Leave me here. I'm. . . going. . ." She weakly pushed him away and leaned over the stool. Harsh, dry heaves convulsed her body.

Trey grabbed a clean washcloth, dampened it, and laid it on the back of her neck. With his other hand he pulled her tangled, damp hair back from her face and watched helplessly until she stopped. He sat with his back against the wall and let her relax against his chest. With another cloth he wiped the sweat and fresh tears from her face.

"If I die"—a shudder coursed through her weary body—"take care of Sophie."

"You're not going to die. You may wish it, but you're going to have to live through this."

She'd gone back to sleep.

He smiled. Being careful, he moved her to the middle of the bathroom, then scooped her from the floor. She moaned and turned her head into his shoulder. He carried her back to the couch. Finding his phone on his bedroom dresser, he pressed the number for the Bryant's house. When Amanda answered on the first ring he breathed a prayer of thanks.

"Were you serious when you said you'd babysit Sophie this weekend?" He walked into the other room and watched his sleeping daughter.

"I wouldn't have offered if I didn't mean it." Her tone was friendly. "Things must be going well if you're calling me this early."

"I need to take Hailey to the doctor. She's really sick." He rubbed the bridge of his nose.

"Oh, I'm so sorry. Mallory wanted to help, so I'll get her up and we'll be right over." The phone went dead.

Forty-five minutes later, a knock sounded on his door. He greeted Amanda Bryant and her eleven-year-old daughter. "Thanks for coming."

"I told the driver to wait. He'll take you to the hospital." She moved past him and stopped beside Hailey. "It looks like she's had a rough night."

"Do you think Sophie will be okay when she wakes up?" Trey scooped Hailey into his arms along with the jacket he'd helped her put on earlier.

"We'll get along fine. Kids love Mallory." Amanda moved to open the door. "Now get going."

"I'll call later."

Amanda smiled as she held the door for him. "Don't worry about Sophie, just take care of her mommy for now."

"Thanks, Amanda." He shouldered past her and took the steps one at a time while he balanced Hailey in his arms.

The ride to St. Elizabeth Hospital seemed impossibly slow. He lost count of the times Hailey gagged. They pulled in front of the emergency room doors just as her body tensed again.

Amanda's driver turned in the seat, concern etched on his already lined face. "What can I do for you, sir? I don't think you can get her in by yourself."

"There should be a wheelchair right inside the door. I'd appreciate it if you could bring it to the car."

The man returned shortly with the chair and opened Trey's door. "Maybe if you can slide this way, I can help get her in. Kinda hard from the inside, isn't it?

Together they managed to get Hailey in the chair. Trey fished in his pocket and handed the driver a folded bill. "Thanks for your help." He pushed the chair down the short hallway to the reception desk.

"May I help you?"

He bit the inside of his cheek. Wasn't it obvious? "Yes. She's been very sick all night."

"Insurance?"

He nodded.

"Please complete these forms." A stack of papers fluttered on the clipboard she handed him.

He scanned the first page.

"Fill out her personal information here. On the back are some questions you'll need to answer. The yellow page is insurance information. We'll need to take a copy of your card. Then sign at the bottom that everything is correct." She took a breath before flipping through the papers to reveal a pink page. "Read this, then sign and date that I gave it to you. It's our privacy policy. Any questions? Please sit down over there and let me know when you get these finished."

Trey handed her his insurance cards then found a spot where he could wheel Hailey's chair beside him while he filled out the papers.

Hailey moaned and turned to lean her head against his shoulder.

If he had to complete all this before they'd see Haley, they would all regret it. Top page finished, he turned the sheet over and began checking the no box beside each question. Do you smoke? No—check. Do you drink? No—check. Are you pregnant? No—ch. . . He straightened up in his chair. She wasn't. He knew Hailey and she would never do that. Did he really know her anymore? He hated the doubt that crept in. He left the box blank.

"Finished?" The receptionist reached for the clip board and handed him his insurance card. She stood and motioned toward the hall behind her. "It's slowed down quite a bit. Why don't you bring her back so she can lie down."

Trey pushed Hailey's chair and followed the receptionist down the hall. Once inside the curtained room, he lifted Hailey onto the bed. Her face was as white as the bed sheet underneath her. It had been one of the longest nights of his life. Somehow, all of the longest nights he'd had were because of this woman.

A nurse stepped into the room and read over the paperwork. "You don't know if she's pregnant? She might be?"

Trey looked at Hailey and wished she'd wake up and answer her own personal questions. "I don't believe she is."

"Do you know the day of her last period?"

He shook his head.

She rolled her eyes. "You are her husband, right?"

"Yes."

"Just making sure because we can't tell just anybody the results of her tests." The woman talked while she took Hailey's vitals and recorded the information. "Lab will be in to get some blood. That will help the doctor know what's going on and how to treat it. It will also answer your question."

Trey smiled at her candidness. Nervous anticipation grew in him while he waited for the doctor. Three times he helped Hailey sit up and heave into the bag he held.

"Mr. Williams, I'm Dr. Clark." The dark-skinned woman shook his hand. "Sounds like you both have had a long night."

"It has been."

Dr. Clark examined Hailey and then looked at the computer screen she'd set on the table. "This seems to be a classic case of food poisoning. She probably won't feel well for several more days. I'm going to prescribe a medicine to control her nausea. You can pick it up at the pharmacy. We'll also keep her here long enough to get some fluids in her." The woman looked up. "Any question?"

He glanced at Hailey to make sure she was still sleeping. "The pregnancy test?"

Dr. Clark held her stylus over the screen. "Negative."

He fell back in the chair as guilt flooded over him.

She raised her eyebrows. "I'm sorry."

"It's fine. This wouldn't be a good time for us." He didn't need to explain their marriage.

"Sometimes the best things come when we don't expect them. I'll send the nurse in to start the IV and meds. Hailey will be here for most of the morning. The day shift will be coming in, so one of the other doctors will discharge her later."

"I'll wait with her. Thank you for your help."

With one arm around Hailey, Trey unlocked the door and pushed it open. The quiet that greeted him was different than it had been since Hailey left years ago. The apartment seemed energized somehow. The toddler bed in the corner and a plastic doll house sitting in the middle of the floor with furniture scattered around might be clutter to some. To him, it was perfect.

"We're making a mess of your space." Hailey grimaced.

"What mess? That's life." He swallowed hard. "I've lived in a clean, orderly apartment too long. Let's get you to bed." Her frame quivered beneath his arm. "Why don't you lie down for a while and then shower?" He escorted her slowly toward the bedroom.

"Did Mrs. Bryant say when they'd bring Sophie back?"

"Mallory thought Sophie would enjoy one of the children's museums. I'll meet them later and bring her home."

Hailey stopped before they got to the bedroom door. "I'd rather be on the couch."

He turned her in that direction. "And I'd rather you be in a bed. You'll feel better."

She sat down in the recliner and looked at the floor. "Please just let me sleep on the couch for now. Maybe later I'll go to the bed."

"All right, we'll try this for now." He unfolded the blankets Amanda had stacked on the arm of the sofa and started making a bed on the couch.

Hailey sniffed. "Sorry I'm ruining your birthday."

"Hey." He stooped down and wiped the tears that ran down her cheek then covered her hand with his. "I've never spent a birthday like this. If you weren't here, I'd be at work. We'll do something when you feel better."

"We leave Monday." She looked down at her hand in his.

Trey helped her stand and move to the couch. Once her head was on the pillow, he lifted her feet up and pulled off her shoes. She watched him with tired eyes.

"I called Todd to let him know what's going on." He covered

her with a quilt. "He said things are fine there."

"You're trying to tell me they don't need me."

He sat on the edge of the couch and took her hand. She was exhausted. He needed to be careful how much he said. "No, I'm sure they need you. But they will manage until you get home. Probably just not on Monday."

"Will you get Sophie soon? Maybe you two could do something fun tonight." She spoke with her eyes closed. "I'm just going to sleep. I'll be fine."

He brushed an errant curl off her forehead. It felt good to be needed again.

Squeals of delight rang across the park as Trey jogged down the grassy slope to the water playground. Sophie tottered from one shooting stream of water to the next, trying to stop the flow with her feet. Mallory Bryant followed her. From the edge of the concrete, Amanda stood with her camera pointed at the two girls. He'd have to ask for some of the prints.

"Daddy!" Sophie ran toward him.

He laughed as he swung her into his arms. "Hey, you're getting me all wet!"

"Pway in water." Water droplets glistened on her skin. "Go pway." She wiggled until her bare feet touched the concrete. She ran back to Mallory.

"How's Hailey?" Amanda stood beside him.

"She's at my place sleeping. Thanks for taking Sophie. It looks like she's had a great time."

Sophie stood over one of the waterless holes in the concrete, hopping from one foot to the other.

"Do you have a moment to talk?" Amanda motioned towards the empty bench under the tree.

The geyser of water exploded, leaving his daughter squealing in delight. He laughed at her antics. Could any child on earth be more adorable? He sat on the bench and waited for Amanda to speak.

"She's a sweet little girl. We've loved having her today." Amanda set the camera between them and leaned back. "Is there any chance you and her mom will get back together?"

Trey leaned forward with his elbows on his knees and smiled at the woman. "Direct and to the point, that's what I've always appreciated about you."

A smile softened her face. "I've lived in this town too long to beat around the bush. If you want the truth, you have to ask for it directly."

He'd be direct, too. "I don't know. This isn't how I'd planned for the weekend to go. My well laid plans to spend hours talking and trying to persuade her to come back are useless."

"Watch, Daddy," Sophie yelled from behind the water cannon. With Mallory's help, they pointed it at the bench and pushed the big, red button. Water hurled in his direction, splattering the ground three feet away.

"Whew. They planned that well," he said to Amanda before hollering at his daughter. "That was close, Sophie, but not close enough."

Sophie cackled and waddled toward him. She threw her wet body over his lap. "You wet, Daddy."

"And I'll tickle you." His fingers moved across her ribs. Peals of delight lifted his mood. "Go play for a couple of minutes, then we have to go see how your mom is doing."

"She needs you to be her dad." Amanda sighed as Sophie ran through an arch of water.

"I will be." He watched his child. "Maybe a miracle will happen and Hailey will come back. If not, I'll figure something out."

"This is a hard business on families." She sat up straight and shrugged. The eyes that met his glistened with tears. "Is your job worth your marriage and having your little girl live halfway across the country?"

He ran his hand over his rough chin. "I hope Rob didn't put you up to this. It sounds like you're trying to get rid of me." The long night was catching up with him.

"Of course not. But even our marriage has had too many rough spots, and I was raised to be a politician's wife." The words she left unspoken hung between them. She rested her hand on his arm. "I just want you to realize there are other options beyond Washington."

"I know." He stood and motioned for Sophie. "Let's go check on your mom." She ran to them and waited while Amanda wrapped a towel around her small body.

"Come see us again." Mallory knelt down and hugged Sophie. "If you live with your dad I'll babysit you all the time."

"Thanks to both of you." Trey picked up the swaddled girl. "I can tell she had the best time with you, Mallory. When Sophie is here, I'll need a good babysitter.

A faint breeze brushed across her face, pulling her from dreamless sleep. The twilight of evening bathed the apartment in a soft glow. The ceiling fan hummed above her, filling the room with soft sound. Hailey rolled to her side. Everything was so familiar, the memories haunted her. Yet she felt like an intruder. So familiar, yet a stranger. The leather recliner where she'd sat earlier was new. The plants she'd tried so hard to grow had either been replaced or had thrived under Trey's green thumb. The memories came to her in waves—meals at the table, working in the kitchen together, watching movies. Why hadn't she come back?

Perhaps a shower would make her feel more human. It would also help her escape her thoughts. She moved on unsteady legs through the living room and down the hall. At the bedroom door, she looked in. Ghosts beckoned her. Stepping in, she switched on the lamp. Hailey gasped in surprise. Their wedding picture stared back at her from the dresser. With shaky hands she picked up the frame. They'd been so young. But even in the photograph, anyone could see the love they shared. On that day, they had been committed to making their marriage great. An example others would see and want. Somewhere along the way, life pulled them in different directions and moved their focus off their marriage.

Hugging the picture to her chest, she explored the room. Unable to stop, she pulled open the closet door. Her clothes hung beside Trey's dress shirts and suits. He hadn't gotten rid of anything. She moved around the bed, looking for something that had changed. A sob caught in her throat at the book on the bedside table. She'd left it there the night before flying home, expecting to finish the last few chapters on her return. For two-and-a-half years, that book had been waiting to be finished.

Hailey fell to her knees. Why hadn't Trey moved? Taken her stuff away? Had she ever considered his need or dreams? She hadn't liked the city. Trey's hours at work increased until he rarely came home before nine each night, and he worked all weekend. They hadn't even taken the time to find a church home. It was more than the accident, her dad, and the pumpkin patch that kept her in Kansas. She had believed no one needed her in D.C.

Fatigue overtook her. Using the last bit of strength, she climbed onto the bed, wrapped her arms around the framed photo and book, and cried.

Trey carried his sleeping daughter into the apartment and propped her stroller against the wall. Only a soft glow from the bedroom shone down the hall. He flipped on the kitchen light and stopped short. The quilt on the couch had been thrown back, revealing the empty space. Apprehension filled him as silence echoed through the room. Sophie turned in his arms, reminding him of her presence.

As gently as he could manage, he laid Sophie on her bed. Sitting at her feet, Trey pulled off her hot pink high-tops and held her tiny foot in his hand. He'd fallen hard for this child of his. Having her and Hailey here gave him hope that they would figure everything out. There had to be a way for them to be a family.

Hailey... Trey looked around the room, half-expecting to see her in the hallway. The glow from the bedroom illuminated the barren space. He tucked the quilt around Sophie and bent to kiss her cheek.

The light drew him like a moth to the bedroom door. The wedding picture was gone, and the closet door stood open. He studied her slender frame curled up on the bed. It was one thing to have Hailey in his living room, sleeping on his couch. Seeing her on their bed reminded him that, for these few days, they'd only pretend to be a family. Soon she'd get on a plane and leave him alone. Trey ran his hand through his hair and rubbed the back of his neck. He moved to the foot of the bed. The silver wedding frame poked out from under her arms. A shudder coursed through Hailey. When coupled with her tearstained cheeks, the action left little doubt of the emotions that had played out earlier.

Moments passed while Trey stood gazing at his sleeping wife. The frustration melted out of his body, leaving him empty. He reached for the double wedding ring quilt folded over the wooden chair in the corner, and spread it over Hailey. The quilt had been a wedding gift from Hailey's mother. Trey breathed a sigh of thanks that Jenny Harper hadn't seen their marriage fall apart.

He backed out of the room. He'd slept on the couch many nights after Hailey had left, not being able to stomach the thought of sleeping in their bed alone. He flung the wrinkled quilt over the couch and fell onto it. Hailey was finally home sleeping in their bed, and he was still on the couch.

CHAPTER NINETEEN

Hailey shut one cabinet door before pulling out a drawer. Even the towels were the same. Not perfectly stacked rows like Trey preferred, but messy with one too many towels crowded into the space like she'd always done. In the bottom drawer she found her cookbooks and loose recipes. Hailey touched the top book cover with shaky fingertips. For two years she'd been away, yet it felt like she'd never been gone. Those things that didn't matter at all—towels in drawers, her clothes in the closet, the recipe books—hadn't changed. Her relationship with Trey—completely different. They'd both grown up these past two years and had experienced the anguish of life because of her choices.

She gripped the top cookbook. Mom had filled it with family favorites and gave it to her for a wedding present. The tightness in her throat grew as she flipped through the handwritten pages. Memories of Mom putting another meal together entwined with the meals Hailey had made in this kitchen for Trey. She stopped at the recipe for bacon-wrapped, basil chicken. Trey's favorite. Judging by the empty refrigerator and outdated cans, he probably didn't eat at home much. What if she made supper tonight? It would be a nice way to thank him for all he'd done this week.

Hailey grabbed a pen and made her list. She'd keep it simple, noodles with the chicken, green beans, and a loaf of French bread.

Better get some sugar and flour. If she still had any energy left, she and Sophie could make cookies.

"Sophie, let's walk to the store." Hailey tucked the paper into her purse.

Sophie looked up from squeezing play dough through a press at the coffee table.

"Let's put this away and you can play with it when we get home."

Sophie's lips formed into a pout. "Go home? Daddy go?"

"Where?" Hailey pressed the yellow play dough together and dropped it into the can. "I mean back here, to Daddy's place. I want to get some things from the store to make supper for Daddy. Don't you think he'd like that?"

"Me, too." She dropped the toy rolling pin and ran into the bedroom, returning with her flowered jacket. "I help."

"I know he'll like that." Hailey finished cleaning up. "You'll have to ride in the stroller. That way you can hold some of the groceries on the way home. Or if I get too much, you can walk and we'll push the groceries in your stroller. What do you think of that?"

"Take car?" Sophie hustled to the door.

"Not here. There's a little market about three blocks down the street. We'll only get what we need. Isn't that different? You'll have to remind me to not get too many things because we have to carry everything home."

After two blocks her legs grew weak and rubbery. Sophie carried on a steady stream of chatter, calling out to the birds that chirped in the trees and pointing at a dog pulling its owner down the street. Once she finished shopping it wouldn't take much to make the meal, but she'd have to pace herself. Otherwise, she'd need another week here to get her strength back. There was no time for that. The pumpkin patch opened on Saturday with or without her. Her dad would never forgive her if she wasn't there.

"Here we are, Sophie. Can you hold the basket and I'll put things in it? That would be a great help to me."

An hour later they were back in the apartment. The groceries cluttered the counter and a tube of refrigerated sugar cookie dough waited in the fridge.

"Cookies?" Sophie hopped around the kitchen.

Hailey pulled a towel from the drawer. "Let's put this apron on you and get your hands washed. I know I have some cookie cutters around here somewhere." The towel wrapped around Sophie's tiny waist three times and hung to the floor. After washing their hands, Hailey found the cutters in the bottom drawer. "It looks like we have Christmas trees, a stocking, or a heart. Which one do you want?"

Sophie studied the choices Hailey offered. She took the heart in one hand and reached for the other two.

"You crawl up on that chair and when I get the dough rolled out you can cut it, okay?" She patted flour on the dough before pressing the rolling pin across its top.

"Now?" Sophie set the cutter on a mound of dough.

"Not yet. Just give me a little time to roll this out."

"Now?" The heart cutter pressed into the thick dough.

"That's going to be a big cookie." Hailey hurried to flatten the rest of the dough. "Now you can cut them." She smiled when the heart cut the top off of the tree, only to have the side of the heart jagged out by the stocking toe. No one would know what the shapes had started as but this little girl, with her tongue between her lips, was having a wonderful time.

Trey stopped on the steps at the sound of giggles coming from the open apartment window. He took a deep breath. How would he ever let them go home? This morning he'd seen a big improvement in Hailey. Judging by the delicious smells permeating the air, she still felt good. She'd be anxious to leave.

This past week had felt like the promise of spring after a long winter. When they left, winter would return and, no doubt, would be worse than before. He gathered his courage and entered the apartment.

"Daddy!" Sophie's squeal carried over Hailey's voice, but the happy sound made him smile.

From the doorway he stared at the cookie covered table. Sophie sat in the middle with her legs crossed. Hailey glanced up from where she sat with an icing covered knife in one hand and a cookie in the other. One look and he knew she'd overdone it.

He set his computer bag by the door and approached the table. A smudge of orange icing graced Hailey's cheek. "What's all this?"

"Cookies!" Sophie picked up several before choosing one and handing it to him.

He took the offered treat and bit into it. "How did you know sugar cookies are my favorite?"

She giggled and picked up another cookie. "Me eat?"

Hailey nodded then gave him a soft smile. "I hoped you wouldn't be late, or Sophie might have eaten all the cookies without you."

"You know what we need, Sophie-girl? Milk. Do you want milk with yours?"

"Uh-huh." Crumbs coated her lips and chin.

Trey popped the rest of the cookie in his mouth and removed his suit coat. He gave it a toss, and it landed on the chair. He rolled up his sleeves on the way to the kitchen. He stopped and scanned the room. Dread filled him. How would he ever go back to being single? "This looks great. I hope you didn't wear yourself out."

"I thought you might like a home-cooked meal." Hailey's arm brushed against his as she stood at his side. "It's a small way to thank you for all you've done to take care of Sophie and me this week."

He touched her cheek with his finger, wiping off the icing. With a grin he licked the sweet confection from his finger. "It means a lot to me. Thank you. If I didn't know better I'd think you were trying to bribe me into letting you stay." He moved to the cupboard.

"Would one meal and cookies be enough?" She handed him a new carton of milk. There was a touch of raw honesty in her eyes.

Did she want to stay? "You wouldn't even need to—"

Sophie tugged his pant leg. "Milk, Daddy."

"Don't give her too much because supper is about ready." Hailey brushed past him and opened the oven door.

—ask. The final word to his comment played through his head. *Just stay.*

"I firsty," the little voice whined.

He held the cup while she took a drink. He needed to get some of those cups with lids.

"You holp me?"

Trey sat down and took the sticky knife she offered. "You think I can do this?" He looked across the cookie covered table and smiled at the contrast between cookies. While the icing on Hailey's cookies was flat with clean edges, Sophie's were multicolored with icing running off some and others were mostly bare. His resembled Sophie's.

Hailey stood at the kitchen sink, her head bowed. Could she see how good they were together as a family?

Hot water sprayed over Hailey's hand as she waited for the sink to fill. Laughter filtered down the hall from the bathroom where Trey gave Sophie a bath. By the time Sophie had iced the final cookie her blonde curls were fused together into colored, sugary chunks.

"I told you I'd clean things up." Trey spoke from behind her. "You've got to be worn out."

She glanced over her shoulder and smiled at him holding Sophie. "I don't mind. You two could go watch one of the movies I brought while I finish."

"I'll help you while Sophie watches it."

The two left, and within minutes the music from "Ballerina Barbie" sounded through the small apartment.

"I wish you'd let me do this." Trey opened the towel drawer. "I'll dry and put away, okay?"

She nodded as he took the dripping glass from her hand. "Did work go okay?"

"I'll be glad when this election is over and we can get back to normal business. I talked to Todd for a few minutes today."

"Why'd he call you instead of me?" She was tired and the words sounded sharper than she'd intended.

"He just wanted to check on how you were getting along."

"He probably wonders how long I'm going to slack off." If Todd wasn't upset, her dad would be.

"Actually, he said to stay as long as you need to. Things are fine."

"He'd say that so I don't worry."

Trey sighed. "I'll check into flights for you tomorrow." He held up the cookie cutters. "I don't have a clue where these go. How'd you find them?"

She pointed. "Bottom drawer by the stove. Do you remember our first Christmas after we got married? We got our tree and then realized we didn't have any ornaments."

"How many cookies did we make to hang on the tree? Do you remember?" His eyes danced at the memory. "I helped cut them out, but you were determined to decorate each one yourself—which wasn't a bad idea if you saw my skills tonight."

She laughed. "I couldn't tell the difference between yours and Sophie's."

"Mine had all the sparkly things on them." His hand brushed against hers when he took the pan she held. "How many projects did you save me from flunking? Sophie took me to the treehouse while I was there. I couldn't believe that paint stain was still there from our history project."

"Mrs. Matthews wasn't very impressed with a lake in the middle of our Civil War scene."

"That was pure genius since all the paint was running down the wall. I think she took pity on you because you were willing to be my partner."

Hailey sighed dramatically. "Someone had to help you out with projects. It was a good trade-off for all the help you gave me in geometry. I'd still be sitting in that class today if it wasn't for you."

"We went together really well." A sad smile finished the sentence.

In the silence, a collage of memories played through her mind, one fading into the next. School projects, hours spent weeding the pumpkin patch, decorating for prom–side-by-side they had accomplished so much.

"You okay?" Trey took the last pan from her and set it in the drainer. "This can air dry. I think you're finished for the day."

She watched the water drain from the sink before taking the towel from him. "I enjoyed being in this kitchen again. It was fun using my things."

"I guess I can't keep you from taking some things back with you, if you want." His voice sounded strained. "Nobody's using–"

"Stop." She held up her hand and faced him. "Let's not spoil tonight. It's been a good evening–I'd like to keep it that way."

His eyes searched her face. "At some point we have to discuss what we're going to do."

"But not tonight." She put her hand on his arm and squeezed gently. "Let's just enjoy the rest of the evening with Sophie."

CHAPTER TWENTY

It seemed the afternoon would never end. Hailey drummed her fingers on the dining room table. For four days she'd been cooped up in this airless room. Trey's entire apartment would fit into the living area of her basement home. The irony that she still lived in a basement hadn't been lost on her. At least on the farm she could walk out the sliding doors onto ground level. Here she could go crazy watching people walk by.

Asleep on the couch, Sophie rolled over and disrupted Hailey's thoughts. It was time to go home. The ever growing list of things she needed to do before Saturday's VIP day overwhelmed her. Did she really want to leave? She'd be walking out on Trey again. How many times would he let her come back if she always left?

The click of the door lock startled her. The door opened and Trey walked in. He smiled. "You look good."

So did he. Her chest fluttered at his few words. She knew exactly how he meant them, but she still enjoyed the casual observation and the way it made her feel. Much longer and she'd beg him to let her stay—even though the city apartment felt cramped and the lack of outdoor space and activity drove her crazy. She had more freedom here than she did at home. The hours spent with Trey were like rain to her parched soul.

"It's only two o'clock. Did the government run out of money

and shut down?" She rested her chin on the palm of her hand.

Trey set his leather computer bag on the table. He shrugged off the gray suit coat and hung it on the back of the chair. "I took off early." His long fingers worked to release knot of the red patterned tie. One tug and it was off and draped over the coat. "I thought Sophie might like to go do something."

Hailey hoped her face didn't belie the pang of regret those words caused. "She'd like that." She looked down at the list she'd been working on and tried to focus on it as Trey unbuttoned his shirt. She cleared her throat, trying to pull her thoughts together. "She's probably slept long enough." She rubbed the scratch on the table, trying to hide her reaction toward him.

"Hailey?"

Her eyes met his. If her face was as red as it felt she probably looked like a stoplight—but she didn't want him to stop.

"If you feel like coming, I'd love to have you join us—unless you'd rather stay here."

The breath she'd been holding rushed out as she pushed the chair back and stood. "No, I'll go. It's time for Sophie to get up."

"Put her swimsuit on. We'll go to the water park then stop for dinner on the way home." His smile grew as he glanced toward the bedroom. "I'll go finish changing."

She bit her bottom lip to stop her grin. "That would be good." It was definitely time to return to Kansas.

Trey scooped Sophie into his arms and dashed through the spouts of water. Delighted giggles erupted.

"I all wet." She wrapped her arms around his neck and pressed close.

Trey closed his eyes. How many weeks until he'd hold her again? He wasn't sure anything was more important to him than this little princess in his arms. He glanced at Hailey. If he could convince her to come back, he would have it all.

Sophie squirmed. "I pway."

"I'm going to talk to Mommy, okay?"

She ran and stood beneath the dumping buckets.

"I can't believe how much she likes this place," Hailey said when he approached the bench. She slid over to make room for him. "I'm glad you brought us."

Trey dropped to the bench and stretched his legs out to dry. "I wanted to bring her before you leave on Thursday."

She gave him a sharp look. "Thursday?"

He'd expected her to be more excited. "I know you need to get back for this weekend." He laid his arm along the back of the bench, resting his hand inches from her shoulder. "The ticket information is back at the apartment. I couldn't get you on any flights tomorrow."

"After a week of playing nurse, you'll be glad to get rid of us."

Sophie dodged under the red bucket after it dumped its water to the ground.

"It's been good having you both here." How long would it take to adjust to being alone? "Next time we'll try to do more together. Just don't eat another chicken sandwich before getting on the plane."

"I won't be eating one for quite a while." She smiled at him. "I can't bring her back until November, you know."

Eight weeks seemed like an eternity. "I know. And with the election, I'm not sure how soon I can come there. We'll see what works out." He moved enough for his hand to rest on her shoulder. She relaxed against his side. "I'd like to spend the holidays with Sophie."

Hailey chewed on the side of her lip. "I know we need to figure this out, but I don't want to. It's selfish, but I don't want to be alone on those days."

"Then you come, too." Every part of him wanted to beg her to come back.

"What happens when you decide to spend the holidays with someone else? She won't want your ex-wife around." Her voice trembled.

"That's not something we need to worry about now." After this week, he couldn't imagine being with anyone else. His thumb caressed her shoulder. "Maybe I could come to Kansas for Thanksgiving and you two could come here between Christmas and the New Year."

She was silent for several beats of his heart. "I could stay in a hotel."

"Yeah, that worked out real well this time. It's something to consider." He forced his mouth into a straight line. His hand dropped away when Hailey shifted on the bench to face him.

"I saw a manual on your shelf from AgMobility. Why do you have that?'

"Todd and I are working on something." He leaned forward and rested his elbows on his legs.

"For Dad?" She turned her body into his side but didn't move away.

Reluctant to share his idea with her, he only nodded. What if they were able to offer Jim a more mobile life and Hailey still didn't want to leave?

"Why didn't you tell me?" Confusion crinkled her brow.

"What's there to tell? Until we get the equipment built, we won't know if things will work or if your dad will accept it."

"Todd hasn't said anything to me. What's your idea?"

He leaned back with a sigh. "He and some guy there are building a chair lift that goes on the bed of a pickup. The lift will raise your dad's chair to the platform of the combine or tractor. We'll make some modifications on certain pieces of equipment that will allow him to use those implements. But it's a gamble on whether or not Jim will accept them."

She leaned back. "Who's paying for this? Nothing you've said is cheap."

"There are some organizations that will help pay for the modifications, and I've applied for a few grants."

Sophie ran towards them, kicking at the water and smiling. "Dwy off."

As soon as the towel was wrapped around her, Trey pulled her onto his lap. She rested against his chest and stuck two fingers in her mouth.

"Why are you doing this?" Tears shimmered in her eyes. "You of all people have been treated worse than anybody by Dad and me."

"I feel sorry for him. He believes he's lost everything and he can't see how much he has to be thankful for. It's hard to stay angry at someone you pity."

She gave him a slight smile. "He would be furious knowing you pity him."

"I know." He knew by Sophie's even breathing she had fallen asleep. "We may have to get take-out for dinner."

"She'll wake up by the time we get somewhere." Hailey picked up her bag and scooted forward on the bench. "That's a lot to do if you only feel sorry for him."

His stomach clinched. Things were too fragile between them for him to admit he want her to leave her dad and come back to him. "I hope it will make things easier for you." That was true. If Jim could work, she'd have more time. He wanted her to see it was time to come home for good.

Together they walked up the incline with Sophie in his arms.

"Since I ruined your birthday and tomorrow's our last day, maybe we could do something special tomorrow night." Hailey readjusted the bag on her shoulder then wrapped her arm through the bend in his elbow. "Do you think that would work?"

"I'm in meetings most of the afternoon, but if you two met me at work, we could go from there." The fact she was reaching out to him gave him a small measure of hope.

CHAPTER TWENTY-ONE

Hailey stared at her reflection in the mirror. She'd found her soft yellow sweater still folded in the bureau drawer. Would Trey remember the night he gave it to her? His birthday, but he bought her the sweater and insisted she wear it when they went to dinner. She ran her hand around the scooped neckline, the memory of his fingers tracing the same contour as fresh as though it happened only yesterday.

"*Always wear yellow, Hailey. It reminds me of sunshine.*" He'd kissed the tip of her nose. "*And you are my sunshine, my only sunshine.*"

They'd laughed at his attempt to sing. But she didn't feel at all like laughing now.

"You pwetty, Mommy." Sophie's giggle broke the reverie. "See Daddy?"

"Yes, we'll go see where he works." Hailey sat on the edge of the bed and covered Sophie's chubby leg with her hand. "We're going home tomorrow, okay?"

Sophie nodded. "Daddy come."

Regret had become a familiar companion. "Not this time. He has to work here, remember? You and I will go home because the pumpkin patch opens this weekend."

"Daddy go." Sophie crawled onto Hailey's lap.

"He's going to visit us soon." Hailey rubbed the child's back. "Remember what we're going to do tonight?"

"Daddy's birfday!" She clapped. "I get pwesent. Go now." She climbed down and toddled into the other room.

Hailey hurried after her daughter. "Let's get you dressed so he doesn't have to wait for us."

Standing under a flaming red maple near the corner of First and Constitution Avenue, Hailey watched the flow of people exiting the Dirksen Building. Sophie squealed and pointed when Trey walked down the steps, deep in conversation with Senator Bryant. Hailey lifted her hand to wave, but let it drop when Trey's eyes met hers, his face tense. Fingers of dread clenched her heart as the two men approached.

"You remember Hailey, and this is my daughter, Sophie." Trey's eyes searched her face while he made the introductions.

The senator shook her hand. "Hailey, it's good to see you again. Amanda and I are looking forward to visiting your pumpkin patch in a couple of weeks." He knelt in front of Sophie. "I've heard a lot about you from Mallory. Now she's begging us for a little sister just like you."

Sophie smiled shyly at the older man then lifted her gaze to Trey's. She held the gift. "Daddy's birfday."

"It's your daddy's birthday?" Senator Bryant stood and clasped Trey on his shoulder. "Happy birthday. I'll meet you inside. Nice to see you again, Hailey."

Trey watched the Senator walk away before facing her. The silence that stretched between them grew heavy.

Biting back her frustration Hailey broke the silence. "Sophie and I will stop at a deli or something on the way home. Will you be late?"

A muscle twitched in his cheek. He rubbed his neck. "Hailey, this wasn't supposed to happen. My meetings got moved back due to a hearing Senator Bryant had to attend. I'm sorry."

"Sophie, why don't you let Daddy open his gift so you don't have to hold it all the way home?" She worked to keep her voice light. She'd come to expect this sort of thing three years ago. Obviously little had changed. Trey glanced at her before he took the gift and pulled off the paper. The first smile she'd seen from him this evening crossed his face as he knelt down in front of the stroller.

"Did you make this?" He held up the frame with two small hand prints stamped on it. "Are you sure your hands are that big?" Sophie giggled and pushed her hands close to his face. "This is the best birthday gift I've ever gotten. Thank you." He kissed her cheek. "Thanks for bringing it to me at work." Standing, he held the frame in both hands and studied the picture. He looked miserable.

Hailey squeezed his arm. "It's okay. You go to your meeting. Sophie and I will see if we can't find a birthday cake somewhere and take it home. We'll celebrate when you get there."

He swallowed hard, eyes never leaving hers. "I might be late."

"We had a nap today, didn't we Sophie-girl?" She kept the smile on her face.

"You look great tonight." He stepped closer.

Hailey gripped the handle of Sophie's stroller to still her shaking hands. "They're going to start without you."

Trey traced the top edge of her sweater, his fingers warm against her skin. "Do you have any idea what seeing you in this does for me?" His voice grew husky with emotion. "I... This isn't how I wanted the evening to go."

"I know."

He took her face in his hands. "I'm so sorry." He bent and kissed the tip of her nose. "Please, Hailey. Please don't take my sunshine away." He took a few steps backwards, his gaze fixed on her face, then turned and walked away.

Hailey swallowed. He remembered. Now, if only she could forget.

Tires splashing on the wet pavement drew Hailey to the window. She raised the blinds and folded her arms on the sill. Even at 3:38 in the morning this city seemed unable to sleep. She knew the feeling. A raindrop trickled down the glass and she followed it with her finger and swallowed the lump in her throat. How often had she stood in this same spot, waiting to catch a glimpse of Trey's shoes as he trod past the eye-level window of their basement apartment? She'd done the same tonight, then scrambled to the couch, her face hid against the loose pillows on the back, as he entered.

He'd stood behind her, so close she could hear him breathe and catch the faint whiff of his cologne. But she feigned sleep then counted his steps away from her with regret. Why was this so hard?

A passing car sent a quick shaft of light past the big tree by the curb. She'd planted flowers around its base the first spring in D.C., but they were no longer visible. Two years of neglect had choked the blooms that brought her such joy as a young bride. She choked back a sob. The untended flowers... Her abandoned marriage...

"Can't sleep?"

Hailey jumped. How long had he been there? Trey stood in the bedroom doorway illumined by the soft glow of Sophie's night light. His hands rested casually on his hips, the blue plaid pajamas she'd given him their first Christmas slung low beneath them. Her breath caught. He'd teased her when he opened them that morning.

"*You don't really expect me to wear these, do you Hailey? I haven't worn jammies since I was in kindergarten.*" He'd kissed the hollow of her neck. "*But if it's me in pj's you want, then that's what you'll get.*"

He leaned against the door frame and folded his arms across his bare chest. He remembered. He knew exactly what he was doing. It was a good thing she was leaving tomorrow. A few more days and she'd beg him to take her back.

She turned to the window. Was the desire in her eyes as visible as in his? "I never sleep well the night before I need to fly somewhere." She ran her hand across the cool window ledge. "Anxious to get home, I guess. I hope I didn't wake you up."

Sophie's bed creaked at the weight of Trey sitting on it.

"I thought I'd check on Sophie one more time."

Hailey swallowed the emotion rising in her throat. "You're welcome to visit anytime and call her when you want." The words stumbled from her mouth. "When you have time I'll bring her to visit. We could even meet you part way or something."

"We'll figure it out." The bed creaked again.

The smell of his soap wafted past. Her senses alert at him standing behind her. "You always hated this view."

"Not always. For a few years I had flowers to look at." Her hand shook as she held the curtain back and continued to stare into the night.

"I tried to keep them alive after you left, but I got too busy." His bare shoulder brushed against hers. "It didn't take long for them to be overgrown."

Just like their marriage. It hadn't taken long for the weeds to choke out anything good. Trey had been busy, and she'd been homesick and lonely.

Hailey needed something safe to think about. "I figured you'd have moved by now. You didn't want to stay here long." She glanced at him.

"I only sleep here. Some nights I don't even do that." Defeat weighted the words. "There wasn't any reason to move."

"Thanks for taking care of Sophie and me this—"

"Remember our first night here?"

Hailey bit back a smile. She never forgot. How many nights had she tossed in her bed with those memories as her only companion? She'd prayed they would fill her dreams, just to relive those moments once more. "That old couch we found and the table with mismatched chairs. It didn't take long to move in, did it?"

"You liked it here, didn't you?" He hesitated. "At least for a while?"

She faced him. "I did like it here at first. But..." Her breath was shaky. "I didn't plan on not coming back. I never dreamed how quickly things would change. Life-altering changes."

The hum of the refrigerator seemed to grow louder. She had to find the right words. How could she apologize for ruining her own marriage? Her lungs were so tight she couldn't force enough air into them. "Trey–"

He tucked a strand of hair behind her ear. "We danced in here our first night."

They had. The lack of furniture had provided a wonderful dance floor while the country radio station played. Her eyes closed, trying to block out the memories. She remembered everything about that night.

"This is our last night together here." His voice was hoarse with emotion.

She opened her eyes and met his gaze. The eyes that twinkled when Sophie was in his arms were dark.

"Dance with me?" He reached for her.

Hailey stared at his hand. How would she keep her heart from shattering.

"Please? For old-time's sake?" The words caught on a short breath.

She slipped her hand into his. "There's no music."

Trey wrapped his arm around her waist and pulled her close. "There hasn't been for a long time." He took a step and she followed. Silence enveloped the dark room.

Hailey shuffled closer when his hand moved up her back. She rested her head on his shoulder. Emotions warred in him. Memories of the old, dried up dreams for their future. Her breath warmed his neck. He brushed his lips across her cheek and felt her body tremble.

Hailey lifted her head and stepped back, moving her left hand to the back of his neck. "I'm sorry you are paying for my choices."

She came willingly when he drew her close again. His steps were heavy, keeping beat with his heart. "I was too busy building my career."

A curl brushed against his cheek when she nodded. Her grip tightened in his hand. "The accident ruined my dad's life. I don't know how to leave him."

"It wasn't your fault, Hailey. The other driver ran that stop sign. Nobody blames you."

She sighed. "Nobody but my dad."

"And you." He turned her so the light caressed her face. "You have to forgive yourself."

Tears in her eyes glittered before they ran down her cheeks. "Maybe someday I'll be able to." Her bottom lip trembled. "I am sorry." She kissed him softly on the cheek.

He turned his head and brushed his lips over hers. The salty taste of tears reminded him how frail she was at the moment. He lifted his head and stared into eyes filled with despair. "Maybe I could make you want to stay."

A sad smile played on her lips. "I have to go back." She rested her forehead on his shoulder as they continued to move as one.

Trey tightened his hold, refusing to let her step away from him and see how raw he felt.

"Do you know what you want?" Her words were muffled against his shoulder.

Of course he knew. He wanted his wife back—his family together. "I'm tired of the separation. No marriage can survive the distance."

She stopped following his lead and stepped out of his arms. He squeezed her hand, unwilling to let it go. In the soft glow of the nightlight her eyes pleaded for him to understand. "I'm still needed at home."

Trey brushed a tear on her cheek. "I need you, Hailey." He wove his fingers through her hair and cradled the back of her head. Anticipation shot through him when her gaze lowered to his mouth. Trey pulled her close and covered her lips with his. What started as a kiss of compassion quickly deepened to a desire he hadn't felt for years. Her hands moved up his back.

"Hailey?" His voice rasped. "What do you want?"

Cool air hit his chest when she backed out of his arms. Her eyes, dark with longing, searched his face. "To spend the rest of the night with you."

Hailey squeezed her eyes shut against the sun streaming into the familiar bedroom. If she closed them tight enough, she could pretend for a few more moments that the past two years had never happened. She opened one eye enough to see the indention on the pillow beside her. Hope that she hadn't had for years filled her. She knew Trey still cared for her. Last night proved it. He wanted to work thing out. With his experience, he could find a job anywhere.

The smell of coffee filtered under the door. She grabbed her old robe that Trey had left at the end of the bed and pulled it on. She spotted Trey at the living room window bathed in pale morning light.

"You're up early," she whispered from the bedroom doorway.

He cocked his head to one side. A lazy smile crossed his face, revealing the dimples in his cheeks. He held out his arm. She closed the distance between them, and he pulled her in front of him with her back resting against his chest, and wrapped his arms around her waist. "It's good to see you in this robe again." He kissed the side of her neck.

Hailey's legs grew weak as she leaned against his body. It took all her will to form a complete sentence. "I thought I might take it back with me. I've missed it."

Trey stilled behind her and then pulled away. "You've missed your robe? Out of everything you left, it's your robe you miss?"

She turned and met the veiled eyes she'd grown accustomed to over the last weeks. "I didn't mean it like that."

He moved to the desk and snapped open his computer.

"Working already?" She followed and slid her arms around his neck, hoping to repair the small rift.

His hand covered hers. "I've been looking at houses."

"Here?" She started to move, but he held her hands tighter to his chest. "Why?"

His chest expanded. "We'll get a house with a yard." He turned his head enough to look her in the eye. "I want you and Sophie to come back and live here…with me."

A knot formed in her stomach. She wrenched away and hurried into the kitchen. She needed some coffee before dealing with Trey. One night and he expected her to move back immediately? Coffee spilled over the edge of the cup, burning her hand.

Trey followed her and picked up a towel. He tenderly wiped the coffee and kissed the red mark.

Hailey threw the towel in the sink. "Is this what our lovemaking was about? You wanted to manipulate me so I'd stay?" She wiped her eyes. "You took advantage of me. I… I thought—"

"No." He stepped to her and took her chin in his hand. "You will not lessen what happened between us by saying I manipulated you. You wanted it as much as I did."

She couldn't deny it, nor did she want to. "But you expect me to come back now just because we slept together?" She pulled the robe tighter around her.

"Because of this whole week. Hailey, I love you. I always have. You are so much a part of me that I will never get over you." He took a ragged breath. "We are supposed to be together. You know it's true or you wouldn't have gotten into bed with me. Come back so we can be a family. Please?" He kissed her forehead. "Please, Hailey. Please—"

She put her fingers against his lips. "Don't say 'stay.' You make it sound so easy, but you don't understand." She didn't either. Why should she have to choose between her father and her husband? It wasn't right or fair. She needed to think, and she couldn't do that with him so close. As long as she could feel him, smell him, see him, she couldn't make the decision. "Our plane leaves at ten and the pumpkin patch opens on Saturday. I have to be there."

"Miss the plane. We'll look at houses today and you can go home tomorrow." His face filled with hope.

She wanted to agree. "I can't make a decision like that so quickly."

He kissed her, and as hard as she tried, she couldn't resist. He took a step back and smiled. "I'll get Sophie up and ready while you shower. Will that give you enough time?"

How many more times would she hurt him? "I don't know." She walked past him and stopped. "Would you move back to Kansas?"

"My job is here." The smile dimmed. "Things will be different this time."

"Like yesterday?"

His smile disappeared completely. "I missed two days of work this week. You have to understand—"

Her cell phone rang, cutting him short. He glanced at it on the table then looked at her, almost daring her to answer.

Hailey stared at the phone for several seconds before answering it. Without a glance at him, she walked into the bedroom. "Hi, Dad."

Trey choked back his annoyance. Soon he'd know where Hailey stood.

A moan from Sophie moved him to her corner bed. Sitting on the end, he listened to Hailey's conversation. It didn't require any imagination to figure out what he couldn't hear.

"Are things ready for Saturday?" She sounded nervous. "I

know, this won't happen again. ... I'm sure Aunt Joni has done fine. I can call her and see what's left for me to do. ... I'm not sure." He heard her take a deep breath. "We might stay today. ... No, I'm not joking. Daddy, calm down. I'd still be there before Saturday." Another pause—a angst-laden one. "I'm not being irresponsible. I– Trey would like us to move here."

Trey smiled. If they looked for houses today, Hailey would come back to him. He heard Jim's voice but couldn't make out the words.

"I know, but I'll never fix everything." Her voice softened. "He's my husband. ... I don't want to." Another long silence, and his confidence withered. "Okay. I'll see you tonight."

Muffled sniffs carried to the living room. He rested his forehead on his hand and steeled himself against the sound. At some point she had to make a choice. The idea that she might have made the final one left him cold.

Sophie rolled over in her sleep. She was so innocent of her parents' mess. He'd never dreamed of being a part-time parent. His body ached with the warring emotions.

He cleared his throat. "We need to leave for the airport in an hour."

"Out, Daddy." Sophie held her hands to him.

Hailey stood fifth in line to check in, so he unhooked the stroller strap and lifted her into his arms. "I'm going to miss you, Sophie." He rubbed his nose against hers. "Will you be a big girl for Mommy?"

She nodded and laid her head on his shoulder.

The small headache he had developed at last night's meeting now pounded, each beat loud enough to be heard over the stifling silence between him and Hailey.

"I've got our tickets." Hailey avoided looking at him as she pushed the papers into her carry-on and reached for the stroller.

"You don't have to wait with us."

He adjusted Sophie on his right arm and reached for Hailey's chin with his left hand. "I want to wait with you. Don't—" The ring of his phone interrupted him. "I need to take this."

"Of course you do." Hailey walked to the elevator that would take them to the second level.

He made the call as short as possible, returned his phone to his coat pocket, then joined her. "It looks like I'll be in Kansas with Bryant the week before the elections. He's scheduled for the last round of meet-and-greets before election day. I would appreciate it if you would bring Sophie to see me?"

"I'll have to see. That's our last week at the patch, but I'll try." She still didn't look at him.

The pounding in his head grew. "Are you sure this is what you want?"

She turned and met his gaze. Her shoulders slumped. "You have never been able to understand this."

He sucked the air in between dry lips, indignant that she still put the blame on him. "I've tried. You are the one who always leaves, and I'm the fool who takes you to the airport every time. It's not about the accident or your dad anymore. You're making your own choices."

Sophie held onto his neck. She understood he wouldn't be going home with them.

The color in Hailey's face rose. "I'm sorry you believe that."

He checked his watch and frowned. They needed to start through security. He walked them to the edge of the line. Hugging Sophie to him, he kissed her. "Be good for Mommy, and remind her to call me when you get home." Trey held her a moment long and whispered, "I love you, Sophie."

Her thin arms stretched around his neck as she buried her head in his shoulder. He closed his eyes when she sniffled. "Love you, Daddy."

"We need to go, Sophie-girl." Hailey touched him on the arm.

He hugged Sophie once more before stooping to put her in the stroller. With one last kiss, Trey straightened and pulled an envelope from his suit pocket. Holding it towards Hailey, he cleared his throat, hoping to dislodge the lump of emotion. "I don't know what else to do. Everything you need is in here. I've changed things to include my expectations with Sophie. If you agree, I'll do my best to keep this from getting messy."

Hailey stared at the envelope and slowly moved her hand over it, but she didn't grasp it with her shaking fingers.

Everything in him screamed against this. Frustrated, he grabbed her hand and pressed her fingers around the paper. "This is what you want, Hailey. It's all up to you."

The sight of her with head bowed was his undoing. While he mentally listed the ways he was a fool, he took her in his arms and drew her to him. "Call me when you get— When your plane lands."

She nodded. Stepping back she studied him. "Do you regret last night?"

Trey stared at the floor. He could fill a book with regrets. "I regret that you answered the phone this morning." He met her gaze. "I'll never regret last night."

Hailey moved behind the stroller. "We'd better go. Thank you for everything." She leaned over Sophie. "Tell Daddy goodbye."

Sophie looked up with pouty lips. "Bye-bye."

Trey stood at the back of the line while they slowly made their way to the front. Hailey pushed Sophie through the security scanner just as Trey's phone rang again. Senator Bryant. He started to answer and stopped. Above the commotion he heard a child's cry. Hailey pushed the stroller out of the way and hurried to unbuckle Sophie. When she lifted her from the stroller Trey realized it was Sophie's cries echoing across the cavernous room. Holding Sophie, Hailey pushed the stroller in front of her and walked toward their gate.

His phone rang again. Trey raised it to his ear. His heart shattered when his gaze met Sophie's, her hands reaching for him over her mother's shoulder, while Hailey hurried to put more distance between them.

CHAPTER TWENTY-TWO

"Coffee ready?"

Hailey jumped at her brother's voice. Since when did he have permission to barge in without so much as a knock? She shoved the papers she'd been reading under the dishtowel. She hoped he hadn't seen them. She had no desire to explain them to Todd.

Her hands shook as she pulled two mugs from the cabinet and poured fresh coffee into each. She pushed Todd's to his chair at the end of the counter, careful not to slosh the contents over the side. It wouldn't do for him to grab the towel. The hot cup burned her hands, but at least it gave her another focus.

"Ellen said your plane was late getting in."

She leaned against the counter. "Storms in Chicago. I appreciated her waiting for us."

"Did Sophie have a good time?" The sugar spoon clanked on the mug as he stirred.

Pictures of Trey and Sophie flashed in her mind. "She loved it. I'm sure she'll tell you all about it tomorrow."

He took a drink. "You okay?"

"Trey wouldn't have let me leave otherwise." An exposed corner of the legal paper stuck out from beneath the towel. She rambled on. "I don't think I've ever been so sick."

"It's a good thing Trey was there." He took another drink, watching her over the rim of the mug. "How are you really doing?"

Hot tears filled her eyes. She blew on the hot beverage. "I don't know." She pushed the honest words past a knot in her throat.

"You spent a week together. How did that go?"

She could still feel Trey's arms around her. "Being sick kind of threw a wrench into the whole trip."

"You weren't sick the whole time." He lifted an eyebrow as his mouth curved into a knowing smile. "Trey called on Tuesday and said you were almost back to normal. How'd you two get along, living together?"

Heat stole up her face. "He went back to work on Monday. I slept on the couch." Except for their last night. Todd's skeptical smile flustered her, and she hurried to explain. "I guess we got along all right. He still lives in the same apartment."

"Why'd you come back?"

"Surely I wasn't gone so long you forgot this is where I belong." She forced a smile. "We're opening this weekend. What other choice did I have?"

Coffee splashed from Todd's mug when he set it down hard. "What choice did you have? You had other choices." He grabbed the dishtowel and blotted the dark liquid spreading across the counter. "You spent a week with your husband. Why would you want to come back here?" He threw the stained towel next to the uncovered papers.

Hailey made a grab for them, but he scooped them from the counter in one motion. SHe held out her hand. "Give them back–they aren't your business."

He pulled the papers to his chest.

"Todd, those aren't yours."

He held them out of her reach and scanned the front page. "Divorce papers? Where did these come from?" Todd slapped the papers on the counter and stared at her. "I talked to Trey yesterday morning, and he thought things were going well. What did you do?"

"Me? If you'd look closer you'd see that he's already signed them."

"I don't believe you. You've done everything you could to ruin this marriage. I appreciate that you stayed around for a while after the accident, but you should have gone back to him. You tried to keep Sophie a secret from her own father." He paused and flipped to the last page of the official papers. "Yesterday Trey told me he thought you two could work things out. What changed?"

Her reasons and excuses twisted together. "He wanted to look at houses today, but I needed to come home."

"Things were going so well that Trey wanted to look at houses?" The chair creaked when he leaned back. "I'm missing something here."

Anger welled inside. "What you're missing is how he manipulated me. He knew I had to come home and–"

"Manipulated you? How in the world did Trey manipulate you?"

"We spent the night together"–the words spewed in a frustrated rush–"and this morning he wanted to find a house for us to move into. What about what I want?"

Todd gawked at her. "You slept with him and then walked out?"

Hailey bit the inside of her cheek, wanting the pain to replace the emptiness she'd felt all day. "I didn't have a choice."

"You're wrong. You don't sleep with your spouse and walk out on him the next morning." Todd walked around the counter and filled his mug with hot coffee before leaning against the counter next to her. "Do you even know what you want? Is this what you want for your life? For Sophie?"

She dumped the lukewarm coffee from her cup and gripped the cool edge of the sink. "I don't know."

Todd took a drink before moving back to his chair in silence. "I don't understand you anymore. Why don't you fight for your marriage? You wouldn't even have to fight–just go back."

"What about Dad?"

"What about him?" Weariness resonated in tone. "It was an accident, Hailey. An unfortunate accident. You can't pay for it for the rest of your life, but you're going to if you don't get out of here."

"You can't take care of this place alone."

"I'm a grown man, not a child. I can run this place or hire the help I need." Todd stood and walked to the door. "You probably don't want to hear this, but I think the only reason you're here is because it's easier to hide than it is to make your marriage work."

She gasped. "How can you say that? I've given up everything to take care of Dad and this farm."

"No, you never went back because you weren't happy in D.C. and your marriage was struggling. The accident gave you an excuse to stay."

She swallowed hard. "I can't believe you're saying this to me." Her marriage had meant everything to her. She never would have left if it weren't for the accident. Even then she hadn't planned to be gone for so long. Her dad needed her and the pumpkin patch wouldn't be successful if she wasn't here. "Get out, Todd."

Todd pushed the door open before facing her again. "It's time someone calls you on this. Trey's a good man—he deserves better."

"Get out!" She wouldn't listen to this in her own home.

His hand hit the doorframe. "You know what, Hailey? I'm surprised he hasn't found someone else. He's probably had plenty of offers. Welcome home."

Trey glanced at his watch. Sophie would already be in bed. In the ten hours since he'd watched them walk away at the airport, his loneliness had become a dull ache in his chest. He'd checked his phone often, but Hailey hadn't called. The time didn't matter. He needed to know they had made it safely.

"If you'll excuse me, gentlemen, I need to make an important call." Trey nodded then turned toward the conference room door. At the end of the hall a bank of windows overlooked the city. He pressed the familiar number on his phone as he strode toward the quiet corner. The breath he'd been holding released when Hailey answered.

"I assume you made it back and just forgot to call."

Her pause spoke volumes. "It's been a busy day."

Trey pulled the sheer curtain away from the window and watched the traffic crawl on the street below him. "Have I missed talking to Sophie tonight?"

"She fell asleep as soon as we got in the car at the airport. I put her to bed early."

"Was she glad to be back there?" Was Hailey?

She sighed. "She misses you."

"I miss both of you." He lowered his head and stared at the taupe colored carpet. "I haven't been home yet, but I know it will be too quiet."

"You're still at work? It's after ten there. Go home."

The empty apartment made working late appealing once again. "Things are wrapping up so I'll be leaving soon. Is being back everything you expected?"

Silence met his question.

"Hailey?"

"Todd's furious with me for coming home." He squeezed his eyes shut to steel himself against the angst in her voice. "I don't remember when he's ever been so angry with me."

A small thread of comfort wove through him. Someone in the family was on his side.

"He saw the divorce papers, and I probably said too much. He figured out what happened last night and couldn't believe I left you again."

So he wasn't alone in his disbelief. Every time he'd thought about it his anger had grown. Each hour at work had felt like two, leaving him exhausted.

"Are you still there?" She broke the silence and brought his thoughts back to the present.

"What do you want me to say, Hailey? You got out of our bed, took your dad's call, and got on an airplane for home. I would be a very happy man if you'd have made different choices." He gripped the phone tighter. Her muffled sobs would be his undoing if he didn't hang up soon. As much as it hurt, she had to decide what she wanted. "I need to go. I'll call Sophie tomorrow. Good night."

"Wait." She took a shuddered breath. "Todd said there had probably been–" Her word caught on another sob.

His patience were gone, causing his tone to be brisk. "Had probably been what?"

"Others." Her voice squeaked the word. "Other women who would want you more than me."

Trey squeezed the curtain in his hand. Maybe he didn't want Todd on his side. At least Hailey cared enough to be upset by the idea. Still, Todd had no business going there. "Todd said that?"

"Is it true?"

That she could even question him after the past week left him disappointed. If he told her the truth would it change anything or leave him more exposed to the pain she could cause? He swallowed hard. "Don't listen to Todd on that one. There's never been any other woman." He turned the phone off before she could say another word and whispered to himself, "Because you're the only woman I've ever loved."

CHAPTER TWENTY-THREE

Grant wove his way through the group of kids running toward the single church van left in the parking lot. The only building with a light on beside the ticket booth was the Snack Shop. A closed sign leaned up against a giant pumpkin. Through the window he saw Hailey behind the counter, flicking through a stack of dollar bills.

"You're out here late." Grant pushed the door shut behind him.

Hailey stacked the money against the old black register before looking up. "Trying to get caught up while waiting for this last group to finish going through the maze." She motioned toward the dessert cooler. "Do you have time for a piece of pumpkin pie?"

He rubbed the back of his neck and smiled sheepishly. "If you have an extra piece. Are you still talking to me?"

"I guess it's your lucky night." She slid a wedge on the plate and added a scoop of whipped cream. "Coffee? You haven't been around for a few weeks. What's up with that?"

"Fall is a busy time." He sat, and she placed a tray holding two slices of pie and mugs of coffee on the table. He nudged the other chair out with his foot. "I needed time to think about things."

She slid into the seat. "Well, I've missed talking with you. I'm glad you came tonight."

Grant ate half his pie before speaking. "How was your trip–

other than being sick?"

"It was okay." She scratched the fork across the top of the pumpkin filling. "Sophie had a great time."

"Did you and Trey figure anything out?"

"Not really. Are you really sure you want to hear this?"

He nodded. "I realized while you were gone that I've been wrong. Somewhere over the last two years I let myself forget that you're another man's wife."

"The fault is mine for letting you believe Trey didn't want Sophie or me." She pushed the plate to the middle of the table.

"He treated you good?"

"Yes." She folded her paper napkin into a smaller triangle. "I didn't stay at a hotel."

"I figured as much when Todd said you were sick." He swallowed his jealousy. Why was doing the right thing so hard? "What's next for you two?"

"I don't know. Trey wants us to move to D.C. again."

"What do you want?"

She gave a short laugh. "To make everyone happy. But I don't see how I can leave Dad, and Trey is not willing to come back here. He sent the divorce papers home with me if that's what I choose." She rested her forehead on her hands. "Everyone else seems to think this is such a black and white decision, but I can't see it."

The last bite of pie became sawdust in his mouth. This was his chance to direct her his way. He swallowed hard. "You know I'd be here for you and Sophie if you got divorced, right?"

Tears glistened in her eyes. "I know, but I don't think I'd ever be ready for that." Her lip quivered. "I've loved Trey since we were twelve. I can't imagine loving anyone else that way."

He took a drink of the lukewarm coffee. Her answer didn't surprise him, but it still twisted inside. "Then what are you doing here? If you know where your happiness is, quit being the martyr and go after it."

"You make it sound easy, but there's still my dad and the

pumpkin patch."

"I don't know if Jim will ever accept you leaving, but you're not happy here. Honestly, I don't see that you being here makes him any easier to get along with either. Joni could run the pumpkin patch if she wanted to stick around."

Hailey stacked their empty plates and carried them to the sink. "I don't want to raise Sophie in the city."

"At some point, Hailey, you have to give a little." He followed her to the sink and set his cup down. "Trey's a better man than me, because I don't know how I'd forgive you for keeping Sophie a secret. I bet if you'd talk with him, you two could find a compromise. But you can't expect him to make all the changes. Does he plan to come to Kansas anytime soon?"

"He said he wouldn't be coming with the Senator next weekend, but I'm hoping he'll change his mind. I can't imagine he wouldn't take the chance to see Sophie."

"Unless he wants to see you moving in his direction."

Hailey reached for the light switch. "Then he's going to be waiting for a few more weeks."

Hailey veered off the main path and jogged between the two metal buildings. If she hurried she might be able to talk with someone from the senator's group about lunch. She'd received a detailed itinerary and plan for the day's events earlier in the week. She knew everything except the one detail that mattered most to her. Did the senator's event coordinator honestly think it more important for her to know Senator Bryant would take three pictures by the tube slides and then receive questions for ten minutes instead of when to serve lunch? The food couldn't magically appear.

Ahead, the camera man adjusted his tripod near the hill encasing the three tube slides. At least someone knew where to be—and when.

"I wish you wouldn't have had those drinks on the plane." Senator Bryant's voice drifted down the narrow alley.

Slowing her steps, Hailey watched the opening at the end of the path.

"It was one drink." A woman answered. "I'm rather surprised you even notice with all the attention you were giving Ms. Morrison."

Hailey halted. The senator and his wife sat on a bench with their back to her.

"You know Caryn is in charge of the campaign ads. I hope you can walk a straight line when they start filming."

"And I hope your phone doesn't ring. We wouldn't want your constituency to think you're anything but a devoted family man."

Hailey backed up quietly. She'd find someone else to answer her question.

The senator's tired voice followed her. "We only have a few more weeks, Amanda. Then things will get better."

"Will they? I have a hard time believing it." Amanda Bryant stood. "They're ready for us."

Hailey peeked around the corner of the building. Before her eyes, the two transformed into a happy couple waiting at the edge of the tube slide for their daughter to appear. If their conversation was any indication of their personal lives, they could both be actors. Big smiles creased their faces while they shared what the world would see as an intimate moment.

"May I help you?"

Hailey jolted. A woman with a clipboard in hand stood near. She cleared her throat. "Yes. Can you tell me when everyone will want lunch? Somehow that information was excluded from my notes."

The woman glanced at her watch then ran a perfect fingernail over the paper on her clipboard. "We should be finished by one. I'll send someone up if it's going to be later." She turned on her heel and seemed to glide to where the couple stood.

Dismissed, Hailey took one more glance at the senator and

his wife. Could this all be for show? Disappointment knotted inside her. The conservative media touted the Bryant marriage as an example for all. If they struggled, how could two people who had been apart for almost three years make it work? Did anyone truly live happily ever after anymore?

With a final look at the couple, she returned to the kitchen.

Two hours later Hailey wiped at a piece of hair stuck to her cheek. "I can't believe that air conditioner chose today to go out. Are you sure you'll be able to handle this?"

Aunt Joni glanced up from where she stood spreading pumpkin spice cupcakes with cream cheese icing. "I grew up without air conditioning, so don't worry about me. I didn't figure you'd even noticed. You seem pretty nervous about today."

"How often have we had a senator here? I'll be glad when it's over." Hailey pulled the mixing bowl from the bleach water and shook some of the water from it.

"It's too bad Trey couldn't come back with them." Aunt Joni set the cupcake with the rest and carried the pan to the walk-in cooler.

Hailey rinsed another bowl. "I thought he might change his mind and come to see Sophie at least. I guess he's giving me time to decide what I want."

"It sounds to me like you need to make some decisions." The older woman swiped her forehead with her arm. "I hope Todd can find a window unit before long. Go finish the tables. It will be cooler out there."

Hailey looked around the hot kitchen to make sure she hadn't left anything out of the fridge. "Come get me if you need anything." She re-tied her apron while walking toward the door.

Outside, the sounds of laughter filled the air. Children made use of the swings and forts in the trees at the edge of the pumpkin patch. Fall foliage gave the trees a festive appearance. Even though the kitchen radiated with heat, outside it was a beautiful day and hundreds of people had turned out to meet Senator Bryant.

She stood at the edge of the pavilion and let the breeze cool her. The hair she'd taken time to fix this morning had escaped the clip and hung limp. She twisted it and tried to catch as much as she could. The apron over her green logo polo shirt was stained and dirty, showing evidence of the hot hours she'd already spent getting ready for this event. She still needed to get the center pieces on each table. Todd had helped put the tablecloths on earlier and now the tables waited for the sunflower arrangements. What started as a simple lunch of hot dogs had morphed into a three-course meal for the senator and other VIPs.

Hailey pulled the cart holding the flowers out of the storage closet and pushed it through the maze, setting one at each table. Her heart sagged with the realization that Trey wasn't with the group from Washington. Even though he told her he wouldn't come, a small part of her kept hoping he'd change his mind.

"Hailey?" A woman spoke from the shadows.

She set a floral arrangement on the closest table. "Yes?"

Amanda Bryant hustled toward her. The woman wore designer jeans that skimmed the top of high dollar red flats. The stark white shirt accentuated the woman's tanned skin, and a colorful scarf draped around her neck. Her loosely braided dark brown hair fell over one shoulder.

Hailey glanced down at her apron and grabbed another arrangement of flowers to hide the largest stain on her apron. She wished the floor would open. It had been years since Hailey had been so self-conscious of her own looks, or the lack thereof. She swallowed. "May I help you?"

"I'm Amanda Bryant. I'm afraid you were very sick the last time I saw you and we weren't properly introduced." She eyed Hailey's apron and smiled. "Looks like you've had a rough day already."

Hailey pulled the flowers closer.

Amanda picked up another arrangement. "One on each table?" She waited for Hailey's nod before moving. "I'm sorry Trey didn't come back with us. I know he has a lot going on right now with the election and coming changes."

Hailey set her flowers on the table and picked up the next container. "I never got to thank you for taking care of Sophie while I was sick."

Amanda pulled out two chairs at the final table. "Do you have time to talk?" Uncertainty clouded her eyes. "I know you're busy, but I wanted to have a few minutes with you alone."

Hailey's chest constricted as she slid onto the chair's seat and crossed her arms. "I assume this is about Trey?"

Amanda glanced down. "Somewhat. I want you to know that I understand your hesitance to come back to Washington." She paused before meeting Hailey's eyes. "I think very highly of Trey, and I know how exciting it is to be involved in politics. But it's a tough business on marriages."

Sympathy spread through Hailey. "You and the senator have made it."

Amanda stared off in the distance. "Some years have been easier than others. Between us, it's not all it appears to be, and the years have definitely taken their toll."

"But you're willing to stay there and make your marriage work."

A sad smile turned up the edges of the woman's lips. "I have been. Both Rob and I keep trying. But there's always another meeting, another school function I have to attend alone, another election, and another woman who would like to have my husband and his power."

"I'm guessing Trey didn't ask you to talk to me?"

"No, and I believe you'll keep this conversation to yourself." She looked around before speaking. "I want you and Trey back together. He's a good man, and I saw when you were sick how much he loves you. I don't think he understands what it's like for the wife."

"Trey doesn't want to come back here." Hailey sighed. "He and my dad don't get along very well."

"I don't know where the answer lies for the two of you, but I wanted to encourage you to be sure you're ready to deal with everything before you come back. No matter what promises of change he agrees to, know that there's so little he actually controls." She stood and stretched out her hand. "I'd better get back before they miss me."

Hailey squeezed the offered hand. "Thank you. I appreciate your candidness."

CHAPTER TWENTY-FOUR

"Let's break for dinner. I'll meet you all back here in an hour." Senator Bryant stood and reached for his suit coat hanging on the back of the desk chair. "Trey, have you seen the finished ad from Harper Farms? I wish you could have joined us. Five weeks is a long time to go without seeing your family. Are they doing okay?"

Trey finished stacking his papers and stood. "I spoke with Hailey for a few minutes last night and everything seems fine. It's a busy time for them."

"They have an impressive business. Mallory is still talking about Sophie."

Trey followed the Senator to the door. He glanced at his phone to see Hailey's number listed three times. Unease struck.

"Coming, Trey?" one of the aids asked.

He looked up and realized the others were already waiting at the elevator.

"I'll catch up. It looks like I need to take care of something first." He hit the send button and waited through the rings. On the sixth one Ellen answered.

"Ellen, it's Trey. I saw that Hailey's trying to get a hold of me."

"I'm so glad you called." The pitch of her voice was higher than he remembered. "Hailey just stepped out of the room, but she needs to talk to you. Can you wait for her to call you right back?"

"Is something wrong?" His anxiety grew. The silence on the other end only increased his fear. "Ellen, is something wrong?" The words came out harsher than he'd intended.

"Hailey needs to talk to you. Please wait for her to call you back."

The line went dead.

Trey squeezed the phone, resisting the urge to throw it against the wall. While he paced up and down the hall, he imagined every horrible thing possible. He walked into the conference room they'd just vacated and slumped into one of the chairs. Time crawled.

He phone buzzed. He punched the connect button. "Hailey? What's going on?"

"Sophie fell out of the treehouse." Hailey's voice caught on a sob. "It happened this afternoon."

Nausea rolled through him. "How bad is she hurt?" His eyes closed, bracing himself for the answer.

"She broke her arm and has a mild concussion."

"Where were you?" He breathed the words.

"I was— She had— It happened so fast."

"You weren't watching her. She got away, didn't she? And you didn't notice."

Her silence fueled his anger.

"It's obvious she isn't as safe with you as you think."

"I—" A shaky breath sounded in his hear. "Anyway, I–I just wanted to tell you." The phone went dead.

Trey slammed his fist on the table.

"Everything okay?" Senator Bryant stood in the doorway. "I thought you'd left with everyone else for dinner."

Trey leaned his head back on the chair. "Sophie had an accident today—fell out of the treehouse."

Senator Bryant pulled another chair out from under the table and sat. "Is she all right?"

"Broken arm and concussion...if you believe Hailey."

"You don't?"

He gave a short laugh. "Would you? She kept my daughter from me for two years. I don't know what to believe anymore."

Hailey propped Sophie on the couch with pillows supporting her cast. The child's tear-stained cheeks and tired eyes were a testament to their last twenty-four hours.

"Please, Sophie. Let Mommy put this in your mouth, then you swallow like a big girl." The plastic medicine dropper shook in Hailey's hand. Between Sophie crying and her own repeated nightmares of Sophie falling, she hadn't slept much, and tiredness made her muscles ache. Sophie's shirt bore the stains of previous failed attempts to get the medicine down the little girl. "Come on, honey. I have a huge group of kids coming this morning and need to get things ready."

"Yucky."

"I know, but you'll feel better if you take this. Aunt Ellen is bringing Jacob over to see you."

The little lips formed a tight, straight line.

Hailey battled frustration and nausea. Why couldn't Sophie just take this medicine? They had tried every flavor from bubble gum to grape and still she refused. "You've got to take this, Sophie. It's almost ten o'clock, and I have to go meet those school groups."

Large tears welled up in the child's eyes. "No go."

A vice twisted inside her. She didn't want to leave Sophie, but she had to go. Wednesday had always been the day Hailey was shorthanded in order to have the staff she needed for the weekends. A glance at the clock showed only twenty minutes remained before three busloads of third graders would arrive.

"Aunt Ellen will be here. Won't you like to see Jacob?"

Sophie shook her head, lips pushed out in a pout.

"Oh, honey." Hailey pulled Sophie onto her lap. "It's supposed to start raining later this evening and continue for a few days. Once these kids leave, we won't be busy all weekend and I'll be here, okay?"

"I stay wif you." Sophie's clear blue eyes--her daddy's eyes–pleaded.

"You'll be more comfortable in the house. It's so cold and windy."

"I go."

"You stay with Aunt Ellen and Jacob this morning. I'll come right before lunch and we'll surprise Aunt Joni in the Snack Shop. Okay?" Hailey waited for her smile.

The kitchen door opened with a creak. Ellen hurried in with Jacob's car seat handle over her arm. "With this wind it was easier to drive over here." She removed the blankets and lifted the baby free. "How are you this morning, Sophie? Look at that pink cast. Uncle Todd said to tell you he's going to write something funny on it at lunch today."

The first giggle of the morning escaped Sophie's mouth.

"Thank you." Hailey smiled over the toddler's head. "We're having a tough time taking the medicine, but I really need to get going."

"I'll see what I can do. Anything else?"

Hailey grabbed her coat from the kitchen chair. "She's not happy with me leaving, so I told her I'd come get her and we'd eat lunch in the Snack Shop. I'll try to be back around noon. Sophie can stay with Aunt Joni or me until the buses leave." At the door she turned. "I really appreciate your help."

"We'll be fine." Ellen smiled as she sunk into the rocking chair, wrapping Jacob's blanket tighter around him. "I'm glad it's you out in this wind and not me."

"I just hope we can get everyone out of here before that rain moves in. It looks like it will be a slow weekend."

"A break will do all of us good. Go, you're going to be late."

A slow weekend would be nice. It didn't help their numbers,

but the dirty dishes piled on the counter and the clean laundry strewn across the table attested to the busyness of the past five weeks.

"How many cookies do you have wrapped over there?" Aunt Joni looked up from the cooling rack where six pans of pumpkin shaped sugar cookies waited.

"Ninety-three." Hailey tied the curling ribbon in a knot around the plastic bag. "We'll need one hundred thirty-five for the school groups."

Aunt Joni slid another pan across the counter and reached for the scissors to curl the ribbon on the tied bags. "Did you let Trey know about Sophie's arm?"

She nodded but didn't look up. "He was glad I called."

"That's all?"

Hailey shrugged. "He sounded pretty upset about it. He'll probably call tonight to talk with Sophie—make sure she's okay."

Aunt Joni stacked the finished cookie sacks into a box, ready to be handed out as each student brought their chosen pumpkin in to be weighed. "How are you feeling about everything? It's too bad it happened with a babysitter."

Hailey finished the knot in the next ribbon and pushed it to Aunt Joni's pile. "It was an accident. Megan didn't have any idea that Sophie would hide in the treehouse. I should have had the ladder removed the first time Sophie crawled up there."

"I'm not sure who felt worse, Megan or her mom." Aunt Joni shook her head. "By the time Dayna got here to pick up Megan, both were in tears."

"I'll call her today so she knows everything is fine and that I don't blame Megan. I know how quickly Sophie gets up there." Hailey glanced at the wall clock. "I told Sophie I'd bring her over here for lunch, so maybe I'll take Dad some coffee on my way to get her. He has to be cold pulling those kids around. When I came in here, there was a long line waiting for him."

"It's good for him to get out and run the train. He could do more around here if he weren't so stubborn."

"Maybe things will get better once Todd finishes the lift he's working on." Hailey tied another sack closed. "The kids were going to eat in the shed, so I'll run down there and make sure everything's going okay." She filled an insulated mug with coffee. "I'll be back in a bit."

"Hot dogs or chili? It's that kind of day, don't you think?"

Hailey's stomach churned. "Sophie would like the hot dog. I'll find something else for myself."

"Stomach still giving you trouble?" Aunt Joni's eyes gleamed with concern. "You need to have that checked out."

"Why? So I can pay someone to tell me I have too much stress in my life?"

"I'm sure yesterday didn't help much." The older woman pushed the lid down on another box and pushed it to to the back of the counter. "I'll make some soup for you."

Several moments later Hailey warmed her hands around the coffee mug and hurried down the hill. The homemade train drove up outside the shed where shouts of laughter rang on the cold wind. The train had been Dad's idea. They'd painted seven plastic barrels, turned them on their sides with a hole cut out, and hooked them into a line. A seat and steering wheel finished off each cart. Dad pulled the homemade train with an ATV. He spent hours driving kids around and seemed to love every minute.

Hailey wove her way through the throng of kids. "Everything okay?" She handed her dad the mug. "I thought you might need this. Aunt Joni is making lunch."

"I'm fine." He took a drink. "How's Sophie this morning?"

"We both had a long night. I told her I'd have lunch with her." Hailey looked into the shed to make sure everything was going well. "You need anything while I'm here?"

"Nope. Thanks for the coffee." He turned in the seat and

spoke above the kids, "Next group ready?" At their shouts of confirmation, he started the engine. "We need to do something about that treehouse."

Hailey frowned at him. "We should take that ladder apart until Sophie is older."

"The whole thing needs to come down. It's an eyesore—always has been. We were careless to leave it up with Sophie around."

"We'll just take the ladder off."

"It needs to go." He started to pull away.

"It's my treehouse, Daddy." She hurried to keep up. "Sophie will be fine. I'll talk to Todd about taking the ladder down. It was an accident."

His lifeless eyes looked at her. "Won't you ever learn? Accidents are caused by carelessness."

He drove away, the tires on the barrel carts rumbling over the path. Dad would have to ask Todd or Grant to tear the treehouse down, and she knew neither of them would agree. Once they removed the ladder, Dad would give up his idea.

In the shed she found the teacher who had organized the field trip. "Is everything going okay?"

"The kids are having a great time. We only have three groups left to go with Mr. Mosier for his class. He always does a wonderful job."

"We're lucky to have him." Hailey pushed her hands into her coat pockets. "Anything I can help with?"

The older lady shook her head. "Nothing I can think of. We'll plan to start bringing groups up at one-thirty so they can weigh their pumpkins."

"I'll be ready. It looks like the rain will hold off until your buses are packed."

"It's certainly gotten colder, but we're thankful it's dry." The teacher turned to help a student open her milk carton, giving Hailey a chance to leave.

Glancing at her watch, she saw it was a few minutes after

noon. Hopefully Sophie wouldn't realize she was late. The thought caused her to hurry her steps. From the path she could see the basement lights were off. Surprising, since it was a cloudy day. Maybe they were watching a movie and Ellen had humored Sophie by turning off the lights.

Stillness greeted her when she stepped through the door. "Ellen? Sophie?"

Where was everyone? Had Ellen misunderstood and taken Sophie to the Snack Shop? The hum of the dishwasher filled the room. Sophie's blankets were folded neatly at one end of the couch. The clothes were still on the table, but three folded piles now waited to be put away. The kitchen counter was cleared, too. Bless Ellen for straightening the house. Maybe if it did rain this weekend, she could take Ellen a meal to thank her.

Several tables in the Snack Shop were occupied. Three moms and their preschool aged boys sat around two tables with their lunches and steaming cups of hot chocolate. An older couple sat at another table, eating pie.

"It's getting colder out there." Hailey spoke as she walked through. "Thank you all for coming out today."

One of the boys jumped from his seat and ran to meet her. "I picked my pumpkin already. It's the biggest one in the patch. Mommy says we'll have to take a wagon back to get it."

"Do you know where the wagons are?"

He nodded.

"I've been needing to get the biggest pumpkin out of the field and haven't found anyone strong enough to lift it. So if you and your buddies can get it up here, I'll give you each a cookie. Is that a deal?"

The boy's eyes sparkled as he looked at his friends. The other two boys jumped in their seats, slapping high-fives.

"We'll take care of it." He shook her hand.

Hailey waved to the moms. "I'll be in the store right after lunch." She pushed open the kitchen door. Sophie, with her arm in the sling, sat in her high chair. Hailey smiled. "Sophie, there you are. I didn't expect Aunt Ellen to bring you over here."

She pointed and giggled. "Daddy."

"Daddy what?"

"Hello, Hailey." Trey stepped from the walk-in pantry. The wariness on his face spoke volumes.

Hailey grabbed for the table. "I... I wasn't... What are you doing here?"

"Is this what you were wanting?" He held up a bag of dried noodles for Aunt Joni.

"Yes." Aunt Joni took the offered bag back to the stove.

"I decided to take a few days of vacation and visit Sophie." He sat beside their daughter. The words he didn't say hovered in the air.

"I'm surprised you can get away, with the elections being so close." She bit her bottom lip. "Have you eaten?" The room was too warm and she was babbling. What must he think?

Aunt Joni tapped the edge of her wooden spoon on the side of the kettle. "I thought chicken noodle soup sounded good today. I'm late because of those cookies, but it will be finished in a few minutes."

Hailey took a deep breath, thankful for the distraction her aunt provided.

"I'm sure it will be worth the wait. We don't mind waiting, do we, sweetie?" Sophie was rewarded with another one of Trey's smiles. When he turned to Hailey, all the smiles vanished. "It's nice you're concerned about my job security, but I have plenty of vacation days. And while this isn't the best time to use them, I do have a boss who understands the importance of family."

Aunt Joni slammed a cabinet door. "Hailey, why don't you get the bowls out and then find those rolls we put in the freezer the other night."

Hailey followed her aunt's direction while the weight of Trey's stare pressed upon her. She stood with the freezer door opened, looking for the bag of rolls and letting the chill cool her face. "How long will you be here?"

"I have to be back to work on Monday morning."

Four days. Rolls found, she needlessly rearranged things in the freezer.

"I was thinking, if Sophie can travel, I'd like to take her to meet my folks. It's their anniversary this weekend, and I can't think of a better gift than meeting their granddaughter."

Hailey stopped arranging. Friction filled the room. He wanted to take Sophie for four days? Take Sophie away from her? The package of rolls slipped from her hands and landed with a *crack*.

"Did you hear me?" Trey gently pulled her away from the freezer and grabbed the bag from the floor. "I want to take Sophie—"

"I heard you." She spat the words. "Just come in here and take her? How many days were you thinking you'd take her away from me?"

"Why don't you discuss this while we eat." Sympathy shone in Aunt Joni's eyes. "I'll warm these rolls while you serve the soup."

Back at the table, Hailey filled Sophie's bowl and then Trey's. She pushed the third bowl aside.

He frowned. "You're not eating?"

"I've lost my appetite."

The bell from the front counter rang. Aunt Joni sighed. "Sounds like someone needs help. You need to eat something, Hailey." She wiped her hands on a towel. "Sophie, make sure your mom and dad say nice things to each other while I'm gone."

Hailey stirred an ice cube into Sophie's soup.

"Do you think Sophie is up to traveling?" He watched her while spooning up some noodles. "We could call her doctor and ask."

"Here, Sophie." She slid the bowl over and watched Sophie pick up a noodle with her fingers. "I need to think about it."

"I'd like to leave in a few hours—drive partway, then stop for the night."

Hailey stood and grabbed her bowl. "I've got to get back to work." She rushed to the sink and dropped her empty bowl. "Give me a little while to get use to the idea, okay?"

"Judging by Hailey's exit, I'd guess that didn't go very well." Joni came through the door a few minutes after Hailey had left. "How did you think she'd take that news?"

Trey pushed his half-eaten meal away and picked up Sophie's spoon to help her. "My parents deserve to know their granddaughter."

"Yes, they do." Joni ladled soup into her bowl and sat. "But do you realize Hailey hasn't ever left Sophie for the night? You told her you were taking Sophie away for several nights. That's been her biggest fear—you taking Sophie and leaving her alone."

He wiped Sophie's hands with his napkin. "I'm not the bad guy, Joni."

"But you are angry with her."

He couldn't deny her observation. "Did she tell you about Washington?"

"Only about the divorce papers you sent home with her."

Trey released the straps holding Sophie in the high chair and carefully pulled her onto his lap. "I was foolish enough to think things were going well—I even suggested she stay another day and look at houses. Then Jim called and she left again. Maybe it's time to figure out how we're going to handle things with Sophie and stop hoping for anything more with our marriage."

"And handling things with Sophie means you come in here and demand to take her away for a few days?" She softened the comment with a gentle smile.

He grimaced. "I probably didn't handle that as well as I should have."

"Usually weekends are very busy and Hailey probably wouldn't miss Sophie as much, but it's going to be rainy and cold. Without Sophie around, it will be a long, lonely weekend for her."

He studied the older woman before speaking. "What did you think would happen when you came to my apartment that morning?"

Joni stirred her soup before meeting his gaze. "I wanted Sophie to know her dad."

"And with Hailey? Did you think we'd be able to start over?"

"No, I hoped you two might realize what you had. But until you forgive her completely, I doubt there's much of a chance."

Trey picked up Sophie's coat and draped it around her. "It looks like Sophie is ready for a nap. Thanks for lunch." He stood and headed for the door. "For the record, I was ready to forgive Hailey, and then she left again."

CHAPTER TWENTY-FIVE

Hailey stopped inside her living room, surprised to see Trey reclined in the chair with Sophie cuddled on his lap. Her pink fleece blanket covered them both. A pile of board books littered the end table. Sophie sucked the first two fingers of her right hand, her eyes closed in sleep.

"I wondered where you two had gone." Hailey set the bag of dirty towels on the kitchen counter.

"Sophie needed a nap. Did all your groups leave?"

"Yes. I'll have time to clean up a little more this weekend. With this rain, we won't be busy. Todd and Dad will make sure everything is shut down."

"Hailey, I know I—"

She shrugged, not ready for another argument. "I've had time to think." She reached out and smoothed Sophie's hair. "I can't stop you from taking Sophie to meet your folks."

"Why don't you come with us?"

She gaped at him. "What?"

"What's keeping you here this weekend? It's supposed to rain for the next three days." He pushed the foot rest down and stood with Sophie cradled in his arms. "Where should I put her?"

Hailey threw the blanket over the couch and arranged the pillows to support her frame. "Do you want my list of why I should stay here?"

Trey gently laid Sophie on the pillows. With a kiss on her forehead, he draped the pink fleece over their daughter. He turned to Hailey and waited until she looked at him. "Will you be okay without Sophie for a few days?"

She stepped back. "I doubt your parents would want me in their home."

"My parents have always loved you like their own daughter. It might be uncomfortable for a while, but maybe you need to talk to them."

"Being in a car with you for hours, while you're angry with me, doesn't sound like a good time."

His quick intake of breath signaled her statement was true.

"I'll try to watch what I say."

"I have a lot of work to do here."

His eyes scanned the room. "I already did the dishes and folded the clothes. Looks to me like things are caught up."

"You did dishes?" What a contradiction this man was.

"I had time while Sophie took her morning nap." He shoved his hands into his jean pockets. "Listen. You can come or not. I can't promise it will be a ton of laughs or that you'll always feel comfortable. It's up to you, but you're welcome to go with us." He reached for his coat on the back of the couch. "I'm meeting Todd in town to see the hydraulic lift we ordered for your dad. I should be back in an hour and I'd like to leave then."

"It's about time you showed up." Todd waved from the far side of the metal building. "David was just showing me how to use this."

Trey shook the other man's hand. "I'm Trey Williams."

"David Philips."

"That's right." Todd grinned. "I forget you two don't know each other." He turned back to the flatbed truck. "If Dad will accept this, it's going to be amazing. Trey, sit in that wheelchair and we'll show you."

As soon as he sat, Todd pushed him onto the metal platform. The hydraulic platform vibrated and hummed, but it raised him high enough to maneuver the chair into the open space of the truck where the captain's seat and console had been removed.

"Okay, now get back on the lift and we'll take you to the combine."

After several attempts and with the two men helping, he soon sat in the combine cab. The mock demonstration had given him a small glimpse into the struggles the older man faced every day. Trey hoped Jim would accept the lift.

"When do you think you'll show this to him?" Trey came down the combine ladder.

"Do you want to be there?" Todd lowered the lift to the truck bed.

"Let it be from you and David."

"But you got things started and found the money to help pay for it. This was your idea."

"For completely selfish reasons." He shook David's hand. "Thanks for your work. If Jim will accept it, I know it will change his life.'"

"I've enjoyed doing it. I wouldn't mind doing more of this type of work."

Trey glanced at his watch. "I need to be going. It's good to meet you, David."

Todd followed him out and leaned on the rental car. "What's your hurry?"

A heavy mist hung in the air. "I'm taking Sophie to meet my parents." Trey opened the door and slid in.

"You're taking Sophie? Hailey's okay with that?" Disbelief colored his tone.

Trey ran his hand down his face. "She's welcome to come along."

"Good luck with that one." Todd pulled up the collar of his coat. "If she does, and I can't imagine she will, you'd better treat her well."

Trey understood. "And if she doesn't go, will you check on her to make sure she's doing okay without Sophie?"

"What's it going to take to get the two of you back together?"

"I don't know—a miracle, maybe."

The wiper blades danced their consistent rhythm, pushing the rain off the windshield. What had compelled him to ask Hailey to go with them? If she agreed, how would they fill the hours? He'd assured her his folks would be fine with her coming. Now he wondered if he should call and make sure. And what if she decided not to go with them? He doubted she would, and he already felt the disappointment.

"Lord, help me accept what she decides."

The storm door on the garage opened a few inches before Hailey rushed out, wearing a red raincoat. She carried a small backpack in one hand and the frog bag in the other. He pressed the button to release the rear door.

"Thanks." Hailey threw the bags in and hurried back to the garage door.

Before he could get out, she returned with the car seat.

"Do you mind hooking this in?" She shoved the seat in behind him. "Sophie is waiting right inside."

He crawled into the back and worked to secure the seat. She really wasn't coming with them. A dark cloud of disappointment settled over him and eclipsed the joy of introducing his daughter to her grandparents.

As he clicked the last clip into place, a flash of red caught his eye. Hailey marched to his side with Sophie cradled beneath an old blanket. Hailey settled Sophie in his outstretched arms and slid the wet covering off the child.

"Just a couple of more things." Hailey dashed through the rain.

Sophie smiled up at him. "Go bye-bye?"

"That's right. I'm going to take you to see Grandpa and

Grandma. They can't wait to meet you." He buckled her in and leaned down to kiss her forehead. "Does your arm hurt?"

"Ouchy." Her lips formed a pout.

"You tell me if it hurts and we'll stop driving, okay?"

Hailey was at the back again and set the familiar suitcase beside Sophie's. Her eyes, filled with hesitation, met his. "You're sure this is okay?" The raised trunk created an umbrella over her.

His heart ignited. "Yes, it's okay."

"I don't want to fight the whole time. Maybe we should make some rules or something."

"Why don't you get out of the rain and we'll discuss it?" He pulled on the carseat's straps before moving to the driver's seat.

Hailey disappeared into the garage once more before emerging without the raincoat and carrying a bag. She slid into the car and busied herself with the bag at her feet. "What are the rules?"

The doors locked when Trey put the car into reverse.

"Don't you want to discuss them before we leave? I might change my mind."

He wanted to get out of there before that happened. "We have plenty of miles to discuss rules." He looked both ways before pulling onto the highway. "Once you closed the door, you were committed."

"What if we get a hundred miles down the road and I don't like your rules?"

"I'll let you out." He kept his tone serious. "That's the first rule—you like my rules or you walk."

"Should I write that down? Cross-stitch it maybe?" She reached for her bag.

"Whatever it takes to remember them." From the corner of his eye he glimpsed her smile. "I didn't expect you to have everything packed and waiting in the garage. I could have helped."

"I knew you wanted to leave quickly. It's a long drive."

"Your dad's okay with you leaving?"

"I'm not sure." She turned in the seat and reached back to Sophie. "How are you doing, Sophie? Do you want a book?"

"Bunny book."

"Let's see if I brought that one." Hailey leaned down and rifled through her tote.

"If you didn't, I almost know it from memory." Trey watched his daughter in the mirror.

"I know. I seriously considered leaving it at home just so I'd have a break from it. Here it is." She propped the open book on the pillow across Sophie's lap. "Need anything else?"

"Jim didn't say anything about you leaving? That's hard to imagine." He drummed his fingers on the steering wheel.

"Shouldn't we discuss those rules?" She tucked a curl behind her ear.

"Second one is honesty. You have to answer everything honestly from now until I bring you back on Sunday."

"Do I have a choice?"

He tapped the brake, effectively slowing the car. His smile grew when he saw her pained expression. The rain on the windshield seemed to grow stronger. "Walk home."

"Okay, I agree about the second rule, but it applies to you, too."

With a nod he agreed. "Now, how upset is your dad?"

"He was busy, and I didn't want him to guilt me into staying."

Trey digested the words before speaking. "So you didn't tell him? Hence the reason you had everything ready to go and waiting in the garage."

"I didn't see him before we left." She shifted in her seat. "Aunt Joni knows, and I left a note for Dad."

"I think it's time for the third rule."

She groaned.

"Your phone has to be turned off for the trip."

"That's crazy. What if—"

He touched the brake again. "Hey, you're riding with me,

right? So we play by my rules. When your dad realizes what you've done, he's going to start calling, and you're going to feel guilty. Then you'll figure out a way to get back home."

"What if they need to get a hold of me?"

"Joni and Todd have my number. They'll call if it's life threatening."

She removed her phone from the bag. "Are the rest of the rules this hard?"

"I'm not sure yet. I'm kind of playing it by ear, you know?" He held out his hand and grinned.

She slapped the phone down, her fingers brushing against his palm. "At least you admit it."

"Honesty's the first rule." He pushed the off button then dropped the phone into a pocket on the door.

"Second." Hailey injected, holding up two fingers. "Need me to keep a list for you?"

His tension released at her impertinence. He met her grin with one of his own. "That might help."

"Read, Mommy."

Hailey glanced over her shoulder at Sophie. "I knew I should have sat back there with her. Hand me the book, sweetie."

"I'll stop so you can move." He looked in the rearview mirror for other traffic. No one else was traveling on this dreary day.

"That would mean unlocking the doors and letting me get out."

He slowed the car and pulled over. "It's going to be a cold, wet walk if you've changed your mind."

Hailey placed her bag on the seat before moving to the back. He pulled onto the road and watched the two in the mirror as Hailey began to read in the singsong voice the words in the book demanded.

His body relaxed into the seat. The fact the Hailey had left without asking permission showed more spunk than he'd seen in a long time. Maybe the woman he'd loved for so long was still in there.

CHAPTER TWENTY-SIX

A steady tapping on her leg woke Hailey.

Trey was turned in the seat watching her. "Hailey, let's get supper here and then we'll travel a few more hours."

She glanced out the window. "McDonald's?"

"You were asleep so Sophie got to choose."

"How long did I sleep?" She unbuckled Sophie and pulled her coat over her good arm. "I didn't realize I was so tired."

"That book almost put me to sleep, too." Trey winked at her before getting out of the car. He jogged around to her side and reached in the open door to take Sophie. "Rule number four, no more bunny book while I'm driving."

Hailey stepped out of the car and straightened. "That's the only rule I've liked so far."

Inside Trey ordered for himself and Sophie then looked expectantly at her.

"I'll get my own." She smiled at the cashier.

"Add hers to mine." Trey's hand pressed against the small of her back, guiding her to the counter. "Rule five is I pay for things."

Frustrated, Hailey ordered then took Sophie to the restroom. When they returned, Trey waited at a table in the corner. Her heart warmed at the sight. He had a booster seat ready, along with napkins and ketchup. Their meals were neatly arranged. She set

Sophie in the booster before sliding into the booth. To anyone else, they'd look like a regular family with an established routine.

"You don't need to pay for everything. I wouldn't feel like such an imposition if you'd let me pay." She reached for Sophie's nuggets and began tearing them in half to cool.

Trey picked up her left hand. His thumb gently rubbed her ring. "See this ring? As long as you wear it, I will pay for things. No matter what we need to work through, we are still a family."

She stared at his hand holding hers, enjoying his touch. Her mind momentarily wandered to their last night in Washington. Warmth spread through her. Afraid he could read her thoughts, she shrugged. "I don't expect you to."

"I want to." He squeezed her hand. "Would you mind if we prayed before eating?" His gaze was fixed on their joined hands. Did he remember how they had held hands before each meal and prayed? It hadn't mattered where they were, Trey would reach across the table for her hand and give thanks.

She nodded, not completely comfortable with praying for the first time in a while. "Daddy wants to pray."

Once Sophie's eyes were scrunched tight, Hailey bowed her head, while keeping her hand inside Trey's tender grasp.

"God, thank You for this food. Keep us safe as we travel." Trey sighed. "You know where our marriage is at and why You have brought us together for this weekend. Make us willing to follow Your will. Amen." With a gentle squeeze he let go of her hand and unwrapped his burger.

Hailey studied the table. Did he think this one weekend would solve everything? "I came for Sophie."

Trey gazed over his burger at her. "I know." He pushed the tray towards her. "Better start eating. I'd like to drive a few more hours before we stop."

She unwrapped the sandwich and gulped back a queasy feeling. Two bites later she put the burger down and folded the wrapper around it.

Trey pulled the wrapper open. "You didn't eat lunch. You need to eat something."

"I'm just not hungry." She laid a napkin over it.

He removed the napkin. "Do you think I can't tell you've lost weight?" His frown challenged her to disagree.

She took a small bite, chewed, and swallowed hard. "I'd rather have your fries."

He pushed them towards her. His eyes, filled with concern, searched hers. "Just eat something. Sophie finished all her nuggets. Do you want some ice cream, honey?"

"I wuv ice cweam." She bobbed her head. "Mommy no ice cweam?"

"I don't care for any. These fries are fine." She shoved another one in her mouth and prayed her stomach would calm.

Back in the car, Sophie watched a movie Trey had downloaded for her on his tablet. A comfortable silence settled around them. They had never needed to fill every moment with talking. She pulled the book she'd thrown in at the last second out of her bag.

"I knew you'd have a book along." Trey lifted it to read the cover. "Is it good?"

"I'm only on the first chapter, but Ellen says it is." She pulled it back.

"Before you get engrossed and I lose you for the rest of the evening, I want to know how Sophie broke her arm. Does anyone keep an eye on her?"

"You've already decided how it happened, so what's there to tell?"

Trey's brows furrowed together. "Humor me. I want to know what happened. Were you busy and she got away? How did she get in that treehouse? She's not even two—someone has to be watching her."

She struggled to keep her voice even. "Do you question what kind of mother I am?"

"No, but a toddler climbed into a treehouse and fell out. Why?

That's all I'm asking. Remember rule number two?"

She studied the ceiling of the car and counted to ten. "I'd hired a neighbor girl to watch her because I had several large school groups and I knew I couldn't keep track of Sophie. Sophie and the sitter were playing hide and seek. When it was Sophie's turn, she hid where she knew Megan would never find her. Sophie must have decided she'd waited long enough, and her ability to get down didn't equal her ability to crawl up the ladder."

"Why didn't you tell me that before?"

"You already knew what had happened, remember? I wasn't keeping track of her. You knew it was my fault."

He had the decency to seem embarrassed. "You could have told me the truth right away. Instead, you let me believe the worst."

"You wanted to believe the worst in me, didn't you? Rule number two..."

His silence stretched long enough she wondered if he would even respond.

"You're right." He laid his hand on hers. "After years of blaming you for everything, it came naturally." He met her gaze. "I'm sorry."

She nodded, not trusting her voice for a moment. "It's okay."

For several miles they rode in silence, his hand holding hers. The joy of his touch left her breaths short. She hoped he wouldn't pull his hand away.

"One more question before you go back to that book." He squeezed her hand.

In mock exasperation Hailey let her head fall back to the headrest and groaned.

"Why have you been losing weight?"

"I haven't lost that much, and I could afford to lose more." If it weren't for his rules she'd make something up. One glance at him and she knew he hadn't accepted her answer. "There's a lot going on and I don't always take time to eat."

"Joni's concerned."

"I haven't felt very good this week–probably a bug I've caught from someone. I'll be fine."

"Have you seen a doctor about it?"

"Of course not. All they'd tell me is to cut out the stress in my life. If you haven't noticed, I have quite a bit." She tried to pull her hand away, but he held tight.

"How bad is it?"

"It's really nothing. Once the pumpkin patch is closed I'll feel much better."

He raised his eyebrows.

"If I don't feel better by the first of November, I'll go see a doctor." His hold on her hand released and she opened the book in her lap. After reading the same paragraph three times and still unaware of what the words said, she closed the book and turned off the overhead light. The glow of the dash light cast just enough light to see Trey's face through the growing darkness.

"I enjoyed meeting Amanda Bryant when they were at the pumpkin patch."

"She's a great lady." Trey pulled into the passing lane and sped around a farm truck. "They both said it had been a good day, and she said she liked meeting you."

"Will a lot change for you with this election?"

"If things play out like they're looking now, Rob will be the Majority Leader. He's asked me to be his Chief-of-Staff." His thumb tapped on the steering wheel.

"Chief-of-Staff?" A thread of pride laced itself with melancholy. "That's what you've always wanted. Congratulations."

Trey nodded. "His seat is uncontested, so it depends on the other elections. But things should go our way."

"I'm really glad for you. You've worked hard for this." It surprised her how much she meant those words. He had worked hard and followed his dream. Since they were in high school, he'd talked about going to Washington and working in politics. At eighteen, it had been a heady dream, one with sacrifices neither of them fully understood. Now it was his reality. But would it become her nightmare?

CHAPTER TWENTY-SEVEN

Trey fumbled with the entry key to their motel room. Would she notice he had to insert it twice? Why did he feel like a naughty school boy? After all, they were married. A night in a motel wasn't wrong. He breathed a sigh of relief when the light flashed green and he could open the door at last. He stepped inside, switched on the light, then turned with a flourish. "Welcome, said the spider to the fly." What a stupid thing to say. The spider's web was a trap.

With Sophie in her arms, Hailey followed him into the room. "Two beds? And what sleeping arrangements did you have in mind? Was this to be covered under rule six?" She laughed nervously and a pink hue grazed her cheeks. "I–I am sorry, that came out wrong."

If he told her what was on his mind, she'd start walking home. Would this be the time to invoke rule number two and find out what she honestly wanted? He shook his head. They had gotten this far, he had to keep it amicable.

He dropped his suitcase on the end of the bed. "Actually, rule six is you need to try and keep your hands off me."

She laughed. "I'll remember that one." She sat Sophie on the nearest bed. "I wouldn't mind paying for another room if you don't want to share with us."

"We're not getting two rooms." Could she hear his frustration?

"If you give me Sophie's nightgown I'll put it on her while you get ready for bed." Trey turned the television to the weather channel and took the pink nightgown Hailey handed him. She disappeared into the bathroom. Within seconds he heard the shower.

"Your mommy sure doesn't make it easy on me, does she?" He cautiously pulled the little shirt sleeve over Sophie's cast. He'd worked hard to be successful, but tonight in this hotel room the satisfaction in living his dream dimmed—he'd lost everything in the process. "Does your arm hurt much tonight, honey?"

"Hurt." She yawned, her eyes heavy with sleep.

"As soon as we get this on, I'll read to you." He pushed the wide opening of the gown over her head.

"Bunny book?" She played with the button on his shirt.

"Don't you have a different one? One about a dog or something?"

A giggle filled the room. "Bunny book."

Why had she been so flippant with her rule number six? Hailey meant it as a joke, an answer to his spider-and-fly remark, but the moment the words were out the two of them returned to dangerous ground. He'd kept the mood light, but she knew all too well the look of emotions stirring in his dark eyes.

Sitting on the edge of the tub, she let the shower run behind her, hoping Trey wouldn't question how long she was taking. She needed time to think—time to put distance between them before crawling into a bed two feet from where he'd be sleeping.

Rules should have been set before leaving the house. Her rules. She'd pay for her things. They'd have two motel rooms. They were pretending to live a normal life—a family taking a little trip for a few days. Hailey stood and wiped the clouded mirror with her towel. Staring at herself, she recognized the truth in her eyes. She wanted them to be a family more than anything else.

After her shower, Hailey crept into the still room. Tears burned her eyes. Trey slept, his arm around Sophie, the bunny book in his hand. Their daughter's head and bright pink cast rested on his chest. Hailey turned off the light above them and slipped between the chilly sheets of the other bed.

"Mommy..." Sophie's whisper drifted across the room. "Sleep wif me."

Hailey rolled to her side. Trey's eyes were closed and his breathing even. "Daddy's sleeping with you tonight."

"Want you." A sob caught on the tired words.

"Shhh. You don't want to wake your daddy. He's had a long day. I'll be right here, okay?"

Sophie's quiet sniffs echoed in Hailey's heart. She'd never get to sleep due to the guilt of a two-year-old. She tossed the covers back, tiptoed to the other side of Sophie's bed, and crawled in. At least the sheets were already warm. She would only lay here long enough for Sophie to fall asleep and then return to the other bed. Sophie would sleep and Trey would never know that she'd followed her own silly rule number six.

Sunlight streamed through the break in the curtain, hitting Hailey in the face. Opening one eye, she noticed the other bed with the blankets thrown back as she'd left them last night. The spot beside Sophie was empty. Hailey rolled onto her back and covered her eyes with her arm. Had she really gone to sleep before moving back to the other bed?

The door clicked open. She pulled the covers up to her chin. Trey stepped around the corner with a paper cup in one hand and a styrofoam plate in the other.

"'Morning." He held the cup up in a mock toast. A smile played about his lips and a twinkle lit his eyes. "Sleep well?"

"I guess." Why hadn't she gotten into the other bed? "You're ready to leave, aren't you?"

Trey shrugged and sat down on the other bed, sliding the plate with the Danish onto the table. "It's still early. I always get up pretty early—like to have time alone, read the paper, and see who crawled into my bed during the night." His smile turned teasing.

Hailey pulled the covers over her face. The mattress gave way beside her, and the jostling caused her stomach to churn.

Trey pulled down the blankets far enough to expose her face. "I knew we didn't need to spend money on two rooms. We didn't even need to spend the extra to get two beds."

"Sophie wanted me to sleep with her." The protest even sounded weak to her.

He chuckled and leaned down. "Whatever you want to believe." His lips brushed over her forehead. "I loved waking up to find you asleep beside me."

"Sophie slept between us." She swallowed against the rising feeling in her throat.

"We can work on that." He touched her forehead again with his hand. "Are you okay?"

"I'm fine." She took a deep breath, praying the nausea would go away. It didn't. She was going to be sick. She shoved Trey out of the way with her feet so she could get out of the bed. He'd thank her later.

Trey opened the bathroom door. Hailey sat on the edge of the tub, her head against the wall. Strands of hair hung limp, framing her pale face. "Hailey?"

"I'm fine." She pressed her hands to her colorless cheeks.

Trey's heart lurched. He'd seen her sick in D.C., but this couldn't be the same. They'd traveled together all yesterday, and she'd hardly eaten a thing. He wet a washcloth with cool water and dabbed at the beads of perspiration glistening on her forehead.

She gave a wan smile. "You always see me at my best."

Trey worked to keep his emotions—fear that something dreadful was wrong, annoyance that she was keeping something from him again—in check. "I could get a complex, seeing as how you seem to be sick whenever we're together."

She stood. "It's not you, Trey. Really. I probably just got car sick." She washed her hands then turned to leave.

He reached and drew her to him, alarmed at her thinness. The memory of their night together hadn't dimmed enough in his memory to forget how she'd felt in his arms. He tipped her head back, but she wouldn't look at him. "This isn't car sickness, Hailey. You haven't been in a car for eight hours. I want the truth. We aren't leaving this room until you tell me what's going on."

She stared at his throat. "I need to get Sophie up. I feel better already."

He glanced in the room and saw Sophie still slept soundly.

"How long, Hailey? This isn't the first time you've been sick, is it?"

She sighed. "What does it matter to you?"

He raised his eyebrows, waiting for her explanation.

"A week or so." She tried to pull away but he wouldn't release her.

"A week, and you don't think you should have things checked out?"

"I've got a lot going on, okay? Between the pumpkin patch, my dad, our marriage falling apart, Sophie's accident—who wouldn't be sick?" She paused. "It's not a big deal. Things will calm down soon."

His hand cupped her chin, forcing her to look at him. "If you aren't better by the first of November, you'll have things checked out. Promise me?"

"I promise."

His thumb traced the contour of her cheek. If only he could trust those words.

"Stop now?" Sophie fidgeted in her seat and threw her plastic sippy cup to the floor. In the last hour her mood had soured.

"You know better than to throw things, Sophie." Hailey retrieved the cup. "We'll be there soon."

"Just a little longer." Trey spoke from the front. "Grandma and Grandpa can't wait to see you."

"Are you sure they're okay with me coming?" Hailey watched his face in the mirror.

His glance met hers in the mirror before he looked back to the road without answering.

Hailey leaned between the gap in the front seats. "They know I'm coming, right? You told them?" She watched his face, panic welling up in her. "Trey, how could you not tell them?"

"It will be okay, Hailey. You'll see."

His voice didn't offer the solid assurance she wanted. She fell back into the seat beside Sophie. "Why didn't you tell them? What if they don't want me there? I can't believe you'd do this to me—to them."

"They want you there, Hailey.""I think I'm going to be sick again."

He slammed on the brakes and turned his head to look at her. "Are you really?"

"Mommy sick?" Sophie felt Hailey's cheek.

Hailey slapped the seat in frustration. "No, but why are you doing this? Why didn't you tell them? What am I going to say? 'I left your son and didn't tell you about your granddaughter. Mind if I stay with you for a few days as a guest?' Really, Trey, what were you thinking?"

"Mommy mad."

Hailey shoved Trey's tablet with the movie playing towards the little girl. "Mommy isn't mad. She just needs to talk to Daddy."

He glanced back at her. "I talked to them before I knew you were coming with us."

"You have a cell phone. Why didn't you call them?"

"Do you want me to call them now?" He held up his phone.

"Yes." What if they really didn't want her there?

Trey glanced at his phone before tossing it into the passenger seat. "No reception. It will be fine, Hailey."

She wanted to scream. She turned in the seat and closed her eyes, letting the miles pass unseen. Every scenario she could imagine played in her mind.

"We're here."

Hailey didn't need Trey's proclamation. When the car quit rolling and his breath whooshed out like he'd been punched, she knew they'd reached their destination. She opened her eyes, no longer able to feign sleep.

Trey turned in his seat and smiled at the little girl. "Look Sophie, that's your grandpa coming to say hello to you." Trey opened his door and came around the car to get Sophie out of her seat. He put his hand on Hailey's knee. "They've missed you. Remember that."

Hailey sat up and ran her hand through her hair, then watched as Sam shook his son's hand, pulling him into an embrace that included Sophie. Behind them, Vicki hurried out of the front door, catching Trey and Sophie in another hug. Vicki pulled away first and looked at Trey. With a slight nod, she walked around the car and opened Hailey's door.

Taking a deep breath to calm her riotous stomach, Hailey stepped from the car and stood with her head bowed.

"Welcome home, Hailey." Vicki embraced her.

Tears coursed down her cheeks, making words impossible. Anything she'd thought of to say escaped her.

"We're glad you're here." Sam spoke as his arms went around the two women. "Why don't we take this inside before we start any neighborhood gossip. They'd never believe this is a wonderful day in our lives."

The small group broke apart and moved around the vehicle to where Trey and Sophie waited.

"Want Mommy." Sophie wiggled to get out of his arms.

Trey set her down and smiled as she wrapped her chubby fingers around Hailey's forefinger. "I'll get our things."

"Have you had breakfast?" his mother asked. "I made cinnamon rolls, just in case you got here before lunch."

"Let me get our bags unloaded, and then I'll be in for your rolls and coffee. That is, if you have coffee made."

"I'll go put on a fresh pot." Mom led the way with Hailey and Sophie following.

The three ladies who meant the most in his life entered the house together. Trey silently prayed it would somehow be a happy family reunion. He handed Sophie's bags to his dad then reached in the car for Hailey's.

"We didn't realize Hailey would be with you." His dad took the small suitcase.

Trey pulled out his bag and set it on the ground, then shut the door and leaned against it. He welcomed this time with his dad. "I know, but I felt like I should ask her to come. The forecast predicted a cold, rainy weekend in Kansas. She surprised me by accepting. I hope you don't mind."

"Mind?" Dad's eyes lit. "I'd say rain is the miracle you're mother and I've been praying for. Are things going okay?"

Trey looked toward the distant peak, thinking of the hidden valley they had hiked to the last time he visited. "Yes, but we have a long way to go." He reached for the bags. "We'd better get inside before Mom quizzes Hailey and scares her off."

Sam picked up the frog bag. "I'm glad you haven't given up on her."

Trey entered the house and followed his mom's voice to the guest bedroom at the end of the hall. He set the bags down against the wall and watched his mom scurry around setting out extra blankets.

"I'm afraid we only have this one guest room." She placed a

stack of towels on the bed. "A family from church loaned us that little bed for Sophie, but. . ."

"It's okay, Mom." Trey put his arm around her. "We'll figure it out later."

"I guess there's always the couch?" She gave an apologetic shrug. "Maybe we shouldn't have downsized to such a small house."

"Don't worry about it. We shared a room last night and Hailey didn't attack me." He winked at his wife standing on the other side of the bed. His smile grew at the blush coloring her cheeks.

Vicki glanced between the two. "She might if you keep teasing her. I'll let you two get settled while I go make a fresh pot of coffee. I want to hear all about your trip." She leaned down to Sophie. "How about it, sweet girl—would you like to help Grandma in the kitchen? You can put some napkins on the table for me."

Sophie pulled her stuffed bunny from the suitcase and tucked it under her arm. "Pink nakkins?" She slid off the bed and took two quick bunny hops toward her grandmother.

A small frown flitted across Hailey's face, followed by a smile when Vicki reached for Sophie's hand. "I bet we can find pink ones. Want to help me look?"

Sophie giggled and nodded. She jabbered as they left the room

Trey turned to Hailey. "No need to worry. Mom raised me and look how well I turned out."

She flung a pillow and hit him on the side of the head. "Did you really have to tell her we shared a room last night? You made it sound so...so... Well, like something happened."

"I almost told her you couldn't stay out of my bed." He raised his eyebrows, laughing when her frown deepened. "I guess you can always sleep on the couch, but I can tell you from experience, it's not the most comfortable piece of furniture."

The color in her cheeks deepened. "I'll sleep on the floor." She stomped toward the door.

Trey caught her arm. "Or you could give in and share the bed with me."

She raised her eyes to meet his. "And what happens when the weekend is over and we both go back to our own homes? Won't that be harder if we pretend like we're a normal family?"

He moved his arms to encircle her waist and pulled her to him. "Come back to Washington with me and we'll be a normal family."

"It's not that easy."

He kissed the tip of her nose. "It could be."

CHAPTER TWENTY-EIGHT

Hailey closed the bedroom door and tiptoed toward the kitchen. Where was Trey when she needed him? Sophie had fought going down for a nap as hard as Hailey fought to stay awake. What would Trey's mother think? Not only had she kept their grandchild from them, but now—from Sophie's squalling—Vicki was probably convinced she beat the child, too. She stifled a yawn as she pulled a chair from the table and dropped into it. "Is Trey around?"

Vicki looked up from the cookbook she was flipping through. "Oh, Hailey, I didn't hear you come in. Trey and his dad are out in the back. I think Sam wanted to show him the patio he built this summer. Did Sophie go to sleep? It sounded like a battle in there."

"Finally. I'm sorry she made such a fuss. She's in a new place, excited and tired—not a good combination for a two-year-old. She wanted me to lay down with her, but I knew I'd fall asleep before she did." Hailey rested her chin on her hand.

"You look like you could use a nap. Don't feel like you have to be in here. I thought I'd get dinner started."

Hailey pulled a napkin from the holder on the table and folded it in half. There was so much she needed to say, but she had no idea how to start.

"It's been an answer to our prayers to meet Sophie." Vicki

continued to pore over the cookbook. "Trey is quite taken with her."

Hailey folded the napkin again. Were they going to have this entire conversation without looking at one another? "She has him wrapped around her finger several times. He's an excellent father." She pushed the napkin away and took a quick breath. "Vicki, I'm very sorry for hurting you and Sam. I was wrong to keep Sophie from you."

"I've tried to understand why you left and never went back to Trey." Vicki pulled the chair out beside Hailey and sat down. "God knows some days I was so angry with you."

"You had every right to be."

Vicki laid her hand over Hailey's. "You've been dealing with a lot. The accident, losing your mom, helping your dad. It's taken me a while, but I think I do understand why you left us."

"That doesn't make keeping Sophie a secret right."

"May I ask what's going to happen now?"

Hailey ran her finger over the wood pattern in the table. "I don't know. I can't get myself to sign the divorce papers. With the exception of these last three years, Trey's been in my life almost as long as I can remember. I can't imagine life without him."

"Then go back to Washington with him."

"I don't know what would happen with the pumpkin patch or my dad. He still needs my help."

"Don't you think he'd understand if you went back with Trey?"

"No. I think he'll always want me to pay for the accident. The pumpkin patch is my responsibility and we really need to keep that going. I can't run it from Washington."

"Sophie needs her daddy."

"I know." Hailey folded the napkin into a small square. "I wish Trey would move back to Kansas. He could farm with Todd."

"Trey's never had an interest in the farm—only in the farmer's daughter." Vicki paused until Hailey looked up from the napkin. "You need to move on with your life. You will always miss your mom and mourn Jim's confinement to a wheelchair. God didn't create us to get stuck in one rough spot and camp out there. He wants you to live again."

Hailey pushed her chair back and walked to the sink to get a drink. Cup filled, she turned and leaned against the cabinet. "I don't want to go back to Washington."

Understanding passed over Vicki's face. "It will be different this time."

"Will it?" She ran her hand through her hair. "Will Trey have more time? Will he spend his weekends with us and come home before supper each night? Or will Sophie and I be alone in a huge city of strangers?"

Vicki took a package of meat from the fridge and set it next to the stove. "I don't know if all those things will change. Have you prayed about this?"

Hailey almost laughed. "When I pray, nothing seems to get beyond the ceiling. I'm not sure God really cares."

"He does, Hailey. I don't know why God seems distant sometimes, but it's usually because we've moved, not him. Ask for His will to be done—either Trey's heart changes about working in Washington or your heart changes about living there. I'll pray with you."

"God didn't save my mom or heal Dad's legs. Why would I think He cares about where I live?" It surprised her to hear the questions she'd never voiced.

"There's a bigger plan that you can't see. You only see a small part, but He sees the entire picture. I don't know why the accident happened, but you have to keep moving forward and put your trust back in Him."

"Does it matter?" A harsh laugh escaped her lips. "Are you ready to throw me out for talking like this?"

Vicki shook her head, giving Hailey an encouraging smile.

"I always thought it mattered if I prayed. I lived a good life and did everything by the book—literally. But what difference did my prayers for Mom or Dad make? I think I'd be in this same place if I didn't believe in God." She gulped in a breath and spoke the thought that had haunted her for years. "My whole life I believed God would take care of me, but where has He been these past three years? When I needed Him most, He left me hanging."

A heavy stillness filled in the kitchen. Perhaps she'd said too much. But if the woman was going to pray for her, didn't she deserve to know the depth to which Hailey had sunk? She wasn't the perfect preacher's daughter-in-law anymore.

Vicki washed her hands in the sink. Slowly she dried them before leaning against the cabinet next to Hailey. "Things happen because of the world we live in. But God has been with you. You weren't hurt in the accident, and you didn't lose Sophie. He placed you and Trey together at the dinner in Washington. He brought Trey back to Kansas. We're not promised a perfect life just because we believe in God. Accidents and death still happen. Marriages get messy. But that doesn't mean God isn't there." She put her arm around Hailey and pulled her close. "Don't you think God has helped you through this? You've grown a lot, and I believe you're stronger because of it."

"Do you think I'm terrible for feeling like this?"

"Never. I'd be more worried if you didn't. We all struggle at times." She stepped away and reached for the frying pan in the drainer.

"I'll do that." Hailey took the pan to the stove and tore the plastic wrap away from the ground beef. Raw and exposed... She knew the feeling all too well.

Trey followed his dad into the kitchen. Relief filled him at the sight of Hailey working alongside his mom.

"Two of my three favorite ladies in one room." He kissed his mother's cheek before moving next to Hailey. One look at her face made him decide against giving her a kiss. Her lips, pressed in a tight line were almost as white as her face. "Is Sophie taking a nap?"

She gave one quick nod.

"You okay?" At his whisper his mom looked over her shoulder at them.

One more nod before Hailey sucked in a short breath.

He reached over to take the spatula she was using to break the browning burger apart. "Hailey?"

The spatula dropped, hit the side of the pan and clattered on the counter. Without looking back, Hailey dodged from the room. The bathroom door slammed seconds later.

Concern etched across his father's face. "What did you do to her?"

He picked up the utensil. "Nothing that I know of. I'm beginning to think she's allergic to me."

Mom turned a worried scowl on Trey. "Is she okay?"

"I don't know anymore. She's been losing weight and didn't feel well this morning."

"How long has this been going on?"

"According to her, not very long." He stirred the meat. "When she brought Sophie to visit she got food poisoning. She–"

"Wait a minute." Mom lean against the counter and crossed her arms. "Hailey and Sophie came to visit you? In Washington?"

"Back in September. They were only going to be there for the weekend, but it turned into a week because Hailey got sick."

"Did she...stay at your apartment during this time?"

Trey fidgeted. "She had food poisoning, Mom. She couldn't take care of Sophie alone. You don't think I'd put them in a hotel, do you?" He wouldn't tell her that was Hailey's original idea.

"No, but I wonder... Well, did you...? Were you...?"

"Oh, for land's sake, Vicki." Dad held his arm wide. "What she's trying to find out, is did you sleep together? Is there any chance she might be...? Did you get...?"

Mom laughed. "See, it isn't as easy as you thought, is it? What your dad is trying to ask is if Hailey could possibly be pregnant."

Trey's face burned with the memory of that one night together. He couldn't look at his parents. He'd never been able to hide anything from them.

He handed his mom the spatula. "I'll check on Hailey."

Pregnant... Pregnant... The word resounded with every footstep to the bathroom. He knocked on the door. "Hailey? Let me in, please."

Hailey opened the door and met his eyes with her own weary look. Did she already know and wasn't telling him? He despised the doubt that crept into his mind.

"Hailey—"

She held her hands up in defense. "Before you say anything, if I'm not better by next week, I'll go to the doctor. Okay?"

He rubbed the back of his neck. "Are you pregnant?" He watched her face for any sign of duplicity. Denial turned to confusion then gave way to concern. Warmth spread through him as Hailey's face displayed each changing thought.

"I..." She tucked a piece of hair behind her ear. "I hadn't... I don't know."

"But it's possible, right?" Would he have a chance to know his child from the very beginning?

She nodded and winced. "That last night in Washington. But we don't know for sure. It really could just be stress."

"Do you want it to just be stress?" The thought saddened him even though he didn't know what his own feelings were.

"You have to admit this isn't the best time—with our marriage in question."

"If I go buy a test, will you take it?"

The muted voices from the living room followed Trey down the hall. The bedroom door was open enough to see the soft glow of nightlight. If Hailey was still awake they could talk. Neither had said anything else about the possibility of her being pregnant once they'd left the room before supper. She had gone back to the kitchen and offered to butter the French bread while he drove to the only store in town that might have a test and scanned the aisles. His search had been successful. When he returned, his family ate dinner together, except Hailey who picked at her food. At bedtime Hailey rejected his offer to lay with Sophie until she went to sleep. He hadn't seen Hailey since.

He sighed when he saw Hailey curled up on the floor, her back to him. "Hailey." He nudged the air mattress with his foot. "Get in the bed."

"I'm fine here." Her words were muffled.

"I am not going to let you sleep down there." He patted the quilt. "Come on, we can share. We did last night." He'd forgotten how stubborn she could be.

"Sophie was between us."

"We'll put a pillow between us." He growled out the words. She didn't budge. "I'm going to go shower. When I come back in, I hope to find you in the bed."

She was still on the floor when he returned. Frustrated, he dropped to his knees beside her. "At least get up and let me sleep down here."

Even though she didn't answer her shallow breathing signaled she wasn't asleep.

"Hailey, take the bed."

She rolled onto her back, a slight smile on her lips. "I'm fine here. Honest. Just turn off the light and go to sleep, okay?"

What else could he do? Short of picking her up and throwing her on the mattress, he was out of ideas. He turned off the light and crawled between the covers.

"Do you like sleeping alone?" Silence hung over the room as his words echoed in his ears. Was it possible that she enjoyed being single? He despised sleeping alone each night. It had taken months before he'd slept through a night after Hailey had left. How many times had he awakened, hoping to find the imprint of her head still pressed into the pillow beside him?

"Once Sophie figured out how to climb out of her crib I've not slept many nights alone." Her blankets rustled when she moved. "When do you think we'll go home?"

He fought a smile at her attempt to change the subject, but continued with his quest. "It took me months to sleep through the night after you left." He rolled to his side. "I have to admit, I don't like it at all."

He didn't know what he'd expected, but the stillness grew thick. After several moments of berating himself, he rolled onto his back and studied the ceiling. He twisted his wedding ring on his finger. No matter how much progress they made each time they were together, it always seemed they took as many steps backwards.

"Trey?" Hailey stood beside him, playing with the edge of the quilt, her head low. "I hate sleeping alone."

Trey stared at her, willing her to look at him. She'd returned his volley, and now he had no clue what to do with the ball. His thoughts raced until the light from Sophie's nightlight caught on a single tear that dripped from her down-turned face.

"What are we going to do?" The words caught on a sob.

He pulled the blanket back and waited. He heard Hailey's shuddered sigh and then the bed dipped gently when she sat on the edge. She kept her back to him and laid along the edge of the mattress. Trey pulled the covers across her shoulders then wondered where to place his hand. Inches separated them. One moment, the distance was too close, and the next those inches seemed like miles. She lay rigid, hardly breathing, as if waiting to see what he'd do. He said a quick prayer for wisdom and extra patience, then gently rested his hand on her waist and pulled her back a little.

"You'll fall off if you stay that close to the edge." The words seemed to echo in the dark. She leaned against him. Trey concentrated on keeping his hand still.

"What are we going to do?" She sniffled.

"We'll figure it out tomorrow. Try to get some sleep, okay?"

Hailey finally fell asleep, and even though hours passed before he joined her, it was the most restful night he'd had in years.

Gray morning light filtering through the windows woke him. From the bed he watched the red numbers on the clock slowly change. How many lines would show up on the test? They'd both been frustrated that the one pregnancy test he could find at the local grocery store could only be done in the morning.

The bed creaked as Hailey turned over and sighed. A rush of cool air hit him when she pushed the blankets back and stood. She grabbed the box from her open suitcase and left the room without looking at him.

If he thought time had gone slow before now, he was wrong. It seemed to completely stop. How long did it take for the lines to show up? He rolled onto his back and listened to Sophie's even breaths. Did Hailey realize he was waiting to find out? He turned to his side and hit the pillow with his hand. What was she doing in there?

He kicked the covers off and sat on the edge of the bed. Elbows propped on his knees, he rested his chin on the palm of his hand. If the test came back positive, one of them would have to give. Would he be willing? He laid down again and tried to take deep breaths. The clock showed only four minutes had passed. Should he check on her?

The bathroom door opened and light spilled into the bedroom before Hailey shut the bedroom door and stood in front of him, tear stains on her cheeks. "Trey, are you awake?"

"Of course." His voice graveled from the long night. He turned on his side, arm propping him up, and pulled the blanket back. "Come here before you get cold."

She slid in and gazed at him with uncertainty filled eyes. She sniffed. "Do you want to know?"

His hand slid to her flat stomach, fingers splayed against the soft fabric of her yellow cami. "I already know."

Another sniff.

"We'll figure this out, Hailey." He kissed her forehead. "This baby will be a blessing."

"You're not angry?"

"I think I had something to do with it. Why would I be angry?" He rested his head on the pillow beside hers.

"It messes everything up."

"Everything was already messed up. I think maybe this will straighten things out."

"I don't want to raise this baby alone." Her gaze speared him.

"You won't. I promise you that."

A tear slid from her eye.

"Why don't you try to sleep for a little bit."

She turned and laid her head on his chest. Soft sniffles told him she was as affected as he was.

He wrapped one of her curls around his finger. They would have a lot to decide and decisions to make that neither would like, but for now he wanted only to be here, in this moment. Not the pain of the past or the uncertainty of the future. Just this—right now. He was going to be a dad again and this time, he'd be there for every moment.

CHAPTER TWENTY-NINE

"My folks had plans with some friends tonight." Trey crossed the patio to Hailey, who sat in a lounge chair in the sun. He hitched his hip on the railing and crossed his arms, glancing across the scenic view behind the house. A small valley gave way to the foothills, green with golden aspen highlights. "They invited us to go along rather than cancel. Are you interested?"

"I…"

"They also offered to take Sophie. I think they want to show her off." He forced a smile, hoping it hid his nervousness. "We could do something on our own. Dinner and a movie, maybe? You know, just us."

She left the cushioned patio chair and leaned on the rail. "Just us sounds really good. I'm not sure I'm ready to face all the questions. How much do you think your folks have said to their church members?"

"As little as possible. I'm sure a few people will be surprised that my folks have a two-year-old granddaughter." He brushed a piece of hair from her face. "I told them we'd probably go out for dinner, especially if they have Sophie. Are you up for a hike? I have a special place I'd like for you to see."

"How long is this trail?" Hailey stopped and took a drink from her water bottle.

"Are you okay?" Trey jogged back to her spot on the path. "It's not much farther, but I don't want to do anything that might—"

"I'm pregnant, Trey. Not sick." She tightened the cap and pushed the bottle back into her jacket pocket. "Let's go."

Trey searched her face. "You'll have to be patient with me. This is new territory."

His smile took away the sting of his words.

He led the way. "Were you sick with Sophie?"

"I don't know. I've tried to remember, but with everything else going on, I didn't pay attention."

Trey stopped at the foot of a boulder. "I'll go up first, okay?"

"Are you sure this is worth it?" Hailey laughed. "We could have taken the other path that the sign showed."

"Nope, that one only goes to a picnic table. There's nothing to see." He reached for her hand. "It's steep here. Let me help you." He pulled her up in front of him and steadied her on the uneven rock. "My dad brought me here the last time I came home. He seemed to think it made a good object lesson."

The warmth of his hands seeped through her light jacket. With each touch she was reminded how much she missed him. "So do I get the same object lesson?"

He threaded his fingers between hers and pulled her to the edge. Mountains dressed in deep reds, greens, and gold surrounded the small valley. A glassy lake reflected the beauty, dazzling the viewer. He shifted slightly, and the two of them sat, feet dangling over the edge. A comfortable peace settled between them.

She leaned against his arm. "Did you and your dad have a good lunch today?"

He nodded. "It's crazy because I knew some of the men from church, but most are business men in the Springs area. I sat across the table from a man whose brother is the director of the regional AgMobility group. He was interested in hearing what we're doing for your dad. Six months ago I didn't even know AgMobility existed. I enjoyed spending some time with Dad." He glanced at her. "Did you and Mom get along okay?"

"You're pretty nervous about us, aren't you?" She rested her head on his shoulder. "Things are fine between us so you don't have to worry. We went to a few of the little shops in town. I think she would have bought Sophie everything the girl picked up if I hadn't been there."

"Mom loves being Grandma. Thanks for letting us all have this weekend." His arm curved around her waist. "I got a text earlier. I need to be in D.C. by Sunday afternoon for a meeting. I'll catch the red-eye tomorrow night out of Wichita."

She sighed. "I guess our time of pretending is over and it's back to reality. Would you rather get a flight from here? Sophie and I can drive your rental back."

"Sorry, but you're stuck with me in the car the whole way to Kansas." He kissed the top of her head. "You're not getting rid of me that quickly."

His tone was teasing, but she considered her next words with care, not wanting to seem flippant or uncaring. "I don't want to get rid of you. I wish we could stay right here and keep pretending everything is okay."

"I'm not pretending, Hailey. We have a lot to work through and some hard decisions to make, but if you're willing, we'll get through this. When Dad brought me up here, I was planning to push the divorce and do whatever I could to get Sophie. The entire time we were hiking I was angry. Not just at you, but at God and myself. I wanted to take the lower path. Dad wanted me to see the beauty of taking the harder path. He said so many people miss the beauty because they're happy with the easy, shorter path."

"What do we do now?" She sat straight and slid over a few inches.

Trey leaned forward, his arms on his legs. "Tell me what you want."

What did she truly want? "I don't want to raise this baby alone."

"Is that it?" He sounded let down. "I doubt you'd have a hard time finding someone to help raise it."

"That's not what I meant." She put her hand on his leg, needing to feel connected to him. "I don't want to raise your children without you in their lives. Or in mine. I miss you—miss being your wife."

He cupped her face with his hands. The depth of understanding she saw brought tears to her eyes. "I need you, Hailey. I need you in my life. Even if there wasn't Sophie and this new baby, I'd need you." He paused. "I don't know how we're going to work all this out, but we will, and it doesn't have to be today. But promise me...we will work it out, yes?"

Cars crowded both sides of the street, creating one lane of traffic. Trey waited for the oncoming car to pass. "Is McMillian's okay for supper? Judging by the vehicles it's a popular place tonight."

"Perfect."

He smiled. Her promise to reconcile sang in his heart. It wouldn't be easy, but at least they were both willing. Tomorrow he'd shred the divorce papers. He pulled into the alley beside the old two-story brick building and parked in the only space remaining. "It sounds like the band is already playing." He jogged around the car and opened Hailey's door. "Remember the first time I brought you here?"

Hailey tucked her hand under his arm and smiled at him. "You warned me the peppers were hot, but I didn't believe you. I wonder how much water I drank that night?"

Trey opened the door. A blast of warm air carried out on the sweet harmony of two fiddles. They followed the hostess to a booth in the back corner.

Hailey slipped off her jacket then slid onto the bench and opened the newspaper menu. "Your mom said the steaks are excellent." She glanced over the menu. "What do you think you'll get?"

He left his menu on the table, content to watch Hailey. So much had happened since the last time they had been on a date. Already he dreaded leaving, knowing it would be several weeks before he'd have time to visit. "I was thinking about the ribeye. I had it when I was here in August."

After giving their order to the waitress, Trey asked about the pumpkin patch.

"It's been one of our best falls." Hailey wrapped the straw-paper around her finger. "All except this weekend the weather's been perfect. If it's too hot people aren't in the mood to visit a pumpkin patch. Once that chill is in the air and you can almost smell the apple cider, people come out."

"You've added some nice improvements to the place."

She smiled. "Thanks. We've tried to come up with new attractions so people will come back each year. I'd say about eighty-five percent of our business is the same people returning year after year. If we add a few new things, it doesn't get old to them."

The waitress slid their plates onto the table.

Hailey stared at her meal. "I will never eat all of this."

"If you eat half of it, I'll buy you dessert. They have the best peach cobbler. Can we pray?"

After praying, they enjoyed light conversation while they ate. Halfway through her meal, Hailey groaned and pushed the plate aside. "I couldn't eat another bite if I had to."

"I thought you wanted some of that peach cobbler."

A sigh escaped her lips. "It doesn't even sound good right now."

"We could take some home."

The band began a song they had danced to in college. He covered her hand with his.

"Maybe if we dance you'll feel better."

She bit her bottom lip, but a slight smile lifted the corners of her mouth. "Don't you remember how the last time we danced turned out? It might be better if we didn't."

Trey stood and pulled her up beside him. She followed willingly to the dance floor and moved into his arms. A perfect fit. "I remember everything about the last time." He whispered against her ear, smiling when she stepped closer. "And you won't hear me complaining if it ends like that tonight."

Head tilted back, her eyes twinkled up at him. "That isn't going to make all our problems better."

"No, but it certainly makes us realize our problems are worth working out, wouldn't you agree?"

Dark eyes studied him. "Yes." She trailed her fingers across the back of his neck. "When did your folks say they'd be home?"

They stepped from the building, and a cold wind rushed around her. Hailey shivered.

Trey slid his hand to her waist and pulled her closer to his side. "It gets cold once the sun goes down."

Despite the chill, Hailey loved this small mountain town. False store fronts lined the block while thousands of clear lights outlined each detail on the old buildings. More lights twinkled in the evergreens. "I've always wondered if you lived here, would you feel like you were always on vacation? Do people even mind working when in a place like this?" At the first snow fall the town would be changed into a winter paradise.

Trey held her car door open while she slid onto the seat. "I'm sure my folks would say a job is still work no matter where you live, but I've never heard either of them say they wished they could move. I think they're planning to retire here." He shut the door, but before he reached the driver's side he stopped and pulled his phone from his pocket.

Hailey leaned her head against her window. The frigid glass

matched the cold dread in the pit of her stomach. The frown on Trey's face, the pacing, the glancing at his watch were all too familiar signs.

He flipped the phone shut and stuffed it in his pocket, then yanked the door open and slid behind the steering wheel, shoulders slumped and sighed. "It's cold in here." Trey started the car and turned the heater on high.

"Problems?" Hailey turned in her seat and pulled her jacket tighter.

Eyes closed, he leaned his head against the head rest and rubbed his forehead. "I need to go back."

"You have a flight tomorrow night, right?" She reached for his hand and pulled it down, holding it in her lap. Her stomach tightened when his eyes studied hers.

"How do you feel about driving home without me?"

Disappointment filled her. "Do I have a choice?"

He shook his head. "They've already got me booked on a flight later tonight. I don't want to do this to you."

"What's going on?"

"You never know in an election year what skeletons someone will find—or plant—in the closet. I need to get back before some things come out in tomorrow's papers. Hopefully it's not all over the nightly news already." He gave her a sad smile. "I'm sorry. This time I'm running out on you."

"Just remember that." She leaned over and kissed his lips. "Sophie and I will be fine getting home. Do you need me to take you to the airport?"

"You're not upset?"

"Disappointed."

"This is why you don't want to come back?"

"Your job demands everything."

"If you come back I'll make things different." His eyes begged her to believe him.

"Is that possible?" She watched another couple walk by and

get in the SUV beside theirs. "You didn't answer about the airport."

Trey put the car in reverse. "I called Dad. They're on their way home so he can take me. So much for our romantic evening at home." Frustration marred his face. He put the gear shift into drive but didn't release it from his hand.

Hailey covered his hand with hers. "I'm sure there will be plenty of other romantic nights." She held her breath and waited.

He brought her hand to his lips and kissed it, then reached across to open the glove compartment. "You were a good sport about the phone rule. I'm thinking I should have given mine up, too." He fished her phone from underneath the Colorado map. "Here, this belongs to you."

She dropped it into her lap. "I didn't miss it much. I think I'll wait until tomorrow to turn it on—just in case."

"Go ahead and check it. I'd rather be here when you do."

She fingered the phone. What would be on it? Had Dad called? "Maybe I'll just check the weather. As long as it was rainy there wasn't much I could do." She waited for it to power up then touched the screen. She groaned. "They were predicting rain all weekend, right?" The knot in her stomach tightened. "It looks like today was clear." She scrolled to the extended forecast. "He'll never talk to me again."

"It will be okay. Even if the pumpkin patch was open today they can handle it without you. We needed this weekend."

"I think you like reminding me that they don't need me." She forced a small laugh.

"They don't, but I do." The look he gave her made her stomach flip. "If there are any messages, listen to them now while I'm here."

Hailey touched the screen again. At the number of messages, dread coursed through her.

"That sigh didn't sound good," Trey pulled the phone from her fingers, looked at the screen, then handed it back. "You could delete them or let me listen to them."

"He left seven messages. They probably don't wish me a good

time, do they?" She stared at the phone.

"You know what? Don't listen to them. Just erase them and I'll call your dad before you get home tomorrow and try to defuse the situation. Maybe he'll take it out on me and will be fine by the time you get there."

"What if something happened?"

"If it were bad, someone would have called me. Since I've had no calls from Kansas, I'm guessing everything is fine and it's just your dad trying to control you." Trey raised his eyebrows. "I don't think you should listen to them. What can you do now?"

Would Dad be more angry that she hadn't listened to the messages? At this point, he probably wouldn't talk to her for months. What if there wasn't anything wrong with the messages? Then she'd be nervous for no reason.

"I'd better listen to them."

Trey's sigh voiced his disappointment.

She turned down the volume so Trey wouldn't hear.

"I don't know what that man did to get you to leave, but you have responsibilities here at home. Call me."

"Hailey, you are being irresponsible. I raised you better than this. You need to get home."

"Call home, Hailey. I don't appreciate whatever statement you think you're making."

"Do you realize how much work you've left for the rest of us? We opened the pumpkin patch without you this morning and everyone is scrambling to cover for you. What were you thinking?"

"That sorry excuse for a husband better bring you home soon. He's worthless—just look at the mess he's put all of us in this weekend. I'll expect your call."

Hailey erased the last message and let the phone drop to her lap before rubbing her eyes with shaky fingers. "Think they could get two more on that plane tonight?"

Trey looked at her so quick the car swerved into the other lane. "We'll make it work if you're serious."

She took a deep breath and released it slowly. "I'd probably be disinherited, if I'm not already."

"I'm serious, Hailey. If you want to go back with me you can."

Why did this have to be such a struggle? A week ago she had no plans to leave and now she wished she could go right now. It wouldn't be right, taking off before the season ended. They'd make different arrangements for next year, but it was her responsibility to stay for the last two weeks.

"There's only two weeks left. I can't walk out now."

"Your dad's the only one who wouldn't understand your decision—and admit it, he might never agree with you about leaving."

"Do you know how bad I feel knowing everyone had to make up for me running off? What would I do in Washington? I'm just going there to stay in your apartment all day with Sophie. There will be plenty of time for that after the pumpkin patch closes and I get things cleaned up."

"You won't be sitting in the apartment every day." Trey's hand on the steering wheel flexed. "We'll find a house and I'll make some changes at work. I promise."

CHAPTER THIRTY

"Almost home, sweetie." Hailey smiled at Sophie over her shoulder as she turned into the familiar driveway. Though Sophie had napped the last two hours, the day had grown incredibly long. It would be good to get out and stretch. She had managed to keep everything in her stomach during the ten hour trip, but the urge to scream grew with each row of cars she passed in the parking lot of the pumpkin patch. The weatherman had been wrong, and it appeared their attendance numbers would set a new record. That wouldn't matter to her dad. She'd been irresponsible by leaving.

Not ready to take the chance of running into him, she parked next to the Snack Shop.

"Mommy may have done it this time, Sophie-girl." She unhooked the car seat straps and lifted Sophie to the ground. "We might be living with your daddy sooner than I thought."

"See Daddy?" Sophie's eyes lit.

"I miss him, too, honey." Hailey held her daughter's hand and walked into the building.

Aunt Joni looked up from the sink where she was elbow deep in dish water. "So you've come home again." She wiped her hands on her floral apron and enfolded Hailey and Sophie in her arms. "Did you have a good time?"

"Is everybody angry with me?"

Aunt Joni shook her head. "We've done fine without you. Ellen wanted to do your things, and it's worked out well." She peered over Hailey's shoulder. "Where's Trey? He didn't want to come in with you?"

"He had to go back last night. Sophie and I drove home by ourselves."

Raised eyebrows provided Aunt Joni's response.

"I'm okay with it. We had a good time and are closer to working things out." Hailey looked around the kitchen once more. "Dad's furious with me."

"So?" Aunt Joni hurried back to the sink and picked up a pan to scrub. "He's always angry at something. If you and Trey are closer to working things out, it will be worth it."

"I hope so. I'll go find Ellen and see what I can do."

"Leave Sophie with me. I want to hear all about her trip."

Sophie had already pulled the wooden stool beside Aunt Joni and had her hands in the sudsy water.

"Thanks for taking over for me." Hailey sat beside Ellen in the ticket booth and tallied the day's attendance.

"Have you seen your dad yet?" Ellen stacked the money into piles.

"Only from a distance. I've been trying to avoid him for as long as possible." She paused and added another column. "Do you think he'll ever talk to me again? I wouldn't have gone if I'd known how wrong the forecast would be."

"It might be a few days, but he will." Ellen shoved the money into a zippered bank bag and handed it to Hailey. "There's one group left going through the corn maze. They should be done soon, and then we can close up."

"I'll close up here and then go check on them. I saw Aunt Joni taking Sophie home about an hour ago."

Minutes after Ellen left, Hailey closed the ledger and scooped it up into her arms. An envelope slipped from the book and landed on the floor. *R&J's Tree Service* and an address from a small town near Wichita was stamped in the upper corner. Probably an advertisement. She slid her finger under the flap and pulled out a pink receipt. She frowned. A bill for service provided? Who requested their service? She scanned the invoice. Four words leaped at her.

Jim Harper, treehouse removal.

Heart racing, she crushed the paper in her hand. Her treehouse? Panic rose within her. She rushed to the back cabinet and dug through the drawer until she found a flashlight. The beam grew dim as she ran down the path carved in the grass. Surely he hadn't done it. The treehouse had to be there.

The dull light rippled through the tree tops before resting on the empty, scarred branch. She staggered the remaining distance. A sob caught in her chest as she knelt next to a pile broken boards. Bitter tears raced down her cheeks. How dare he do this to her?

Warmth covered her shoulder seconds before she was pulled into an embrace. "Oh, honey…" Aunt Joni rocked her from side to side. "If I'd have known he planned to do this, I'd have paid more attention to the truck I saw out here. We've had so many people in and out all day, I guess I figured someone needed a place to park where they wouldn't get hemmed in."

"Why would he tear it down?" Her hands tightened into fists.

"He'll have to answer that himself."

Hailey pulled back and panned the light above her. "He didn't leave anything. It's all a pile of scraps."

"Your dad never does anything part way."

"He had no right. That treehouse is mine—mine and Trey's. I'll never forgive him." The flashlight faded, leaving them in the dark.

"Then you'll be just like him."

"I'm nothing like him. I refuse to be like that." Hailey glared at her aunt and saw her slight smile and raised eyebrows. "I'd never destroy something of Sophie's."

"Jim wouldn't have twenty years ago either." Joni folded her arms over her chest. "I know you're angry and have the right to be, but if you hold onto your anger, you will be like him. He's bitter to the point he can't even live."

"What he's done is wrong."

Joni nodded. "He's justified it in his mind. You may never understand it, but you're going to have to forgive him and get on with your own life. A life away from here."

"I don't want to forgive him. He should experience what it feels like to be held responsible for hurting others."

"You think he's going to notice or care? You're the only one who will be miserable and each day will be worse. Not forgiving someone is like leprosy—it eats away at you until there's nothing good left. Jim's the best example of that. Why would you want to join him in living that way?"

"He doesn't deserve to be forgiven."

"None of us do, but forgiveness is a great gift God has given us, and we need to offer the same gift to others."

Hailey hung her head. "I knew somehow you'd bring God into this."

"That's who I am and who your mom was." Aunt Joni hugged Hailey. "She'd be so disappointed to see how your faith has struggled since the accident. I think she would have wanted her accident to result in something good, not ruin your faith and your marriage."

The ground suddenly felt crowded and less comfortable. "I thought you were here for me to cry on your shoulder."

Aunt Joni stepped aside. "I'm here to make sure you become the woman your mother prayed for, not the female version of Jim Harper."

Hailey straightened her shoulders. "Rest assured, I'll never be like him."

"What's always been the most important thing to him? The

thing he'd give up anything else for?"

"This farm."

"Your mom often joked that the farm was his mistress. I think it always bothered her because she knew Jim would choose the farm over her. You're a lot like your dad, but you don't have to be."

The words faded into the night. A solitary coyote cry stirred up the howls of a distant pack. The loneliness of her life covered her as she absorbed the words of truth. "Only you could be so honest."

"I want you to be happy, but you're not going to find contentment here."

The phone's beep woke Trey from a fitful sleep. He grabbed it from the table and fell into the pillows. "This is Trey."

"The treehouse is gone."

He struggled to hear the broken whisper. He pulled the phone away to see who had called him. Hailey. He pushed himself up on one elbow and leaned his head against the headboard. "What?"

"Our treehouse is gone."

"Gone? Where did it go?" This wasn't an easy conversation to follow at midnight. He'd been working since getting back early yesterday morning to unravel the rumors circulating about the state of the Bryants' marriage.

"He had someone tear it down before I got home today."

Images flashed through his mind of the two of them building it. In the wooden hideaway friendship had turned into love. "Did he tell you why?"

"I don't even want to talk to him."

"Do you think he did it because of Sophie's accident?"

She sighed. "I don't know. He told me the day we left for Colorado he wanted to take it down because it wasn't safe with her around. I said we'd take the ladder off like you suggested. I guess going with you was all the motivation he needed."

Trey sat up and pinched the bridge of his nose. "I shouldn't have let you go home by yourself."

"I don't know if I should have even come home. I've given up three years of my life for him. My marriage is in shambles—"

"No, it's not." He shoved the covers back and stood. "Our marriage was in shambles, but we're working on it. Don't let your dad make you question anything that's between us. Do you hear me, Hailey? We're going to make it. If there would have been another option I'd have taken you home and faced him with you. I'm sorry you were alone."

"The treehouse was already gone. You couldn't have changed it." She took a breath. "Did you get the problem solved?"

"I hope so. It's amazing what people will say in order to hurt someone's reputation. I've known Rob and Amanda for years and I've never seen him treat any woman in a questionable way. For this to come out now screams of deceit."

"But his race isn't even close, is it?"

"No, but it's a way to question if he should be the House Leader. Also if he ever wants to run for president this would be something people would remember—regardless of the truth. We'll see how the Sunday morning news shows spin it, but I think we've found enough evidence for them to question the woman who's making the accusations."

"You like being a part of all of that, don't you?"

"I do." But was it worth the cost? He couldn't voice the words until he found some other way to support his family. For now Washington still had a grip on him.

"I'll let you go. I shouldn't have called so late."

"You can call me anytime." He wasn't ready to hang up yet. How long would it be before they would live together again? At least on the phone he could pretend she was there with him. "I miss you."

"I wish we were still at your folks. Thanks for taking me with you and Sophie."

"Hailey, try to forgive your dad. You don't need the anger or the stress. Those things can't be good for our baby."

"I know, but it isn't easy. Good night." The phone went dead.

He slid his phone back on the table. Why had he sent her home alone?

CHAPTER THIRTY-ONE

A chilly breeze blew through the metal shed where Hailey worked. One more week and another year would be finished. As much as she loved this business, it was time to hang up the CLOSED sign. Regardless of everything else, it had been a good year for business. The weather had given them perfect fall days—cool and crisp but sunny.

She ran a gloved finger down the ledger column. If things continued this way for the last week, they'd top their previous record number crowds. A shiver ran down her spine. The building offered protection from the wind, but the cold still seeped inside.

The side door slammed shut. Ellen wove her way around the shelves of decorations and snacks and picked up a miniature pumpkin from the basket on the counter.. "That wind is really picking up. It's a good thing you have school groups scheduled from now till we close. I can't imagine adults wanting to be out in this cold."

"They'll still come. People love it when it feels like fall. I bet this weekend will be one of our busiest." Hailey closed the book and set it in the wire rack. "I'll make sure we have plenty of hot drinks on hand. They sell better than anything else right now."

"Todd just called." Ellen rubbed her finger over the pumpkin, not looking at Hailey. "They'll be here in a few minutes. I'm going to get your dad now."

"Where is Dad? I haven't seen him this morning." She grabbed the feather duster from the shelf beneath the counter and ran it over the display closest to her.

Ellen tossed the pumpkin into the basket and jammed her hands into her coat pockets. "The message is for you, not your dad. Todd wanted you to know they're almost here. He wants you out there, too."

"What does it matter? I didn't have anything to do with the life." One of the painted gourds fell off the shelf and broke on the cement floor.

"Keep that up and we won't have any gourds to sell." Ellen snatched the duster away. "Todd needs you there. They've been working on this for weeks, and it's important to him."

Hailey took off her stocking hat and ruffled her hair. "What if Dad doesn't accept it? I'm already so angry with him for tearing down the treehouse. I don't know what I'd do if he's mean about this."

"There's a good chance he won't like it, but you need to be there for Todd. It's a big deal to him. I'd think you would want to be there since Trey can't be. Won't you want to tell him how Jim reacts?" She held the duster towards Hailey. "I'm going to take Jim to the parking lot. They'll be here any minute."

Hailey knelt to sweep the broken gourd into her hand. Ellen was right—Trey knew Todd was showing the equipment to Dad today and would want to hear how he responded.

The combine's roar carried over the wind. Hailey stood and threw the pieces of the shattered gourd into the trash. "Let this make a difference." She whispered the prayer. "Don't let him be mean to Todd."

Zipping her coat to her chin, she hurried out the door before she could change her mind.

"What's this all about?" Dad's voice drifted down the sidewalk to where Hailey stood in the parking lot. Ellen laid her hand on his shoulder and said something that seemed to calm him for the moment.

By the nervous smile on Todd's face, Hailey knew he shared her concerns. This could turn into a huge disaster. Their dad didn't like anyone interfering with his life or plans. Confusion covered the older man's face as he looked at the combine and the pickup he hadn't driven in three years parked beside it.

Todd motioned for Hailey to come closer. She wanted to refuse, but the hope on his face drew her forward. "We decided it's time for you to get in the field." Todd stopped in front of Dad and hooked his thumbs on his belt loops. "David and I have reworked some things on your combine and truck so you can farm again."

Dad's knuckles gripped the side of his chair and he stared at the equipment. Hailey wished she knew what he was thinking.

"The lift on the truck will raise you up to the combine cab." Todd's words were rushed. "Do you want me to show you?" He flicked a glance at Hailey.

She couldn't breathe, but forced a smile to her lips and hoped it would encourage him. Even the wind seemed to hold its breath while they waited long moments for a reply.

Dad cleared his throat. "You did this?"

Todd nodded. His eyes filled with apprehension. "I had some help."

"Go ahead and show me how it works."

Almost as one with the wind, they all released a collective breath. Todd's face broke into a smile as he stepped behind the wheelchair and pushed it forward. Ellen squeezed Hailey's hand. Together they watched Todd demonstrate and then guide Jim through each step, answering the questions with a grin that continued to grow.

Jim slid from the wheelchair and into the combine seat. Todd crawled in the cab and explained the harness system that would keep Dad fastened to the seat. Hailey's throat tightened when she saw tears coursing down her father's weathered cheeks.

"I think he likes it." Ellen breathed the words.

"It looks that way." Hailey tried to swallow the painful lump. "Thanks for making me come out here."

Ellen squeezed her hand again. "Now you'll be able to tell Trey all about it."

"I'll call him later tonight." If she called him now, she'd cry and he wouldn't know if things had turned out well or not.

"I wouldn't wait too long." Ellen's voice broke. She nodded to the father and son. Dad's arm stretched around Todd's back. "Todd might beat you to the call."

Scared to hope, she asked the question that burned in her mind. "Do you think this will change things? Change him?"

"I don't know. Maybe the question is, does it change you, Hailey?" Ellen never took her eyes off the two men. "Does it free you to leave and go back to Trey?"

"We're trying to make things work. I'm not sure..."

"Jim might be the one with the new equipment, but you're the one they all did this for. As much as we love you, it's time for you to leave. You don't belong here with us."

Stunned by the blunt words, Hailey gaped at her sister-in-law. "I'm glad to know how you feel."

A slight smile crossed Ellen's face. "You've got an incredible husband. From the stories Todd has told, you and Trey were meant for each other. Each one of the guys had their reasons for working on this project for Jim, but their main goal was to free you from this place. Don't let their efforts be for nothing. Besides..." Her smile grew. "Sophie and the new baby need their dad."

Hailey took a short breath. "Did Trey...? How did...?"

Laughter rang. Ellen hugged her. "I just had a baby. I noticed all the times you've run to the bathroom. It didn't take much to figure out that more than food poisoning had gone on when you visited Washington." Her voice grew serious. "Go back to him. We'll be fine, and so will the Harper Farm Pumpkin Patch."

CHAPTER THIRTY-TWO

Hailey rested her forehead on the steering wheel and took a deep breath. "Give me the words to say that he'll understand."

The roar of the combine eating its path through the burgundy heads of milo drifted across the dark field to the grain truck. The lights from the mammoth machine flashed across the cab as it turned at the end of the row and lumbered to the truck, heavy with grain waiting to be unloaded.

The sight of her dad in the driver's seat brought tears to her eyes. The accident had changed his life, but maybe now he'd find a new type of normal. She hoped he would remember how instrumental Trey had been in his return to farming.

The light shower of grain from the auger signaled an empty bin on the machine. Hailey climbed from the truck and hurried up the combine ladder. She opened the door and scooted into the extra seat. "Mind if I ride for a round?"

The smile on her father's gave agreement. "As long as it's not dewy, I'll keep cutting. What happened to Todd?"

"Ellen had a meeting tonight, so he ran home to put Jake to bed. He'll come back out once she gets home." Thank goodness for the darkness that hid her shaking hands. "Aunt Joni is baking cookies with Sophie."

"Is she staying around much longer?" He leaned against the harness that held him in the seat.

"She might. We're her only family and it's great to have her here." This wasn't a good lead for what she came to tell him. "You must be glad to be back up here driving."

"Yep." He paused. "The lift on my truck sure opens up some options for me. Todd rode with me today, and we discussed some other modifications we could make on the 7400 and maybe the swather."

"I know he'll be glad to have you back out here."

He cleared his throat. "I appreciate what he's done."

"I hope you told him."

He gave a slight nod.

"He and Trey worked hard to make this possible." He needed to remember the man who started this.

"I'm grateful to him, too."

Hailey took a deep breath. She was jumping into a deep pool, not sure if she even knew how to swim. "Trey wanted to give you your life back."

"This is only part of what I lost." He never looked away from the rows of grain feeding into the header.

She bit her lip, trying to keep her emotions under control. "Daddy, I can never give you Mom back. I live with the regret every day. If I could go back to that night, I'd take the way home that you always took. Or you could have driven." She took a short breath. "I can't change Mom's death, but I've tried to make up for it by sacrificing my own marriage."

He speared her with a glance. "You haven't sacrificed anything."

"Mom stood by you through everything. The night before my wedding she drove home from the church with me. You know how Mom was, always giving words of wisdom. She told me you were a hard man and she didn't always agree with you. But she never considered leaving because she had made a vow to stay with you forever."

He raised the header at the end of the row and turned the combine.

"It's time for me to go back to my marriage. I can't make restitution for the accident the rest of my life. Mom wouldn't agree with the way I've treated Trey, and she'd be so disappointed if I divorced him."

"So you're leaving?"

"I am." The words caught on a sniff. "I'm flying to D.C. tomorrow to tell him. We'll probably look for a house."

The combine stopped, pitching her forward.

"It's the last week for the pumpkin patch. You can't leave now." The lights from the dash glowed, revealing the annoyance on his face.

"I'll be back on Thursday evening. Aunt Joni and Ellen can handle everything while I'm gone."

"I didn't raise you to be irresponsible."

"And Mom didn't raise me to walk out on my husband."

He pushed the gear back into DRIVE. "You're abandoning me and the business. We may have to close."

She almost smiled at the drama. "Maybe I can come back in the fall."

"You know there's more to be done than that."

"Aunt Joni might be willing to do more. She could move here and take over. She'd do a great job."

"I won't have that woman around all the time. She'd drive me crazy."

"You'll have time to find a replacement for me. Sophie and I won't leave until we close and things are cleaned up for the winter."

Other than the roar of the machine it was silent. The combine inched to the end of the row at the same time the beeper screamed, announcing another full bin. Todd's pickup pulled up behind the grain truck.

"I'll leave Sophie here tomorrow with Aunt Joni." She turned to face him. "Daddy, I love you. If I didn't, I wouldn't have stayed. But

I want to be with Trey more than anything else. I've lived almost three years alone, and I don't want to live the rest of my life without him. You'll be fine without me."

His gaze never left the front window, but his jaw twitched. She knew him well enough to know enough had been said. The pop of the door unlatching broke the silence.

Hailey stepped onto the ladder. "Thanks for letting me ride." She slammed the door and gave a small wave before crawling down and trotting to her brother.

"You okay?" Todd perched on the tailgate. "How did he take it?"

Hailey slid onto the tailgate beside him. "Better than I thought he would."

"You're doing the right thing." He put his arm around her shoulder.

"It's the worst time to go."

"And Trey will appreciate that. Are you ready for your flight?"

"I think I've been ready for weeks—I just didn't realize it."

The parking lot was full when Trey pulled in. Seven school buses attested to the fact that the pumpkin patch season was almost over. He stopped in front of the house and reached behind the seat for the bouquet of flowers he'd picked up before leaving Wichita. If it took too much longer to find Hailey, they would be a wilted offering.

He jogged around the house and down to Hailey's door. It was a long shot that she'd be in the house, but it gave him a place to start. When the knock was unanswered, he looked around until his gaze settled on the scarred tree, empty of the weight it had borne for years.

The pile of broken boards drew him to the base of the tree. He had little doubt why Jim had destroyed it, but what kind of father did that to his daughter? Trey nudged a plank with his shoe. If Jim was trying to protect Sophie, taking the ladder down would have been sufficient. Jim wasn't just getting rid of the hazard—he wanted to get rid of the memories.

He stood and looked around the yard then hurried toward the busy buildings. Two high school-aged girls manned the admissions booth, both texting. "Excuse me." He bit his lip to disguise his smile as they tucked their phones under the counter. "Do either of you know where I might find Hailey?"

They blushed and shrugged. The shorter one answered. "You'll have to ask Joni. We just take the money."

"I see." He smiled. "And where might I find Joni?"

"Oh, sorry." She pointed over her shoulder. "She's probably in the Snack Shop."

"Wait." The older one withdrew a map and laid it in front of him. "You are here." She made an X at the spot marked *Admission Booth*. "And the Snack Shop is—" She turned the map so she could see it. "Oh, yeah, the Snack Shop is right here." She drew a line to connect the two landmarks. "I hope that helps."

"Thanks for the information and the map." He grinned. Their giggles followed him up the path while squeals of delighted school kids echoed through the trees. Groups of children dodged around him. This had worked out better than he'd hoped. No one knew he was coming and Hailey would be surprised. Now if she'd accept his offer to start over.

"Daddy!" Sophie squealed from her stroller in front of the craft barn.

Trey waved then stopped short. Grant was on his haunches, talking with Sophie. What was he doing here? Trey's anticipation turned to anxiety.

Pointing furiously, she shrieked again, "Daddy!"

Grant's gaze settled on Trey. A look of concern crossed his face as he pushed Sophie towards him. "What are you doing here?"

"Someday I hope you find a different question to ask me."

Trey knelt and unhooked the strap. He stuffed the flowers into the stroller pocket. "Come here, honey." He held Sophie. He couldn't stop the wide grin on his face while Sophie gave him kisses, squeezing his neck tight.

Grant's forehead furrowed. "It wasn't meant the way it sounded, Trey. It's just that you're not supposed to be here. Hailey left a couple of hours ago."

Trey kissed Sophie on the nose. "I can wait. Sophie and I will have a great time." She giggled and bounced in his arms.

"You'll be waiting a few days." A smile creased the other man's face.

Trey looked up sharply. "What do you mean?"

"This is classic." Grant laughed. "I don't know if I should tell you or not. Hailey wanted to keep it a secret."

A group of little boys, each holding a pumpkin, jostled between them.

"What's going on?"

Grant put his hand on Sophie's back. "Sophie, where's Mommy is going?"

"See Daddy."

Trey looked back and forth between the two. "She's coming to see me?"

They nodded in unison.

"When did she leave?"

"At eleven. Her flight leaves at one-twenty."

"Why was she coming?"

"I've already said enough." Grant yanked the flowers from the pocket and traded them for Sophie. "There are some things you and Hailey need to discuss." He glanced at his watch. "If you hurry, you might catch her and save you a trip back to Washington tonight."

Trey pivoted and started back to his car. Then he whirled and hurried back. He gave Sophie a kiss, and then he held out his hand and waited until the other man grasped it. "Thank you."

"She's a good woman. Treat her well."

Most of the chairs were filled when Hailey got to her gate, leaving her to stand against the far wall. She took out her phone and called Ellen. "Hi. I'm about to board the plane and wanted to check on Sophie."

"Grant came by about an hour ago and took her with him. He had several things to do and she wanted to get out of the house. I hope that's okay."

"They'll have fun. I'll call back tonight when I know more."

"You don't need to be nervous. Trey will be thrilled to see you."

Her phone beeped, and she glanced at it. "Trey's trying to call me again."

"Have you talked to him?"

"I'm afraid if I answer his call I'll tell him what I'm doing." She shifted to the corner for a small bit of privacy. "What if I tell him and he says not to come?"

"Do you really think he'd do that? He's going to be thrilled. I doubt he'll want you to come back to Kansas on Thursday. Did you see your dad this morning?"

"He didn't come to see me off, but when I drove past the field he waved."

The phone beeped again.

"Maybe that's his way of letting you know things are okay."

The boarding announcement blared.

"They're calling my row number so I'd better go. I'll call you when I arrive." She studied the missed number on the screen while reaching into her bag for her boarding pass.

Trey glanced at his watch as he pushed through the door and ran to the ticket counter.

The airline worker looked over her glasses. "May I help you?"

"Flight 2313—has it left?" He gasped, trying to get his breath.

"I'm sorry, that flight left the gate at 1:20. It's in line for takeoff. Is there a problem?"

He sat the flower bundle on the counter and leaned his head against his hand. "Can you stop it? My wife is on there." He'd flown too many times to expect a positive answer.

"Are you the President of the U.S.?" She raised one eyebrow.

"I've met him." He released the breath he'd been holding and ran a hand over his face. He'd missed her by six minutes.

The woman smiled for the first time. "Unless you can get him on the phone in the next thirty seconds, you might want to consider your other options. A different flight, maybe?" Her hands traveled over the keyboard. "We do have one open seat on the seven-fourteen flight."

Frustrated, he rubbed the back of his neck, trying to release some of the built up tension. At the moment, he couldn't think past his disappointment. "I already have a ticket on a five thirty flight." Exhausted, he stumbled to the row of vinyl chairs and slumped into the one facing the window. The plans he'd made to surprise Hailey now warred with the images of her walking into an empty apartment.

Six lousy minutes. Tomorrow he might see the humor in this, but right now it rankled. If she would have told him it would have saved them both. He pushed back the truth of his own secret trip to Kansas. At least she could have answered her phone. He'd lost count of the times he had hit redial.

Perhaps Amanda could meet Hailey's plane and keep her until he got back. There had to be an earlier flight. He slapped the wilted bouquet against his leg. Six minutes...

"Waiting for a flight or meeting someone?"

He jerked around at the familiar voice and pushed himself out of the chair. "You tell me."

Hailey's eyes twinkled. "They won't let those flowers through security so you'd better be meeting someone. She's a lucky woman."

"I'm the lucky one." He lifted the wrapped offering and grimaced at the mangled, wilted blooms. "I should find some new ones—these have been through a lot."

She stepped closer and enfolded his hand in her warm one. "I'm sure she'll love these."

Flowers between them Trey pulled her to him. The built up tension from the past hour fell away. "That was too close." He took a deep breath of her familiar shampoo then stepped back. "How did you get off that plane? Why didn't you answer your phone? I don't know how many times I called."

Hailey turned her face up. An innocent smile played across her lips. "Seventeen. Grant called right before I walked onto the plane. I didn't answer yours because I wanted to surprise you."

"Telling me would have been bad?"

Uncertainty washed her features. "I didn't want you to tell me not to come."

Hope for their future expanded in his chest. "I guess I'm not sure why you were coming." He needed to hear her say the words he'd waited years for.

"To ask if you would let me come back—for us to be a family."

Trey pulled his hand from the flowers and cupped her cheek. "You're willing to move to D.C.?"

"I want to be with you. Maybe I'll be so busy with the kids I won't even notice your long hours." Her eyes still showed concern. She tilted her head to once side. "What are you doing here?"

"I had a job interview last night."

Confusion clouded her face. "An interview...for a job?"

He smiled. "Would you be too disappointed if we didn't live in D.C.?"

She pulled back and sat on the arm rest of the chair. "I don't understand what's happened."

"Would you be willing to move to Colorado?"

"Are you serious?" She paused for his nod. "You got a job there? Doing what?"

"Do you remember me telling you I met several of Dad's friends at that prayer lunch last week, and one of the men is the brother of the director of AgMobility? The brother called me Monday morning to see if I'd be interested in working for them. I had an interview yesterday, and before I left he offered me the job. I'll be an advocate for disabled farmers and ranchers, and help them decide what equipment or alterations they need as well as the funding to pay for it."

"You're sure you want to leave Washington? I don't want you to ever regret it." Her eyes were dark with emotion.

"I'll regret it if I don't. This whole time I've expected you to make all the changes. The other night when I left you at my folks, I realized what my job demanded." He took a breath. "It won't be easy to rebuild our marriage, but if you're willing to walk away from your dad and I'm willing to leave my job, then we'll have a fresh start. Will you do this with me?"

"Yes." She rose and slid her arms around his neck. "No one's expecting me back until Thursday night."

He released the breath he'd been holding. For three years his world had been off-balanced. Now it righted itself. He held her at arm's length and allowed his gaze to follow every inch of her. He wanted to remember every detail of this moment. "Come back with me. My plane leaves late this afternoon." He reached for the handle of her suitcase. "I'd hate for you to disappoint everyone by going back to the farm early." He kissed the tip of her nose.

"I'd like that." She cradled the wilted bouquet. "What will we do till then?"

"I'm sure we'll think of something." He slid his arm around her waist. "As long as we're together, it doesn't matter to me."

EPILOGUE

Christmas Eve

Trey stopped the car in front of the two story brick home. Soft snow floated from the black sky. "It looks like the contractors got everything cleaned up."

Hailey tugged her stocking hat over her ears. "It's like a picture on a Christmas card. Next year we'll decorate the porch with greenery and bows. Come on." She jumped from the car. "I can't wait to see how that old fireplace they found in the kitchen looks now. Even when I was in college and visited your family, I loved this old house. Think of the history it's seen."

Trey met her at the sidewalk and took her gloved hand in his. "I hope you're as happy with it once we move in. A new house would have been more logical and efficient." His smile softened the words.

"Logical, efficient, but no history and no character." She went up on tiptoe and kissed him. "We'll just have to snuggle at night if it gets too cold."

"That's definitely a plus for the place." He kissed her on the nose. "Let's see if the inside is ready for us to move in next week."

Hailey had dreamed for weeks about this home. She stepped inside and turned slowly, observing every minute detail from floor to ceiling. If only she'd remembered to bring her notebook filled with pictures and decorating ideas. She touched the empty walls that begged for fresh color and photographs of their family. When she closed her eyes she imagined the sweet cinnamon fragrance of fresh baked delicacies that would waft from her kitchen. This old home offered them a place to rebuild their marriage and grow their family.

"There's more to see than the foyer." Trey pulled on her hand.

In the kitchen new stainless steel appliances gleamed against the dark countertop and white cabinets. "I wish we could celebrate Christmas here." Hailey ran her hand over the smooth counter and then squealed. "Look at that fireplace. The stove fits right into it. I knew it would look fabulous. You love it, don't you?"

Trey leaned against the counter and watched her. "I never had any doubts."

"That's not how I remember it." She laughed. "Think we could have Christmas here tomorrow? I don't want to leave."

"Next year. Mom would be disappointed if we changed plans now." He pointed toward the living room. "Let's see what else they've done."

"Maybe I could bake something here for tomorrow." She backed out of the kitchen and through the living room door. "It looks like they left some lights– Oh, my. . ." A tall, slender Christmas tree stood in the middle of the room. Hundreds of lights twinkled among the ornament laden branches.

She blinked back tears. "Did you do this?" Taking a step closer, she recognized the delicate painted glass balls they'd bought at an art gallery in D.C. and the carved wooden skis from Winter Park the Christmas they got engaged. "When did you...?"

Trey stepped behind her and wrapped his arms around her waist. "My folks did it. I sent them the box you labeled *Christmas Decorations–Keep Forever.*"

"It's beautiful. There's even a present. Is it from your folks, too?""

He released her. "That's from me. Merry Christmas, Hailey."

She knelt beside the tree and pulled the flat packaged toward her. "May I open it now?" She pressed the ribbon bow onto the lapel of her winter coat before tearing the wrapping. Tears blurred the words on the wood sign. She bit her bottom lip to keep it from trembling.

SENIOR PROM 4-21-02

FIRST KISS 4-22-02

ENGAGED 12-31-08

MARRIED 6-23-09

SOPHIE BORN 12-04-14

FRESH START IN COLORADO 12-24-16

"How did you get this?"

"I found it in the pile. I figure your dad never went up in that treehouse or he wouldn't have left the boards for someone to find."

She traced the bottom line. "I love it that you added Sophie and Colorado." She wiped her cheek on her shoulder. "I hated the thought that all these memories and dates had been lost."

"Nothing can make us lose the memories. They will always be ours, with or without the boards." He cupped her face in her hands. "Want to see where I thought we could hang that?"

"It will look wonderful anywhere in here."

He helped her up then led her to the French doors overlooking the backyard. A flashlight rested on the windowsill. "I hoped Dad would remember to leave this light." He grabbed it and ushered her onto the patio. Fluffy snowflakes floated to the white ground. "The snow is beginning to pick up." He fanned the beam across the trees before letting it settle on an old cottonwood tree. "What do you think?"

Hailey followed the flow of light and gasped. "That wasn't there before, was it? I'd have noticed it."

Trey put his arm around her and pulled her to him. "My dad

and a friend of his built it. It's not exactly the same as the old one, but we're not the same either. Hopefully, both the treehouse and our marriage are stronger."

No words needed to be said. She rested her head on his shoulder and listened to the stillness for several minutes. Then she stepped away from him. "Do you hear music?" With hands raised to catch the snow, she tilted her head and turned in a slow circle.

Trey caught her hand. "I do." He raised her hand to his mouth and kissed it. "May I have this dance?"

A hushed silence on this holiest of nights blanketed them while they danced to the song that played in their hearts.

ACKNOWLEDGEMENTS

If I have learned anything on this journey, it is how priceless encouragement is. When I first started putting my stories on paper, I didn't tell anyone because I wasn't sure what people would think. Instead, I've been so blessed by many of you and your encouraging words. I could fill pages with your kindness.

Mark: Not once have I heard you complain about eating out or a messy house while I'm writing. You've done so much to make sure I had time to write and the chance to go to conferences and meetings. Thank you for being an amazing man and husband.

Caleb, **Bryce**, and **Isaac:** I am blessed to be the mom of three young men who have cheered me on with their words and have shown interest in my writing for all these years. I pray daily that each of you will follow the dream God has put in you.

Logan VandenHoek, **Seth Roe**, **Amy Schoonover**, **Paul Matzek:** Thank you for remembering the stories I wrote in high school and years later letting God use you to encourage me to continue this journey. Your interest after so many years felt like God was telling me to trust Him and try.

Mom and Dad: I think I learned my love of reading from both of you. Thank you for believing I could do this, for praying for me, and celebrating the accomplishments along the way. I am honored to be your daughter.

Julane Hiebert: Who would have thought in 1984 that God would bring us back together years later for this! God knew I could not be in a better boat than yours for this journey. What a blessing it has been. Thank you, my dear sweet friend, for every moment you have shared with me.

Cherie Gagnon, Susie Wallace, Kathy Terral: You've read, listened, critiqued, and suggested. I would not have Autumn's Grace without you. More than anything, I thank God for bringing us together to write and then He grew sweet friendships.

Becky Walters (www.thewaltersfarm.com): I wanted to write a story on a farm and your pumpkin patch became home for the Harper family. Thank you for taking the time to answer my questions, explain what it's like to run such a business, and show me around. Whenever I drive by I feel like I own a small part of your beautiful place!

Paula Patton: Thank you for sharing your knowledge of Washington D.C. Your maps and suggestions made writing those scenes easier.

Kim Sawyer, Connie Stevens, and **Wings of Hope Publishing:** Thank you for giving Autumn's Grace and me a chance. You have made this process so enjoyable. Your help and suggestions have made my story stronger.

Deb Raney: You not only offered your writing expertise, but also a sweet friendship. Thank you for always asking about my stories, encouraging me with ideas, and sharing your wisdom for being a wife and mom.

My Berean Family: So many of you have encouraged me and cheered me on. Your love and friendships make going to work a true blessing. Thank you for showing so much excitement for Autumn's Grace. When our family came back to Berean, I knew I was home.

And finally, I have seen the **hand of God** guiding and directing me on this journey. I am in awe that He placed the love of story in my heart and gave me a dream to write. He has directed this entire journey and it has been amazing.

TO CONTACT THE AUTHOR

FACEBOOK
www.facebook.com/sarameisingerauthor

WEBSITE
www.sarameisingerauthor.com

Wings of Hope

Est. 2013

Wings of Hope Publishing is committed to providing quality Christian reading material in both the fiction and non-fiction markets.